MARKED ONES
ANTHONY AND LARRY
BY
JULIA MATTHEWS

Prologue

Anthony

Ugh! Mirrors told exactly what one's day was like. Rough didn't describe it. Took hours for a simple decision to be made. Okay, I understood. Sort of. David and Bryan were newly pledged and had only been on their honeymoon for a couple of hours when the President called. Man sounded desperate. Understandable. Someone had taken his son. Held him hostage for something the President could never give. Or so the man claimed. Still, took hours to convince David to go and rescue the young man. Even after David heard the predicament he still refused. Wasn't sure how Caleb and Theodor managed to work with David for so many years. Aggravating didn't fit the man's attitude. Who had to be bribed to go and rescue someone? David's who.

I gave my already standing out hair another yank and rolled my eyes at myself before dropping my leather tote beside the door. David's arguments about being newly married might have held more merit if David found a Protector. Least they could have legally gotten married. Humans hadn't gotten their thumbs out of their ass far enough to realize that love didn't take into account sex, race, or other issues the humans could come up with. Love only cared about emotions. Hell, what was I thinking, for years the Royal Leaders of the Bombardians had been bigots.

Three former Royal Leaders had been kicked out for having found a Keeper, instead of a Protector. There should have been no issue about a Royal Leaders being given a man instead of a woman to calm his beast side. Yes, Protectors could give them a child, but no guarantee that the child will be a Bombardian. Okay, a male child would carry more royal blood than any other Bombardian with royal blood. Still, that shouldn't have . . .Okay, a Royal Leader being paired with a male, a Keeper, to calm his beast side was very rare, but not impossible. Not even sure why the former Royal Leaders thought it would be. I mean Bombardian's are blessed with Keepers all the time. Why would they have thought the Royal Leaders would be different. They were Bombardians. Okay, we carried more skills than the other Bombardians and were closer related to the first Bombardian than the rest, but still . . . When it came down to it . . . Underneath we are Bombardians. Must abide by all the laws that we set up for our kind. Why had it been so hard for the former Royal Leaders to believe that?

Their thinking might have made more sense if new royal blood Bombardians were born only to Royal Leaders, but not the case. Studies showed one out of five Bombardians carried royal blood. Not the same amount as a child born to a Royal Leader, but that shouldn't matter. Why had the former Royal Leaders been such bigots? Had they truly feared their family line dying out?

What the hell! Ugh! I'd been over and over these very thoughts with Theodor, Caleb, and Franklin. Why rehash them with myself? Did no good.

A tilt of my head had my neck popping as I stumbled down the hallway. Needed to pack my carry along bag and get some sleep. That's what I needed. Best possible answer. Dream of the upcoming free time. Five days spent curled up with my lover. Ahhhhh . . . Nothing better in the world.

Chapter 1

Larry

My glass slipped around the pull-down tray as the stewardess braced her hands against the seats on both sides of her. The speaker crackled as the pilot's voice filled the air.

"It'll be okay. Just a little turbulence." David, the muscle-bound rescuer, said.

I couldn't respond, so I faced the window and replayed the last few days.

I'd been on my way home from the last class of the day when someone rear ended my dad's limo. Secret service jumped into action like good little robots. Driver went to deal with whoever hit us. The two newer guards watched the driver like a hawk. All seemed ridiculous to me until . . .

A loud hissing consumed the inside of the car. My hand went over my head as I ducked into the floorboard. A loud thump and little pings ricocheted around the inside of the limo. Small grunts of pain drew my head up far enough to see the smallest of the two guards wiggle through the window. The door handle rattled as something banged against the window. I could hear someone talking in a foreign language, but hell if I knew which one. Then a light breeze and the voices grew louder for a split second before I heard another shot.

"Fuck!" the guard beside me shouted.

I whipped my head up just as the guard who'd been shimming through the window disappeared into the front of the limo. A muzzle appeared in the middle of the partition.

"Open the door, or I'll shoot him." The gunman trained his weapon on my forehead. "I'm not kidding." The guy's finger pulled back the trigger, which spurred the guard into action.

The click of the handle barely happened before the door was jerked open and the gunman fired. I ducked, but the shot hadn't been aimed at me. It landed right where the guy wanted. Dead center of the last secret service guy. A hand gripped my forearm and jerked me out of the limo. A coolness appeared against the side of my neck and things went black. When I woke, I'd been gagged and tied to a chair. The room had been pitch black and stank of stale urine. I could hear others moving, even picked up some chatter, but had no idea what they said. Minutes faded into hours and days. I never once saw anyone. Was sure they were going to kill me. Might have if my rescuer hadn't arrived. The guy came alone but took out everyone. From the different voices I'd heard while tied up there had been at least twelve people watching me. Odd. The people spoke a strange language, but their voices were identifiable. Each had a different tone or level, allowing me to pinpoint how many was around. Twelve was way more than one person should have been able to destroy.

"Need to buckle up, Larry. We are landing." A soft female voice broke me away from the image of a naked, blood-soaked David. I'd asked where his clothes were, even asked him where he was injured. The man refused to answer. Hadn't even spoken until they were enclosed inside what appeared to be a military tank style Hummer. Was the first sign David had been sent by my father. The car held two bags of clothes. One held mine, another proved that the guy was military. Military was bad ass, but from what I knew none were sent alone without backup. David had no ear com or anything.

"Who are all those people?" David shook his head as he glanced outside the small plane window.

"Secret Service." I answered before looking out the window. Mistake on my part. I had no idea why there were so many suit bearing people around my father.

"Why so many?" David unbuckled soon as the seatbelt light flickered off.

My heart raced as my hands filled with sweat. "I can't go out there." I pushed the shutter down, leaning my head against the headrest. Why had father brought all those people to the airport? I'd explained some of what happened. Told him I'd explain all when I got home, but . . . The man . . . Couldn't give me a freaking day to visit with him before sicking the entire world on me.

"How will you get home?" David's calm tone had me laughing.

"What's funny?"

"I won't be able to." An inward groan filled my already throbbing head. "Will you do me a favor?"

"Depends."

"Let my father know I'm not leaving the plane until everyone is gone."

David's lips lifted as he hesitated before he glanced out the window. "Okay. See why all those people are a bit scary. They look like vultures ready to pounce on day old prey."

Accurate description. "They are. I'm the prey, except . . . I'm not dead. Yet. Or . . . Don't think I am. Might be stuck in a dream, but the blood oozing from you seemed pretty real. The flight turbulence felt natural."

"Don't go freaking on me." David touched my shoulder and headed towards the plane door.

He stopped the stewardess and whispered something to her. She handed him a phone, but I couldn't hear what was said. Bet David spoke to one of dad's liaison. David could handle his dad. Gave me a bit more time to process what all had gone down and decide a few more things. Like how in the world to get dad to assign David as my new and only Secret Service guy. The rest could go to hell, or back into the academy.

"Larry, son." Dad's voice drew me away from internal working. "Mr. Lincoln said you refused to leave the plane. Care to tell me why."

One look told me all the suit wearing people that came with dad was not around. Boded well for the next phase of my plan. Another glance told me David was gone as well.

"Where's David?"

"I suppose he's headed towards his other flight. Why?"

"He can't . . . No . . . I won't stay where . . ."

"Son," dad laid a hand on my arm, "relax. Breath. I can't understand a word you are saying."

I shook my head, taking a deep breath. "He can't leave. You need to assign him as my guard. No one else. I won't allow it."

"Son, I've got the best guards in the world. You will be fine. Promise."

"Yeah, like the three dead ones." Hadn't meant to be cold-hearted, but I struggled to think. When David was around . . . I was calm, stable, and able to work through emotions. "David, or no one. I won't speak to anyone about anything that went down." Didn't really know much.

"Son, he's not one of my guys. I can't order him around."

"Why not? He's military. Has to be. He took out twelve guys to rescue me."

"He did!" the light blue faded from my dad's eyes. "Did he tell you he's military?"

"No. Assumed. You mean he's not?"

Dad's sigh was answer enough.

"Then what is he?"

"I can't say."

Right. Father kept many secrets, but never anything that pertained to my life. The guy had to be trustworthy or father wouldn't have sent him in.

"I don't care. I feel safe with him. I meant what I said. He's my guard or I speak to no one."

Dad's shoulders slumped and he pulled out his phone. I listened as he talked with someone, calmly before the shouting started. The phone struggle went on for about half an hour. Was about to give up when dad gave me a weak smile.

"He's going to speak with us, no promises."

Workable. All I needed was time to explain. One thing David showed me since he rescued me was kindness and patients.

Moments later David walked in. His body posture was loose and easy. No sight of tightness stretched across his face. No fear of facing the big bad President of the United States. None of the star gaze eyes. Nope. He walked with an air of supremacy, but I saw through the fake smile. David's eyes appeared to be glowing and it had dad taking a step back. Intimidation clung to each breath father released, but he stood up taller and offered his hand.

"Thanks for returning. I know - -"

"President Wells, I'm not keen on people who attempt blackmail. They irk me as much as people who kidnap others because of whose son they are. I returned because you said Larry was agitated. If I can be of help, then move aside. Let me see if I can convince him to leave the plane. I'd like to get home to my man."

His man? Um . . .

"Mr. Lincoln, my son has requested you - -"

"Move aside. Let me speak to him or I leave."

Wow. Man cut father off twice. No one did that. More David talked more I felt like my decision was the best.

"Dad, step aside." Wasn't going to lose my chance because dad's macho posturing.

"Larry," David gave me a questioning eyebrow.

"I'd like for you to remain as my guard. I can pay you for your time away. You may even bring your partner if you'd like. Or I can go where you live if you don't mind." How much more of a babbling fool could I have been. I was an educated, rational young man. Even if I didn't show it.

David crossed his arms and darted his eyes towards dad, who was frowning. "I'm sure this isn't your idea."

"No. It's his." Dad sharp and snappish tone didn't make David flinch like it did most.

"Why are you asking this of me?" David returned his full attention to me.

I hung my head and laid it all out. "The men took me while I was with three Secret Service guys. I no longer trust them or feel safe anywhere. Except . . . When you are around. The moment I found you left the plane my heart sped up. I couldn't think clearly. I wanted to crawl under the seat and hide."

Hated hearing my weakness. Worse was dad was present for it. I was a strong-willed man, but like most . . . Limits existed. Mine had been breached and the only way to regain them was to take care of myself. Not worry about what others thought. How they saw me. What they believed me to be. Not what the world thought about the President's son being a weak man. Nope. Had to take care of myself so I could live a healthy life.

David looked as if he was a second away from telling me to grow up. He focused on the roof of the plane while taking one deep breath after another. I knew I needed to take charge of my life. What did that mean? Lots. What stood out the most? Mmmmm . . . What I needed was time for the fear to subside. All the trauma case studies I examined for my psychology degree stated the fear was natural and could be overcome with time. I'd seen it first handed. The knowledge was engrained in me. I could do it. With time. Space. NO PRESS.

"Larry," okay my fate was in David's hands and he was delivering. I kept my shoulders straight and sat up taller. "If I agree to this you will have to accompany me some where I can protect you better. There will be no press or sight seers able to come within twenty miles of you. There will be rules you must follow for your safety and mine and my mans. First and most important is that whatever you see, learn, or hear never crosses your lips in front of anyone other than the ones in my home. We clear?"

I nodded and stood, gathering my bag, but dad blocked my path.

"That's not acceptable. He will have to speak to the press and the others. There is no way I can keep him from having to."

"Good for him I can."

David's calmness soothed the rising nerves my father's response created. I'd expected David to be the hardest to convince. Looked like I'd been wrong. Dad's arms were crossed and his *stone-cold do not cross me stance* was in full mode.

"Let me be clearer." David took two steps forward and looked down at father. "If Larry Wells request my assistance, I will provide it the best way I can. If he agrees to my terms, then I will do what I can to make him comfortable enough to be around others."

Knew my mouth had to be hanging open. I'd never seen anyone dare talk to father in such a manner. Most were freaked by his status. David didn't seem phased by it. Either the man had balls of steel or held something major over dad. Most likely the other. Intriguing, but not enough for me to outright ask.

"You are treading on thin ice. One word and all . . ."

David remained hovering over my dad. My dad's eyes closed, and his entire body lifted and fell with each inhale he took. Too bad it did little to rid dad of his cocky attitude. His words only seemed to make things worse.

"Mr. Lincoln, you best remember who you are talking to. In a blink of an eye - -"

"You can what? Do away with the lie your species spread?

Species? What the hell?

"Uh . . . Dad . . ."

David took a step back and leaned against the seat behind him. "Larry, do you wish my help?"

Had. Still did. David could provide me the time to heal. David scared dad . . . Was I safe with David? Yes. He rescued me at dad's request. What was there in it for him?

"Did he promise you something to come after me?" I knew the answer before I asked. Typical. Promise things to achieve ultimate goal. He'd done the same during his campaigns.

"We asked for nothing when he approached us, but he promised to reconsider our original request."

Asking more would have done no good. David said more than expected. If I went with David. I'd most likely find out more by watching. Way it worked with dad.

"Son, you are seriously considering leaving with him. You know nothing about him."

"How much did you know when you sent him after me?" Dad jerked back at my harsh tone. "I'm sure you wouldn't send a man after me you did not trust to some extent." Would have sent someone he believed expendable and anyone who held something over dad was expendable.

I faced David. "I agree to your terms."

"Larry," his dad gasped, "do not do this. You can't. I need you to speak with the press and - -"

"I know everyone wants to know all the little details about who took the President's son and where I was held and why. Well . . . It's not happening in person. I will write my statement and mail it to you."

Dad started to speak, but I shook my head, grabbed my bag, and moved to David's side. "I'm ready to go wherever."

"Then hang on." David wrapped his arms around my waist, and everything went black. Again.

Chapter 2

Larry

"Oh . . . Fudge."

My knees gave way, but I never fell. My eyes opened, but white floating dots filled them.

"What the heck?"

"Breath. It will fade." Something hit the back of my knees. "Sit. I won't let you fall."

David guided me back until I was on my ass and then he pushed my head down until it was between my knees.

"David . . ." A light airy voice squealed as feet slapped against the floor. "You're home."

"Babe."

Silence consumed the air. Didn't have to look to know David and his man was lipped locked. Part of me longed for someone to greet me in a deep loving manner. As a child my main goal had been growing up and finding love like my parents had. Too bad their entire marriage had been a scam. Was fifteen when I realized the truth. My parents lived a television life. Mom was a typical money grubber woman who married dad for the money and prestige of his family name. Dad married mom to gain a picture-perfect wife. Sure they sated each other at some point, but then . . .their life dissolved. Those revelation hadn't detoured me from wanting the life they portrayed.

"Who's this?" The airy voice said.

"Babe, this is Larry Wells. He's going to be staying with us for awhile." David replied.

"Uh . . .what's wrong with him?"

"I transported him here."

"Oh . . . I'll get him some juice. It always helps me."

Footsteps moved away, returning as quickly.

"Can you lift your head, yet?"

Wasn't sure but tried. The room spun, but nowhere near as bad as earlier. The spots disappeared, but a deep throbbed replaced them.

"Here's some juice and Aspirin. Magical Transportation always gives me a massive headache."

My hands shook, but I took the glass and tossed the pills back. "Thanks." The coolness felt heavenly.

"No problem. My name's Bryan. Nice to meet you."

I took his offered hand. "Nice to meet you. I'm assuming you are David's man."

"Ah, let me guess my . . ."

"Babe," David's voice held a bit of warning and made Bryan lift an eyebrow.

"Don't you Babe me. I won't censor myself in our home."

My lips stung from pressing them into one another when Bryan marched up to David and pressed his finger into the man's huge chest. More comical than Bryan barely reaching David's shoulder was the way David hung his head. That had me ducking. Never saw a bulky man cave to someone so much weaker. Or one who appeared weaker. Bryan's tone held all the power my father wielded each day of his life.

"I wasn't going to ask you to." David's little frown told me he'd been about to, or something similar. "I was going to request time to explain. Larry's agreed to keep our secret, but I would rather him not get a full crash course at once."

"Let me interpret your words." Bryan grinned, propping his hands on his hips. "You've yet to tell Theodor you brought the President of the United States' son home to protect him from the terrorist who are after him."

Damn. Bryan was amazing. He'd nailed the truth down in seconds. Wasn't sure about the Theodor part. Dead terrorist wasn't after me. Press was. Okay. Press . . . Type of terrorist. Dang people were as evil as suicide bombers.

"Oh . . . Going to love seeing Theodor's reaction. Please let me tag along." Bryan clapped his hands like a little boy. Entire interaction was comical and proved how right I'd been to ask David to protect me. Or would be once I figured out who Theodor was and why it mattered what David did.

"Can't. William coming today. Right?"

The sparkling eyes and huge smile lasted until Bryan gave David a doe caught in the headlights look. The look would have brought me to my knees. Not only was it cute and sexy, but man it made me warm from the pits of my stomach.

"Fine. Fine. I'll call Theodor. That will allow you to listen. Least you'll hear some of . . ."

A deep breath eased my burning lungs as the two lovers bickered back and forth as they walked down the hallway. Alone time. Perfect. Gave me time to recoup from the unusual method of travel. I could just imagine what my dad looked like. Doubtful the plane was usable again. Press agents would have a field day covering up whatever fit my father threw. Not to mention the spin they'd have to give the press about my delayed appearance. How would dad explain it? Not that it mattered. The press would write whatever they wanted. No matter what I said. I couldn't tell them the name of each men who stole me after killing my Secret Service guys. Some of those butchers would still print that I swore blue Martians took me to space.

A shrill pulled a jerk from me. David appeared in front of me so fast that I sprang up, sending the chair I sat in into a black cabinet.

"Where'd you get that?" He pointed at my pocket.

Good question. "No idea. Those guys didn't take mine. It was in the limo seat." I pulled the strange yellow flat smartphone from my pocket. So not my taste. Dad's photo filled the screen. "Guess dad put it in my pocket."

"Can't let you keep it." David held his hand out. "Your father has too many people who could trace you with one push of a button."

Had no problem giving it to him. Not like I wanted to talk to my dad.

The second David took the phone it vanished.

"Wow! How did . . . Where did . . ."

"Magic." David shrugged. "Your dad knows how to get in touch with me if he wishes to talk to you before you request to call him."

Had that phone disappeared? Did David say Magic? He had. Oh boy! No denying what I saw. Unbelievable. Explained leaving the airplane. Shit! What a secret dad kept from the world.

"Come on." David motioned towards a dark brown door on the left. "Go take a seat before you fall over. Bryan and I will be back in a few minutes. A call needs making."

One foot moved in front of the other, but I saw nothing. Not even what I sat on. Took several seconds before the features of the room came into focus. The room could hold at least a hundred people with the furniture and there was plenty of that.

I pretty much melted into the large gray fluffy sofa I sat on. On each side of me sat two matching recliners. Two other sofas surrounded the large bay window overlooking the front yard. Photos of David and Bryan consumed the walls. There were several pictures of five men in royal blue robes. A photo of Bryan and three other men hung to the left of an extra-large hand-painted photo of Bryan and David. On the right side stood Bryan and another man that had to be Bryan's father. The resemblance blew me away. On the mantle sat photos of what I assumed to be David and his family. Some including Bryan and some without. There were also photos of the five men in blue robes with Bryan in the middle of the group. It was clear whoever these people were, they were family. Something I'd longed for.

Oh boy! What had I gotten myself into? Had I made the right decision? I'd gone with a man dad sent to rescue me. A man who held something major over my dad. Let a stranger take me to an undisclosed location. Stupid. Right? Man! Had I landed myself into something worse than the terrorist? Nope. Magic was lots better than dead. Magic . . . Fuck!

Magical man unknown to the world. Magical man who could disappear equaled . . . Cult? Had to be. Right? What else could it be? Why had I not thought this through? Didn't have to. David rescued me. Saved me. Equaled safety. Healing. Avoidance. Time for myself. That's what mattered. Not being around a man who could transport people or make a phone disappear.

"I'll stay with him." Bryan patted my shoulder as he walked by and took a seat on the sofa circling the bay window.

How old was . . . Didn't need to ask. Bryan was near my age. David was bulky, like the photos of the Red Hooded Guy I'd seen. Yep. I'd landed myself in the home . . . Was this a Destroyer Hermitage? Nope. No others seemed to live here. Where was I? A Cult member's house? Did they have houses? Thought they lived together in those homes? Most of those who became marked ended up in them. Some ended up on the arms of . . . Yep. A Cult members home. Bryan was a Marked One.

"Thanks, Babe. He's still a bit shaky."

David's voice faded, but David's departure didn't send me into a tailspin like it had on the plane. Where'd the ease come from? David's interaction with Bryan. The fact that Bryan sounded compassionate while he bantered with David. Wasn't sure. My mind was a mess. Still not as bad as it had been on the plane. Or at the idea of facing the hoard of press. Whatever the case was, I felt safe with Bryan. Might apply to anyone David let in his home.

"Nice place."

"It's huge, but nice and safe." Bryan stared outside.

Rudeness? Nope. Didn't get that vibe from him. Nope. Bryan was giving me space to explore the new surroundings. Unnecessary. Usually the minute after I entered a room everyone pointed out who

I was and began interrogating me. Bryan hadn't. Felt good not to be bombarded with stupid questions about what it was like being the president's son. Worst was when people told me it must be a fairytale life to live in the White House.

Bryan's kindness gave me the strength to take up Bryan's unspoken offer. I stood and moved to the shelf of DVDs, running a finger over each movie. I'd gotten lost among the different movies and the vast range of genre. The chime of the doorbell sent my feet two feet off the floor.

"It's okay. Just William, my father. We've recently met, and he comes on his day off to visit. If it will make you uneasy, I can ask him to come by another day."

Kind, but not necessary. David and his partner did not need to rearrange their lives for me. I had to adjust to being around others. Come to terms with what happened to me. Best way to do so was to live. Not shut myself down, or bury myself inside one room. Nope. That wasn't who I was. I faced challenges and beat them.

"No. Please, visit with your father. If you will point me towards a room, I'll give you some privacy."

"Not necessary, but if you want some time to yourself the first room on the left is an extra room. I'm not sure which room David will want you to use while you're here, but feel free to escape into that one if you want to."

Bryan made his way into the hallway and discreetly whispered to his father, William. When they entered William offered his hand and introduced himself. The man had a caring tone and manner. Better than William's kindness was how he never made note of who I was or asked why I was there. Bryan and his father had not been in the hallway long enough to discuss me in any detail. Doubtful that Bryan would have done so without David's permission. William appeared to be as kind as his son.

"Nice to meet you." I shook William's hand. Once again, no unease arose. No sudden urge to scream for David. No urge to rush from the room. To hide. To curl into a tight ball. My mind knew I was safe. Just like I had known I would be. Oh, I was sure William could be deadly if the situation required.

William lifted the boxes of pizza. "There's plenty if you are hungry. Bryan loves double sausage and jalapeno. For some reason, but half is all meat."

Odd combination. Who was I to critique what Bryan ate? Not like I'd been given a choice in what I ate. Dad sure never encourage me to do anything than put on a prefect face for the press and to stay out of trouble. Wasn't quite sure how to respond to sharing a pizza so I did what I did best.

"I'm going . . ." I pointed towards the hallway.

"Not necessary, but if it's what you want then we understand." William sat the box on the coffee table and flipped the lid open. "I've not had the privilege to meet any of my son's friends."

"Hey." Bryan rolled his eyes. "What's Tommy, chop liver?"

"Your brother."

"Oh God!" Larry and Bryan whined at the same time.

"How lame can you get." David said from the doorway.

William busted into a round of belly laughter. Bryan joined in. David snorted a couple of times. Before I knew it, I was holding my stomach, doubling over. Next time I looked up, David was in the recliner with Bryan in his lap. William had taken over the matching love seat against the far wall. One of them had cut the television onto some college basketball game. Each held a slice of pizza. The short-lived fitting in moment had passed and I once again felt out of place.

"You best grab and stuff." Bryan took a huge bite, before swallowing. "These two will demolish their half in two seconds and you'll be stuck with gorging on my half."

"Hey . . . No talking with your mouth full." William grinned around his own bite of pizza.

David groaned, taking a second to wash down his food. "Don't pay these two barbarians any attention. I can account that William knowns better. Bryan does to, but I've not convinced him of the decorum of following social etiquette."

Wow! How much more down to earth could someone get? I'd never been in a room with such. Not even in college. People bent over to ensure they minded their Ps and Qs when I was in the room. Mom and dad would have fallen over dead if they saw someone offer me something as simple as pizza. The one time I'd snuck off with some friends I'd embarrassed myself when a friend offered me a French-fry. I'd never seen one and asked what it was.

They hadn't laughed at me, but I got some exasperated looks. Later my friend inquired as to how come I'd been clueless. If it'd been anyone other than Shawn, I would have played it off as a joke, but Shawn and I were more than friends. Most considered them more like brothers, until they'd told their family and friends about being gay. From then on, they'd been a couple. Still would be if Shawn . . .

"You okay?" David's question drew me away from depressing memories.

"Yes. Think the flying is catching up to me." Larry heard the lie.

William covered his face with his hands.

David tilted his head.

"These guys can sniff out a lie in less than a heartbeat." Bryan said.

"Uh . . ." Can someone shout true meaning hidden behind those words. "Don't try to evade someone whose fathers makes a living of avoiding saying the truth."

William's eyes darted towards David, whose face had gone blank and tight. Red flashed across David's eyes. Anger, but the expression didn't put me on edge. A sense of peace came across David's entire body when Bryan patted his arm and shot him a grin wider than any man could pull off. Soon as David relaxed, William did to.

What was going on? What had Bryan done to change the entire atmosphere? What had I said that caused it to change?

"Did I say something wrong?"

"Nope." Bryan rubbed David's chest. "Big guy here forgets people can get snippy sounding."

Larry hadn't meant to come across rude, or to upset David. I'd been kidding. What in the world? Didn't David know what a joke was? Even I did. My words ran across my mind. How could David had taken my words. Tone hadn't been sharp. Had it?

A glance at Bryan revealed that him and David was once again engrossed in the ballgame. William on the other hand stared at me like he could see through me. Might could have. David did magic. From what Bryan said William and David could decipher lies. Seeing the core of someone should be easy. Right?

"Bryan," William's fatherly tone reminded me of Shawn's father when the two of us had an argument over some small trivial thing and we missed the bigger picture.

"What?" Bryan kept on watching the game.

"You're being an ass." William's words had pulled a growl from David.

Bryan whipped his head around to him.

Oh boy. Not good. Or . . . Deep growl emanating from David was directed at William. Not me. What would it take for William to dig himself out of the hole he'd dug? Narrowed eyes. Glowing eyes. Tight lips. Anger. Protector. That's it. David was in protect mode that screamed, I'm death and will deliver. Would and could if needed. He'd done it to save me. Bet David would rip someone in half in a flash for Bryan.

"Just why is my Keeper being an ass?" David rumbled instead of talking.

"Actually," William sat a bit straighter, but lost the harshness and took on a tentative, yet strong tone. "I think it was you who missed the most, Commander." Commander? What in the world? "I think Bryan might have picked up on it and assumed you snatched it from his mind."

Laughter stuck in my throat, but I refused to clear it. William was treading carefully. Didn't need to make things worse.

"Just what did I miss?" David rubbed Bryan's legs and glanced towards Bryan.

"Larry was joking with Bryan." William said.

David's jaw dropped opened and Bryan leaned in, licking his lower lip before kissing David. I was sure Bryan meant it to be a peck, but David cupped his head and took the kiss to what looked like to be a toe-curling one. William grunted and muttered something about a father being in the room.

"They always like this?" I hoped to give William a reprieve from watching his son be ravished.

"Each time I'm around." William made it sound like a hardship, but the bright smile contradicted himself.

"What can I say . . . It's hard to keep my hands off my Keeper." David pinched Bryan's ass, enticing a little squeak from Bryan.

"Keeper?" I held my hand up. "Never mind. Where can I sleep and how will I get some of my clothes?"

"Theodor is taking care of that. He'll have them by tomorrow. He's going to touch base with your dad tonight." David sighed. "My well-meaning cousin swears he'll have to play patcher-up since I'm such a caveman."

"Caveman?" Dad wouldn't call David's action anything like that. More like disrespectful.

"Theodor thinks I was rude to transport you like I did."

"Was neat. After I got over the aftereffects." I chuckled when an image of dad standing there gaping at an empty spot. "Second thought . . . My dad might be a bit miffed. I won't let him cause you any trouble. Promise."

"As if he could." David shrugged and patted Bryan's leg. "Will you show him to the room you mentioned earlier?"

"Come on. I'll make sure you've got everything you need until your stuff arrives." Bryan snatched his drink off the coffee table and motioned down the hallway. "It's going to be nice to have someone other than Tommy to talk to."

Wasn't sure who Tommy was. Doubted Bryan was lacking for anyone to talk to, but once again there was an air of an underlying message.

Chapter 3

Anthony

I tugged the cover over my head as the blaring roared to life again. Didn't cease the God-awful noise. Would pulling my pillow over my face help? Worth a try. If only it had worked to eradicate the third, or was if fourth, didn't matter. The unwanted disturbance continued.

I slapped the nightstand until I felt the phone vibrate under my hand. "Shit." I knew that ring tone. If it had been any other caller . . .

"Hey, sexy."

I rubbed my eyes, inwardly wishing Kevin had waited a couple more hours. Theodor's emergency meeting had been excruciating. David's rash action brought up loads of topics, all of which Theodor was dead set on hashing out before deciding what to do about David's promise to protect the President's son and magically zapping them off the plane in front of the President. Most of their time was spent rehashing how wrong the former Royal Leaders had been. Nothing they could change. What had been done had been done. All they could do was move forward. Make better decisions. David's rash actions hadn't fallen into that category. All agreed on that. Or they had until . . . The new situation gave us an advantage. We could use it to apply more pressure onto the President. Get him to reconsider some of the restriction placed on the Bombaridans and the Destroyer's Hermitages.

"Sorry if I woke you."

My eyes flew open. "What's wrong?"

"You know me so well."

Damn. I shoved my free hand under my legs, refusing to bite my cuticles. "I do. When you avoid answering and become polite you've got news I'm not going to be happy about."

"What you been up to?"

Ugh! Not how I wanted my day to start, but . . . Nothing to do about it. I scooted up so my back was against the headboard. Couldn't push Kevin into telling me what was up. One option, go with the flow until he was ready to open up.

"Long ass meeting."

"Why working so late when you are flying out in four hours?"

"Not flying. Going to pop over. Didn't you get my text?"

"Right. Forgot. Why working beforehand?"

"No choice. Last minute issue came up. Don't worry. It's taken care of. I've got the next five days free."

"Unless another emergency comes up."

Couldn't dispute that. David had tried to take his honeymoon a few days ago and been interrupted. Royal Leaders never had days off. Completely. Fact indisputable. Irked me. Irked David. Irked all the Royal Leaders, but it was just one downfall of having royal blood. Being a leader. Being a stronger Bombardian. As much as I hated it, I enjoyed some of the benefits it gave me as well. Or . . . I hoped I would. Still all new to me.

The lite tapping I'd been hearing through the phone was growing louder, meaning my lover was getting aggravated. Wouldn't be much longer before he spilled the reason behind his early call.

"Don't matter." My lack of knowledge of my skillset had allowed me to gain a promise from the other four Royal Leaders. Even David agreed. "Been promised uninterrupted time so I can help you arrange your move to my place."

Taken me a week and half to convince Kevin to move in with me. Hadn't expected it to be so hard. We'd been lovers for five years and I'd been planning on moving in with him before the attack on the Royal Leaders took two Royal Leader's lives, throwing me into the new phase of my life. Royal Leader. Not like I had much choice. I was the next in line. It was my place to take over for one of the two fallen Royal Leaders. Kevin knew this. He was a Bombardian. Knew the importance of a Royal Leader. Crap. What if Kevin changed his mind? Nope. What if he . . . No way. He could have. Had he? What would happen if Kevin had ran across his Keeper or Protector. Fuck . . . That would . . .

"Uh . . . Sexy . . . What is it you need to tell me? My mind conjured up a bad image." Understatement and half. My heart resembled a blender on the fastest speed possible.

"You won't like it."

"Oh my . . . You found . . . Keeper? Protector?"

"No!" Dang. I jerked the phone from my ear. "Why would you think that? You wouldn't hold that against me. Would you?"

"Lord no. Would hurt to know I could never hold you again."

Lame, but Kevin was the person I could be my true self around. He never expected me to be a solid rock no matter what was going on. Others did, after all I was a Royal Leader. Before I took on the title, I held royal blood, which made my family place me as head of the family. Hard roll to fill. One I never wanted. One I despised. Did what people expected.

"I'm leaving for France tomorrow."

Huh? Where had the air gone? I shook my head.

"You there?"

Why was my phone laying on my bed? I was holding it when . . .

"Hey? You okay? Anthony, answer me."

I'd heard wrong. That was it. I picked up the phone, shaking my head harder, hoping to squash the fuzziness from my mind. "I'm here. Phone slipped. What did you say?"

"Anthony, you heard me. The phone wouldn't have landed in your lap if you hadn't."

This wasn't happening. Couldn't be. Breath in. One. Breath out. Two. Breath in. Three. Breath out. Four. Okay. Options. What where they? Always had some. Something could be done. All I needed was the basic facts.

Time frame? One day. Not long, but some was better than none. Why? Not sure.

"Why?"

"Mr. Kimbler offered me the CFO position."

When had Kevin applied for the job in France? Why had he not told me? Chill out, Anthony. Stick to the basis.

"You have to leave tomorrow?"

"Yes. I put it off for a week."

"What?" He knew a week ago. "You knew a week ago?"

"You couldn't get away." Shit. Kevin's animosity earlier made more sense. "I understand how important your job is."

"A week ago?"

"Don't go getting all kinds of mad. What would you have done if I told you a week ago?"

Zapped my royal ass to you and fucked your brains until you refused to go that far away. Found someone in the United States to give you such a grand job. Yeah right, Anthony. You would not have done any of the such. Would have entered my mind, but Kevin would have stomped me into the ground for trying to run his life. All I could have done was . . .

"I could've spent the last week hold up in your bed, showing you how much you mean to me."

"It would have made things harder. Plus, I had lots of shit to straighten out."

Course he did. Packing to leave for another country . . . "How long will it be before you can come for a visit?" Small bump in the road. One they'd faced when I'd been promoted to the Royal Leaders seat. Not that different. Airplanes could bring Kevin back to the states. Or Kevin could zap himself in for a visit. Just like we'd planned to do before Kevin agreed to move in with me. No biggie. Right?

Quietness consumed the phone. Silent Kevin was worse than polite Kevin. Politeness meant an issue we could work through. Most of the time. Silent Kevin equaled decision made. Without me and Kevin didn't care if I liked it or not. Last time my lover did such had been when he'd gotten tired of being a hidden lover. Resulted in Kevin moving to California out of defiance. Kevin pretty much left my ass, but gave me a way to gain him back. Told me if I wanted a relationship that I'd have to come to him. That he wasn't going to continue to hide who he was just so my family didn't think I was gay.

"I think . . ." Kevin's *I thinks* meant mind made up. "It would be best if we parted ways. Long distance wasn't in the cards for me when I moved out west. The purpose had been to live an open life. You're now a Royal Leader, so we are once again back to me being a closest lover."

"We aren't. I told you this." Multiple times. "You witness the Pledging Ceremony between David and Bryan." Best news I ever received was when I found out that the law forbidding Royal Leaders from having Keepers was abolished. "We can live a wonderful life."

Long breathy sigh told me all I needed to know. My lover's mind was made up. Our relationship was over. No matter what I wanted or said. I'd always feared being a Royal Leader would destroy my life. Just not like that.

"I'm sorry. You will always have a bit of my heart, but I've got to live my life. If I don't . . . I might . . . Never have a chance at finding my Keeper or Protector."

Damn those two words. Keepers and Protectors might be sacred people among Bombardians, but at that moment I never wanted to meet mine. Protector or Keepers were to calm the wolf side and most of the time the Bombardian fell head over hill for the one who did, but my heart belonged to Kevin. A fact I doubted even a Keeper or Protector could change. Many among the Bombardian had their calmer as well as lovers. I'd always figured Kevin and I would fall into that category. Looked like Kevin had other plans. Kevin left me out of the decision that affected my life in the most primal way.

"You can't. Won't. Your family would have a shit fit. Not to mention no sane royal blood Bombardian would willingly give up their spot. It's an honor."

Felt like a death sentence. Had since the moment I realized I preferred men. My family condemned same sex partners. A lesson I'd been taught since I started school.

"Every Bombardian in the United States needs the correct Royal Leaders in place. It keeps our world from crumbling."

What about my world? It's tumbled and been burnt into a huge pile of nothingness. No sense in saying so. Kevin's words were true. I could never be happy giving up my Royal Leader position, even if I disliked it. It was in my blood, whether I liked it or not. It was as thick as my love for Kevin. Giving up the Royal Leader seat meant I might as well go ahead and move into the confinement house and live among the one whose lost their Keeper or Protector. Those stuck in half wolf, half human form. I'd become as wild and uncontrollable as the Mélange. I might not be stuck in half wolf, half human form, but I would require the stability that came from living in the confinement houses.

"Anthony, just wish me luck. Keep yourself safe and live your life."

Rough spoken words told the story of the amount of pain lacing those words. Kevin believed he was doing what was best. Some sense, he might be, but didn't mean his heart wasn't breaking right alongside mine.

"Can you do this for me?"

No. How can he ask such? "I will." Liar.

"Promise me you won't hide yourself away from everything, but necessity."

Can't. You know I will. You are the only one who knows the true me. "I won't." Liar.

"Swear it, by your oath as my Royal Leader."

"What!" Why in the world would Kevin put me in such a spot. I couldn't.

"If you don't . . . You will shut yourself in your bedroom, leaving only for work related issues. You will forget to eat. I know you. Don't tell me you won't."

"I can't swear it to you." If I did, I'd have to uphold it and I wouldn't be able to.

"Then I'll have to call Commander Theodor and have him check in on you every day."

"That's low." More than low. If Theodor and Caleb found out Kevin left my ass, they'd never let me leave their sides. My cousins were like vultures when one of the others were upset, or unhappy. I'd heard the stories of how Caleb and Theodor kept track of David until Bryan accepted him completely. From the way Bryan and David described it, it was worse than parents.

"Swear or I'll call Commander Theodor and Commander David." No breakage in Kevin's voice. He'd live up to his words. "What will he say after the little fit you had when you met Bryan?"

"You are cruel." Should have expected Kevin to have all his ducks in a row. How could I be pissed at him when all Kevin wanted was to ensure I remained healthy and happy. "Fine. Fine. You win." I exhaled and rushed through the oath. "I Commander Anthony Lincoln swear by my royal blood that I will continue to live my life to the fullest without Kevin at my side."

"Thank you, my love."

Kissing sounds filled the line for a second then silence shattered my heart into a million and one pieces. Not even my cousins would be able to piece it back together. Laying the phone down felt like an end. Couldn't do it. Nope. Doing so signaled the end of my relationship with the man who owned my heart. I scooted down on the bed and rolled onto my side, laying my head over the phone as the tears fell.

What was I going to do?

Chapter 4

Larry

Watching David pace the living room and rub his chin had become a habit of mine. David growled with each step he took. When he wasn't walking the living room, he was throwing things. It'd been three straight day and nights. Not that I could blame David. Bryan hadn't kept anything down, not even water.

What I wouldn't give for someone to care that much about me. Someone so devoted to me. The first night Bryan woke up throwing up David wrapped him in a blanket and fretted over him. Placed Bryan in bed and told him not to get up for anything, not even to go to the bathroom. Kind of overboard on that, but David had been serious. Each time Bryan got sick David held the trashcan for him and then washed his face and cleaned up after him. The man did everything I would have done, except . . . After the third day of keeping nothing down I would have loaded him into the car and rushed him to the hospital, demanding treatment. Might have been an overboard reaction on my part since Bryan had regained his appetite. Then again . . . Might not have been since soon as Bryan ate, he was tossing his cookies again.

A week had passed, Bryan was no better. David swore no doctor could help Bryan. Stupid. He could at least give him something to calm his stomach. A doctor would have been able to pinpoint what was making Bryan so sick. I offered to call in a famous doctor, but David snarled. I was sure if Bryan hadn't grabbed for the trashcan that David would have bitten my head off. Literally. Could have . . . Was sure David's teeth had changed into sharp canine like teeth. Was not the only unusual things I'd saw since arriving, which told me not to shove what I saw aside. David and Bryan had a bad habit of sealing their lips when I walked into the room. I didn't take it personally.

Knew David had secrets that I wasn't privy to, but Bryan and I had become friends. Friends shared. Shawn and I always did.

Shit. Bryan wasn't Shawn. Our friendship wasn't old enough for sharing. Shit. Shit. Still, didn't mean David should ignore me about taking Bryan to a doctor.

"Hey," Bryan waved David away when he began moving towards him. "I can walk." Not well, but Bryan was up and moving and had begun fussing at David for hovering, who was wisely giving him space. Not much, but enough to calm Bryan's ire "One worry wort is enough."

"Easier said than done." I huffed and glanced at David as he resumed his pacing. "Why won't he call a doctor?"

"They can't help."

"Why the fuck not!"

"Just can't. Trust me. David will figure out what is wrong with me. The best people he can get on it is on top of it. Believe me."

Ugh! What was wrong with Bryan? Why was Bryan so adamant about the best people working on it? No one had looked at him. I had to figure out . . . What had I seen over the years that might relate to . . . Constant throwing up. Not keeping food down. Smells making . . .

"I swear to God." My hand flew up, knocking my hair from my eyes. "You remind me of Shawn's mom when she was pregnant."

David sudden stop and wide eyes had me cringing back into the sofa. For the first time since David rescued me, fear zoomed through me.

"David, honey," Bryan rushed to his side, "what is . . ." Bryan's words faded as he heaved.

I ran for the thrash can. David scooped Bryan into his arms and rushed down the hallway. All of our actions were null. Bryan had nothing in his stomach to lose. He gagged and heaved for ten minutes, while David murmured one apology after another and mixed in an explanation. By the time David grew quiet Bryan glared up at David and I was unsure if I heard him correctly. One thing was clear, the secret my dad kept was bigger than I ever dreamed possible.

"I'm tired." Bryan slumped against David, who had been holding him up.

"Come on. Let's get you sat down. I've got some calls to make." David stood, taking Bryan back to the living room.

"Think you need to repeat yourself a bit before you make calls." Bryan laid his hand over his half-closed eyes as David laid him on the sofa.

"Just read my mind, babe." David went to leave the room, but Bryan's words halted him and had me silently blessing the man.

"Not for me. I'm sure Larry caught part of what you said. I'm sure he's baffled. I would be if I heard you."

"Bryan . . ." David groaned. "I can't."

"You can. You brought him here. Had him promise to never repeat what he heard. You trusted him, or you would not have brought him here."

No raised voice, but I heard the *or else* in Bryan's voice. David must have too, because the tension in his back faded. The small grin changed to relief as he flopped onto the floor beside Bryan. I wasn't sure what to do. Part of me wanted to tell David he didn't own me an explanation. And he didn't. Yet . . . The curious side of me wanted to know what secret dad and the rest of the government had buried.

"Take a seat. This won't be short."

"Make it short as possible. Bryan need to keep food, or liquids down."

David leaned his head on the arm of the sofa and Bryan weaved his hand through his partner's hair. The creases on Bryan's face didn't mesh with the little grin he sported.

"Listen," Larry sat in the recliner, letting it ease some of his own tension as he glanced between David and Bryan. "I want a full explanation, more for curiosity than needing one, but what I want more is Bryan well. If you know what is causing the sickness, then find a solution and then explain if you still want to."

"Might not be an easy solution. Some people need tracking down. I'm in new territory. Even for me." David's shoulder tightened so much his shirt wrinkled. "I'll let Bryan fill you in on what we are most likely looking at while I make some calls. Then . . . I'll answer any lingering questions to the best of my ability. Remember your promise. What you are going to hear is big. I need it to remain a secret for everyone's sake. Not to mention Bryan's."

Oh boy. What in the world? Did I want to hear it? Did. Enlightenment into why Bryan was so sick would ease my mind. I hoped.

"What do you mean tracking down?" Bryan rubbed his throat. "I love you, David, but I can't stand upchucking anymore."

If what I heard was true . . . There might be ways to help . . . I knew all kind of home remedies. A hobby of mine was to learn new ones each week. Something I picked up from Shawn's mother. She swore that home grown medicine was the answer to everything. She used quite a few when she was pregnant. No way . . . Lord . . . What was I thinking? David had muttered it, but . . . How was it . . . Didn't matter. If the things Shawn's mother done helped Bryan that what mattered. Think Larry. What had she . . . Ginger-ale. Saltines.

Would they help Bryan? Doubtful. Bryan couldn't be expecting. Still . . . Worth a shot.

"Why don't you try some ginger-ale or ginger tea?"

Bryan frowned at the mention of either, but David nodded and rushed from the room. Moments later he came back sporting two glasses of fizzling ginger-ale. David held the glass as Bryan took small sips of the drink. Ice clanked as Bryan sat back, sighing.

"That's feels good on my throat."

"How's your stomach feel?" David ran his finger over Bryan's cheek as he took a sip from the other glass. "I'm so sorry, babe."

I felt like an intruder, but it warmed me to see someone so in love that it oozed from them. What I always wanted. Longed for. Hoped for. Dreamed for. One day I would have it. I hoped.

"Do you really think . . ." Putting words to my thoughts seemed like bringing it to life. "Why would you think . . ." Okay the word was not going to exit my mouth. I could not put the thought into the universe.

"I'll let Bryan tell you after he settles down." David kissed Bryan's forehead. "Is it working?"

"It's staying down longer than the water." Bryan's grin shined from his eyes. "What made you think of that?"

"Shawn's mother stayed sick when she was expecting his little sister." Many days Shawn and I cleaned house and did the dishes for her. The woman swore she'd been as sick with Shawn as she was then. I had just wondered why she seemed thrilled about puking her guts up. Sure hadn't liked her being sick.

"I've got to make the calls."

Intruder. Leave the room. Those thoughts occurred to me, but I remained still and watched as David wrapped his much larger hand around Bryan's.

"Keep trying to sip it. If you need anything think of me and I'll come."

"Go. I'm sure Larry won't mind helping me if I need it."

Bryan was right. I would do anything if it helped eased Bryan. I hated seeing him so sick. It'd been a long time since I'd felt a kinship with another. Sure, didn't want to lose him, because David failed to tend to him.

"Find out what you can and get some answers for us. Then we'll discuss why you failed to clue me in."

David's frown had me sucking my lower lip between my teeth, but his words had me biting it until warm metallic taste consumed my mouth.

"Can we skip that part?"

"Not hardly, mister."

A quiet chuckle slipped from me when Bryan smiled up at David.

"Didn't think so. Worth a shot, babe."

"Long shots never pay off." I winked at Bryan. "Learned that a long time ago."

"Me to." David nodded and left the room.

"Is that really helping, or did you say it was to appease your man?"

"It's helping." Bryan took another small sip. "It has a taste to me. None of the other stuff has. My stomach isn't rebelling it the moment it reaches it. That's good."

Sure was. "Want to try some crackers?"

"Don't think so."

"Are you sure?"

"Yes." Bryan rubbed the toe of his sock over the hardwood floor. "Don't worry so hard over me."

"Why not?"

"David won't let anything hurt me. Plus, what this is . . . Let's just say there might not be much anyone can do."

"Is he . . ." Serious? "Does he really . . ." Think you are pregnant. "Do you really . . ." Would hearing it from Bryan's mouth make it more realistic?

"You won't believe me." Bryan shot me a small grin and gripped the small pillow beside him. "I'm not sure if I believe it and I was able to hear David. Even heard the conversation he had with his family."

What family? No one had been there but them. If Bryan knew of a conversation, why hadn't he thought about it.

"I'm not following."

"Promise to keep what I tell you to yourself. No matter what is done to you?" Bryan's look of death would have zipped a zombies' mouth shut.

I held up two fingers. "Promise on Shawn's grave." Okay. I'd gone a bit farther than I meant, but I would never tell something a friend told me. No matter what was done to me.

"Simple promise would've done." Bryan nodded. "I know how much you cared about him." He tossed his pillow towards me. "You know David has . . . Um . . . Special skills."

Boy did I. Those skills saved my life.

"Those skills somehow guarantee he will reproduce."

Damn it. I gripped my forehead, hoping to hold it still when it wasn't moving. I'd heard right. No way. Couldn't be. Not possible. Men could not . . . Wrong. Wasn't it? No stranger than David zapping me from a plane. Taking out twelve terrorist. The fang like teeth I'd seen. There'd been . . . Irregularities heard and seen. None was logical. Rational. All had happened. I'd played them off, just like I'd done David's initial mention of Bryan being pregnant, but . . .

"Your saying . . . David really thinks . . . Pregnant?" Explained why David flipped when I mentioned Bryan acting like Shawn's mother.

"Apparently. He didn't know such was possible until our Pledging Ceremony."

"What? Huh?" I rubbed my temple. "I'm not following. Course he didn't know it was possible for a man to get another man pregnant." Did I say that? I had.

"Such a loaded statement." Bryan reached for the trashcan and heaved.

I rushed around the coffee table and rubbed Bryan's back, hoping to ease him in some small manner.

"Want to try some more ginger-ale?"

"Least the cold soothes my aching throat."

A grunt had us looking at the doorway. David stood with his hands tucked in his pockets, rocking back and forth.

"Spill." I ordered then winced when David's eyes shifted to one huge eye instead of two. "Sorry. Please enlighten us."

Bryan's little half huff, half snort made me shake my head as David gave Bryan the softest grin I'd seen them share. Their love filled eyes put a full-on ache in my stomach but warmed me at the same time. One day I hoped to have the same with someone.

"Babe," David moved to Bryan's side, resting his hand on the back of his neck. "Theodor trying to locate them. They left without giving us contact information."

"Why did you let that happen?"

David flinched when Bryan pinched his arm. "I was more interested in getting down the aisle." David's bright-eyed wink was followed up by a kiss to Bryan's cheek. "Not sure what the others were thinking. You can give them all the hell you want when they arrive. Per Theodor's orders. He's not pleased about being in the dark about something concerning our entire species. Not to mention when there's a chance of all four of them running into their own Keeper."

Species? Keeper? What in the world?

"I don't want to be a test subject. Find your damn uncle." Bryan jumped up and stormed down the hallway, slamming the door.

David fell onto the sofa and slammed his head into the back, sending a crack throughout the room, but it did not appear to faze him, so I kept quiet and watched as his eyes fluttered shut and lines formed across his brow. I didn't know what to say to him. It appeared that David was indeed on new ground.

"You are clueless, aren't you?" David's nod made my stomach churn. "Doctors . . . I mean what I know as Doctors can't help him. Can they?" Another nod. "What can I do to help him? You?"

"I'm not sure. Don't even know what to expect. I'm not sure if he is. If he is . . . I'm not sure if it would be like a Protector's or not."

I jerked when the coffee table slid an inch close to me.

"I'm going . . . I don't know what . . ."

"David," I leaned across and laid my hand on his knee, "go. Hold Bryan. Both of you need some rest. You can think clearer when rested." Wasn't sure if the picture would be clearer with sleep, couldn't be worse. "When you wake up, I'll have some food for you both. Least I can do."

Chapter 5

Anthony

What in the . . . My feet jarred as I landed on the cool floor. Who had the balls to enter my home? How did they get past the Combatants?

"You best be dressed."

Theodor? Splintering wood could be heard as the door flew into the wall.

"What the hell you doing barging into my bedroom?" I crossed my arms, shivering a bit as my nice and warm arms landed against my cool bare chest.

"Not your bedroom." Theodor mocked my stance.

"Of course . . ." Blue wallpaper? Wrong. Where? Damn it. "I did it again."

"Yep." Theodor exhale rattled my eardrums. "My General is getting pissed at having his night interrupted every time you transport yourself here."

"Sorry." What else could I say. Had no clue why I was zapping into Theodor's house.

"What was it this time?"

Theodor sat down in a designer chair in the corner of one of his six guest bedrooms. Never understood why Theodor had such antique furniture. I mean there were always arguments taking place between him, Caleb, and David. Franklin even got into it sometimes. One or more time these arguments came to blows. Even more confusing was that every bedroom I'd seen was small. My shoulders barely fit into the doorway. Me and Theodor in the same room equaled a crowd and gave little room to breathe. And why did Theodor need such a huge house. I mean he lived alone. Had no Keeper or Protector. I had a couple of big homes, but the one I used only had two huge bedrooms. One living room and a conference room.

"Why do you have such a big house?" I flopped onto the bed, crossing my legs. "It's just you."

"To make my irrational, magical-poofing cousin ask questions instead of answering me." Theodor winked.

Nice. Just what I needed. Not sure I would have behaved that way if Theodor was the one popping in and out of my home. First time I might have understood, but two months was beyond bonkers. I mean Royal Leaders had more control than that. Or should have. Sort of why I never wanted to take my place among the Royal Leaders. I lacked the typical knowledge of most royal blood carriers. If Michael and Reginald hadn't been killed in the explosion me and Franklin would still be living a normal life. Franklin didn't care that he'd been called to assist the other three Royal Leader in ruling over the Bombardians. Me on the other hand . . . Didn't matter. It was what it was. I'd been called up in time to get revenge and take out a major enemy. Also witnessed something I never thought would occur. A Royal Leader's Pledging Ceremony to a Keeper. Before David found his Bryan, a male that kept his beast side under control, a Royal Leader had to ensure his blood line continued by having a child, which men could not do. Meant I would have had to bed a woman. Not something I could have done. Least we known that Royal Leaders indeed can find a Keeper, meaning my reason for despising being a Royal Leader no longer was a true problem. Plus, we recently found out that a Royal Leader's Keeper could produce a child. Little was known about this new issue, because the former Royal Leaders, who told us this, failed to leave contact information. We'd been stupid and not thought about asking them either. We'd all been too caught up in David's Pledging Ceremony.

"What happened to make you pay me a middle of the night visit?"

Oh boy. Might have rolled my eyes if it would have done me any good, but it wouldn't. Theodor wanted an answer and all I could tell him was that it was my own stupidity. "Not sure. Went to bed. Woke up when you threw the door open."

The tilt of Theodor's head made it clear he wasn't buying my answer. Not to mention that small action always led to me relaying more than I wanted to.

"You don't recall my Combatants storming the room, or me opening the door like a calm person?"

Had they? Oh boy. I'm losing my mind.

"Don't get pissy with me but answer me truthfully."

"What?" Failed at not sounding pissy, but I knew whatever question he was going to ask would tick me off. If it wouldn't he wouldn't have told me not to get pissy.

"Would this Kevin guy do a spell to ensure your own safety?"

"What the fuck!" I lunged only to be stopped by a wall of fire. "Stop it. You'll burn us up."

"No, I won't." Theodor pointed to the floor. "It's not even touching the floor. I wouldn't do something that would endanger me, or anyone else. Plus, you could snap your fingers and put it out with a spray of water."

Could I? God, I'm a piss poor Royal Leader. If only . . . I should have studied all those books that each royal blood carrier is given.

"Shit." Theodor ran a hand through his hair. "Time for a truth session."

"Why?" No one else needed to know how pathetic I was. Right. The winy tone I used was really going to keep Theodor from thinking such. The intense glare coming my way told me I was not getting out of truth time. Double shit. "Fine. Ask away."

"Were you born knowing about our world?"

No toying around from Theodor. He went straight to the gut of things. "Yes."

"Were you raised by your birth family?"

Ah . . . The question I feared. "No." My upper teeth scraped across the bottom ones to keep me from giving my normal response of *shove your question up the ass.*

"Per our laws you had to be someway related to Michael's family, or they couldn't have accepted you as a child of their royal blood family line."

A law I hated. Zane Lincoln, my father, had been a hound dog and slept with anyone who spread their legs. He'd had six children before he ran into his Protector. He knew about every one of them, but lacked interest in them, which in the end resulted in him turning into a Mélange when his Protector rejected him. One drawback for all Bombardians was if they didn't care about their children then the half human, half wolf state overtook them if they lost the one who calmed their second side. Sucked for Zane and all his children. Me more than my two younger brothers, who the royal blood skipped. My three half-sisters were clueless about their brother's other side since women did not carry the Bombardian gene. Because of that his three sisters were placed into the human foster care system. My two brothers were placed with a Bombardian family that bore no royal blood. I'd been the special one. The one that Zane's brother took in and treated like one of his own sons.

"My father was Zane."

There it was. The sour expression that said it all. Theodor knew about Zane.

"I'm sure your Uncle ensured you had the required material about being a royal blood gene carrier." Theodor sighed. "Why don't you know how to use your affinity?"

Theodor was right. My Uncle gave me all the material. Hadn't meant much to me. I'd not gave it a second glance. Even thinking about being a Royal Leader sickened me. Far as I cared that special blood could be stripped from me and given to someone else.

"Anthony."

"Because I was fucked up. Despised what I was from the day I was old enough to understand it. Uncle knew Michael outranked me, so he didn't push me. His son was more important. A fact I was perfectly fine with."

Damn. Hadn't meant to go off at the mouth. Okay, entire subject was touchy for me. Most nights as a child I prayed that one of my brothers had really been given more royal blood than me and it was overlooked to start with, but second blood test revealed the truth. Knew back then that wasn't possible, but . . . I was a child.

"I get it." Theodor sat back. "Michael went through a rebellious stage. We each do. Being a royal blood carrier isn't all it's cracked up to be, especially if you were not pleased with your life. Why not reject the position when it was offered to you." Theodor waved off his question. "Sorry. Stupid question. Listen . . . If you don't want the position . . . tell us. We'll find another."

If only it was that easy. I might hate the spot I was in, but I didn't want . . . Made no sense to me, so it would not make any sense to Theodor.

"I want it. I have nothing else. I think that might be why I keep popping over."

Theodor lifted his eye.

"I've been trying to find a proper way to request some assistance in understanding things. I re-read the books, but I was never a bookworm. The words . . . Twist on me." Uncle told me it was due to my mother being an improper human for his brother.

"That we can help with" Theodor leaned forward, propping his elbows on his knees. "You'll have to start staying at your house or popping into someone else's. I had company last night. Wasn't easy to explain how you got into my house, or why I had guards rushing in with weapons."

Oh boy. "Shit. I'm sorry."

"Forget it. I did some mojo on him and wiped his mind. He wasn't a good lay."

A deep chuckle slipped from me as I stood. "Guess I'll zap myself home and dress."

"Do." Theodor slapped his leg. "Then go to David's. He's got a lead he needs to check out."

"Solid or weak?"

"Solid. Hopeful. I'm not sure if David and Bryan can stand much more of the sickness. Bryan's about at his breaking point from what I've seen."

Hated that for Bryan and David. They were good people. "I'll go bother him for awhile."

"David only. No pissing off Bryan. He pulled on David's power yesterday and made a tree grow in the middle of the living room."

"Damn." I lifted my hand to weave the pattern I used to zap me from one spot to the next but paused. "Do you think Kevin could have spelled me?" Hated thinking such, but . . .

Theodor shrugged. "Don't know him well enough. If he did . . . Doesn't seem like one hell bent on revenge."

"He doesn't believe in revenge." Had been one feature that drew me to him. Kevin grew up with an abusive alcoholic mother until the day his Bombardian mark was spotted and his father's family rescued him from that life. They were way better, but his birth mother's abuse done him in by the age of twelve.

"What does he believe in?"

"He believes in peace and . . ." Shit. Kevin. Why in the world . . . So kindhearted even as his own heart broke.

"What is it?"

"He spelled me. Not for revenge."

Theodor's forehead formed funky twisted V. Weird but made him look less burly.

"He did so to protect me from my own downward spiral."

"Sounds like a good man. Now you know what is causing you to poof in. Can you quit it? Or counter spell it?"

"Yep. Might take me a day or two, but I'll get it fixed. Promise." Finding a way might take more than a day or two.

"For now, go help David and Bryan." Theodor gave his typical dismissive wave before he snapped his fingers and the bed was made up. "Start working on your natural born talent as well."

* * *

Theodor's question worked its way under my skin. My reasoning for avoiding my natural born skills were deeper than I'd admitted. Stupid was what it had been. I'd gained no revenge. Dismissing my true skills over my father's selfish actions . . . I fell into self-loathing deeper than any human's hell.

I slapped the steering wheel as I pulled onto the hidden road leading to David's house. Ridiculous thinking.

I was starting my second round of self-berating when a red-haired guy materialized in front of my car.

"Stupid Combatant." I rolled the window down.

The guy came up to it. "Commander Anthony, I was not alerted to your arrival. I'll have to call General Thompson."

"How long you worked for David?" I knew the answer would be less than a month. Looked like I'd have to have a talk with David about his Combatants playing childish games like mine had. A few days after I'd taken my position three Combatants resigned and some of the old ones thought it wise to play a welcoming prank on the new ones.

"Two weeks, Commander Anthony."

"Word of advice, Combatants behave just like college frat boys." I pressed my lips together when the guy stood up and looked behind him at a bush where I assumed his partner was. "Who's stationed at the gate with you?"

Travis, David's fourth ranked Combatant, stepped from behind the bush. "Sorry, Commander Anthony. Please forgive my actions. It will not happen again."

It would, but I wasted my breath anyway. "Make sure it doesn't. I will be reporting this. Would you rather I went to General Thompson or David?"

Travis took a small step back and dropped his head. "Commander Anthony, please do not bother David with something so trivial. There's way too much on his plate at the moment."

"Good choice." I pushed the small silver button, shutting Travis and the other Combatant away.

Moments later I pulled up beside the large black military style Hummer that each Royal Leader had access to. Most Combatants called it BASS for Bad Ass Shit-kicker Security. Fitting name. From what I'd been told the only thing that ever took the huge ass machine down was the attack on Bryan right before the Ghoulians set off the bomb at Theodor's house.

"Bout time you arrived."

Foul mood one oh one. "Hi." I shut the car door. "Theodor said you had a lead and needed some help."

"Yes. Needed to leave an hour ago. What took you so damn long."

I took in a deep breath. Travis had been right. Too much on David's mind. No wonder he chose General Thompson over David. Such a joke would not have gone over well with David in his state of mind. That was all that kept me from getting testy back.

"Had some issues to take care of." The small hitch in my voice rang loud to my ear, but David didn't seem to notice. Good thing. It had been harder to make the call than I expected. Kevin admitted to casting a spell to ease the separation. He hadn't expected it to disrupt my sleep. It'd been meant to make me feel loved and wanted whenever I experienced loneliness. Apparently, I became that way during the night. Made sense. Best time I had with Kevin had been in our bed when we fell asleep after exhausting, amazing rounds of lovemaking. I had no idea why the spell transported me to Theodor's. I'd have to know the exact words Kevin used and . . . Kevin refused to give them. Odd. Unusual. Kevin never hid anything before.

"Huh, more important than . . ." David tugged the end of his hair, groaning. "Sorry. I'm a bit stressed and acting like a bear who lost his shit."

How did bear and shit fit into the very rational frustration David was suffering? Not much I could do, but help David find his Uncle. "Don't worry. Tell me what you need me to do."

"You may not like it." David darted his eyes towards the window, where Bryan stared out at them.

Shit. David was going to ask him to watch over his pregnant Keeper. Damn, Theodor. He was so dead. Fucking payback sucked. Popping over a couple . . . Okay, several times, in the middle of the night didn't warrant such. Did it?

"See you realized why Theodor sent you."

"No." I wasn't sure what I said no to. Watching over Bryan or why Theodor sent me. Neither seemed wise.

David's deep, rich chuckle put a knot in my stomach. "Bryan insisted you be the one to watch over him."

"Uh . . . I verbally attacked him when I met him." Another low moment of my life. My anger hadn't been at Bryan, but at having to take a spot among the Royal Leaders and leave the new era of life I'd been about to start.

"Yeah, Neither me or Theodor understands the reasoning, but . . ."

Fuck! "Theodor fudged on how long you've prolonged following up on this lead. Didn't he?"

David nodded.

"The tree was when you suggest someone else. Wasn't it?"

Another nod.

"Damn, David. You best answer my next question with words." I inhaled as water spewed from the ground. "Shit."

David stepped back under the safety of the front porch. His faint smile and glittering eyes screamed, "Theodor told me you were untrained."

"Instead of smirking tell me how to stop the spewing." I shouted louder than I meant to, which had a couple of Combatants rounding the corner of the house.

David walked over to the wooden swing and sat down.

"Fine. Let it water your precious earth."

"Earth loves water." David huffed as he swung back twice before he stood. "Once you stop the water show . . . Join me inside. Word of advice . . . Don't keep my Keeper waiting long. He'll make the ground toss you inside. Promise."

Didn't doubt it, but I had no freaking idea how to stop the water. My head fell back as I groaned. "What the hell did I do to deserve this?"

No answer, but my verbal fit did cease the spouting water. Too bad it was replaced with a down pour, which fell only over the tree sprouting dead center of the cemented pathway. I took one last look at the rain, which didn't look as strange as the tree growing in the oddest spot, then walked inside.

Chapter 6

Anthony

I pushed the door closed, taking one last look at the rain falling over the bright orange and red leaves. Bryan sure had been in a good mood when he created the pretty fall tree. Thought . . . thought Theodor said it was in the middle of the house. David must have transported there. Looked natural with the matching mountain treetops in the background. Growing through the walkway made it stand out, making David's house being hidden that much better. Reminded me it was time for me to find a place off the beaten path. Staying in my townhouse was no longer wise. It was harder to defend and if someone attacked the entire neighborhood would be in danger.

"Thought you said he was here to help."

Wow! Sexy, deep voice.

"He is." David said.

The husky voice had me moving closer to the doorway, but I remained out of sight. I had to hear more of that voice, even if he was badgering David for answers. That didn't bother me. Didn't appear to David either. He sounded like he took the interrogation with a grain of salt. Not sure I could have done so, even if the voice drew me in.

I moved so I stood in the doorway. I propped myself against the door frame. I could see David's face, but all I could see of the other was . . . Nice, round ass. Bet it was as firm as a rock. Had my cock plumping up at warp speed. Had my wolf howling so loud my brain rattled.

Shit. It was . . . Shit. . . What do I do? How . . . Was it possible? Couldn't be. Was.

My wolf snarled the moment David stepped towards the way to skinny, hunky man. A low warning howl slipped past by lips, catching David's attention like I'd hoped.

"See, he's . . ."

I shook my head at David. Didn't need the hunky man noticing me until I had a conversation with the rest of the Royal Leaders. I had no idea what to do. Wanted my Keeper, but never expected to find one. Why? I knew David found one. Proof was right in front of me. That meant I had a chance to find one. So did Theodor, Caleb, and Franklin.

"Keep Bryan company." David waved Bryan to his side and kissed his forehead. "I need to go and discuss a few things with my cousin before we track down this lead."

I stepped out of the line of sight and made my way into the kitchen. Way safer than the hallway. Soon as I walked in there a sense of dread consumed me. My breath faded as my mind screamed, "I can't protect him if I'm away from him. I can't ensure his happiness if he's not at my side. I don't know how to be a Bombardian to a Keeper. I was trained for a Protector."

I ran my hand through my hair and forced air through my lungs.

"That's it. Breathe." David laid a hand on my shoulder. "Unexpected turn of events."

"Can say that again." I yanked a chair out and flopped down. "What the heck do I do next?"

David tugged another chair out. "Depends. You want your Keeper?"

Ugh. I banged my head against the tabletop. "Thought I hid my reaction better than that."

"Listen," David kicked his legs out in front of him, "you've been an open book to me since the day you joined the Royal Leaders. I'm not sure if Theodor and the others caught on, but you revealed your true self when you verbally attacked Bryan."

Piss poor reaction on my part. It'd been a stupid move, but my life had been full of those. This was one aspect of life that I couldn't afford to screw up. I was so fucked. The only person I'd ever been comfortable around was Kevin. Going to him for advice on drawing in my Keeper wouldn't go over well with Kevin or my Keeper.

"Want me to call the others so you can move onto the next phase?"

Could I direct my own life? My Keeper was mere feet away and instead of running to don the Red Hooded Guy I'd escaped to sulk at my cousin's kitchen table.

"Yes." I'm so screwed. "I guess it needs doing."

"You want to? Neither of you will be happy if you don't." David's concern confused and shocked me. "Don't give me that have you lost your freaking mind look. It will do no Bombardian any good if one of their leaders is distressed over being attached to a Keeper when he doesn't want to be."

I wanted my Keeper. I'd messed up my entire life. It was yet another thing for me to destroy. "It's not that I don't. I do, believe me." I shifted in the chair, trying to ease my aching dick.

"I believe you, but that's the physical response. You know that. There has to be an emotional one as well. You have to have it figured out before you approach him as the Red Hooded Guy."

Boy did I. David's reminder was appreciated, but I'd let Kevin go in order to take my rightful spot among the Bombardians. No way I'd rejected my Keeper forcing myself to a life as a Mélange. A loveless life with my Keeper was more rewarding than becoming a monster stuck in half wolf, half human form.

"I'm assuming this is the infamous Larry Wells, the son of the President of the United States."

David nodded.

"How traumatized is he?"

My wolf snarled and pushed closer and closer to the foreground. The wolf wanted revenge for the assault done to its Keeper. I knew David killed each terrorist, but the wolf demanded it gain revenge for its Keeper. It was its job to protect their Keeper. Not David's. I could all but feel the fur sprouting across my arms. Not even the desire for revenge drowned out the wolf's insistence of claiming what belonged to them. Stronger than I'd dreamed possible.

"Larry seems fine here. He didn't handle the idea of the shit storm his father's position brought to him."

Bet so. I'd read the human history books. Saw the massive amount of press coverage an event with the President carried. A day did not go by that him or his family wasn't in the press. Most of the time it was made up bull crap to gain readers.

"He's a smart man. Intuitive."

Nice ass. Shorter than I expected. Wouldn't mind seeing what else the man had to offer. How would he feel about me? Not all Keepers were attracted to their Bombardian.

Crap. Why did I choose this shirt? I tugged at the hem of the awful blue button down. His favorite black one was needed. It showed off his thick muscles. Made my green eyes shine brighter, even when I was upset.

"Curious, but don't push for answers. In fact, he's more interested in gaining help for Bryan than finding out the whole truth about what I am."

Kind. Caring. Great attributes. But if . . . Crap. Worse than I thought. "If Bryan and him are friends . . . I'm screwed nine ways to never." I grinned at David, who chuckled. "I'm fucking serious. Your Keeper will take me out using your powers if I screw things up."

David shrugged, not bothering to hide his huge smile. "Might, but I'd fear Theodor doing so before my pregnant Keeper."

Huh? What did that mean? I hadn't made my mine up, yet. Right. Who was I kidding? Larry belonged to me.

"Go to the conference." David stood and came behind me, pulling me up by the collar of my shirt. "I'll call and tell the others to join us."

* * *

Each step towards the conference room was like a bullet ripping through my chest, but I managed to ignore the urge to rush back to the living room. I longed to hear the deep voice again. Longed to . . . Couldn't think that way. Had to keep my mind on the next step. Don't get ahead of yourself, Anthony. Keep control.

Damn. How had my life gotten so out of control? Why was I worrying? Finding a Keeper was a joyous time. Some Bombardians never found them. Others were rejected. I could be. Doubted I would be. My wolf refused to think along that line. My wolf deemed the turn of events the best thing in their lives. Was it luck finding Larry? Yes. No. Sort of. What to do?

I loved Kevin. Had for my entire life. He's the only man I slept with.

"He doesn't look like a man who just found his Keeper." Caleb's appeared in the middle of David's light brown carpeted conference room.

Didn't really want to know what I looked like. Could be white as a ghost, or red as a pickle beat, or ten other damn clichés. All they would do was piss me off. Right then . . . Hearing one would have had me throwing punches.

"Thought you said he found his Keeper." Theodor tossed his head my way. "What's got you in such a twist over this?"

"You have to ask." I winced and took a huge step back when Theodor growled.

"Let's think." Theodor lifted one finger. "You never learned to control your water affinity, as evident from excessive water over

David's new tree." Another finger shot up. "You never wanted to be a Royal Leader, per evidence of your verbal attack on Bryan."

A fact I would never live down. My own fault.

Theodor lifted another finger, making me feel like he hammered a nail in my coffin. "You've been paying me nightly visit without knowing it because your ex-lover chose his job over you."

Could I strangle Theodor? Nope. The man would set me on fire, and I wouldn't be able to douse myself in water.

Franklin walked in, carrying five special blended coffees. "Figured this wouldn't be a short meeting. I grabbed us some drinks." He winked at David. "Even brought one for the two Keepers stashed away safely in the living room."

I rolled my shoulders and let the grin I'd been holding in free. As much as the idea of a Keeper frustrated me, my wolf side was pleased and wanted its Keeper like any Bombardian would.

"Ah . . . He is one of us." Caleb chuckled and used a small burst of wind to push the chair beside me back. "Take a load off. Let the newness sink in. Sure, this is a major shock to your system."

"Shut the hell up." I flopped into the chair, rubbing my temple. "Go on. Have the rest of your fun. I'll take my medicine like I should." Should have expected it. It was the Royal Leader's MO.

"What's he talking about?" Franklin sat a cup of steaming coffee in front of me. "Extra milk."

"Thanks."

"Not sure." David grabbed one of the drinks. "This mine, right?"

"Yep. Black and stout."

Never understood how anyone could drink coffee black. David was even worse, he preferred it so strong it would wake the dead.

"You didn't give Bryan coffee did you?"

"Yes. He requested it when I called him. Was I not suppose to?"

"Oh fuck!" Theodor said.

David dematerialized.

Uh . . . What in the . . . I glanced at Caleb, who bore bright gold eyes.

Theodor shook his head.

"What'd I do wrong?" Franklin passed Theodor his cup.

"Bryan's not able to keep it down, but the man is craving it." Caleb took the last cup.

I half listened as they conversed while I silently kicked my own ass. Theodor had been right on all his points. Even some he didn't get a chance to mention. Still, I wouldn't give up my Keeper for any reason. I needed the Red Hooded Guy and quick. My wolf was all but pushing through my skin. Hell, my claws were digging into my palms.

"Can I become the Red Hooded Guy?" I hadn't meant to blurt it, which might be why Caleb spit coffee as he chuckled. "What? Thought that's why I called you here."

"It was." Theodor passed Caleb a roll of paper towels. "Caleb's just being his normal stupid self."

"Can't be anyone else."

"Then what was so funny?" I tapped the side of my cup.

"Your face. It shifted when you asked and it was . . ."

"Caleb, shut up. You only making things worse."

Might have laughed at the sour expression Caleb shot Theodor, if Theodor hadn't been correct. Caleb was being himself, but it was making my wolf push harder.

"I need permission to don the Red Hooded Guy costume. Now." I hoped that's what I said. The wolf was so close I growled.

"Fuck. What did you do to him?"

Think David stood in the doorway, but my eyes were shifting back and forth so fast I couldn't grab onto a solid image.

"Caleb," Theodor's voice was gruff.

"Oh." David's head moved back and forth, or so I thought. The movement sort of blurred together since I was seeing double.

"Franklin, Larry says he's going to kick your ass for making Bryan upchuck again."

Ah .. Wonderful name. Wonderful person. My vision cleared for a second, but fur covered my arms and neck. I'd have to meet my Keeper soon.

"Uh . . . Guess I have to let him." Franklin huffed. "Can't have Bryan sick. That's plain out dangerous. Can't have Anthony's wolf running around trying to kick my ass for upsetting his Keeper." The chuckle pulled another growl from me. "I say let him cast the spell. What we got to lose?"

"Loads."

Predictable. Didn't need Theodor analyzing every small detail. Vote was simple. A three-letter word. No discussion required. Yet . . . There would be a long and drawn out one. Sickened me to think it, but I could only let them have their talk. One thing I'd learned over the last few months was that Theodor spoke until his point was made. Quicker I heard him out the quicker I'd be able to show myself to my Keeper. Would happen soon, even if I had to take out the other four Royal Leaders.

"What?"

"He's the President's son. David was to protect him. Not play match maker. How do you think his father is going to react to you inducting his son into the Cult lifestyle?" Theodor kicked his legs onto the tabletop, enticing a low menacing growl from David.

"There's not a God Damn Cult." David knocked Theodor's legs down.

"I know this. Every Bombardian knows this. The President knows this. The humans will see it as their elected leader's son rebelling into the one thing his father has continuously spoken against but allowed because the Senate and House made him."

Leave it to Theodor to throw cold water on me. Too bad it did little to settle my wolf down. The wolf didn't care what the humans saw or said. All the wolf understood was that I was a Bombardian. Created by humans. They have to live with the results of their decision. When it comes right down to it, I didn't give a flying fuck what the humans thought either. Larry Wells was my Keeper, the one my wolf craved. The one my body, mind, and soul longed to hold close and lavish with affection. The one who would replace Kevin. The one I'd promised Kevin I'd accept if I found.

Wrong. I promised to accept a Protector and to let him accept a Keeper if he found one. Semitics. Kevin would kick my ass if I rejected my Keeper and ended up a Mélange.

"None of this matters." Might have spoken too soon. I had no counterpoint.

"Why not? You asked to don the Red Hooded Guy costume." Theodor crossed his arms.

"I did. Want to. Will. We don't even know if Larry Wells will accept me as a Bombardian. He could outright refuse me."

"Yeah, erasing his memory and relocating the President's son will be so easy." Caleb huffed and shook his head. "You are stupid if you think this Keeper can be given that option."

"Has to be." David chimed in with a mischievous grin. "It's our law that the Royal Leader Keepers be given the exact same options and treatment as any other Keeper and Protector."

"Fuck you." Caleb slammed his coffee down, splashing some over the edge. "Don't be throwing the laws at me. You know this Keeper has to be handled different than yours."

"You are cleaning that up." David pointed at the mess, then faced Theodor. "How are we going to handle this. Caleb is partially right. We won't be able to relocate Larry after zapping his memories."

Right. Great points. My Keeper was to well-known. No matter where he was stashed, he'd be noticed. "Fate hates me." I dropped my head against my chest. "I have no options. I have to give my Keeper a choice. I gave my word to Kevin. Promised him I'd continue to live my life to the fullest. I'm sure rejecting my Keeper doesn't fit into my promise."

Franklin's little snicker had me shooting him a finger.

Caleb snort earned him one as well and so did David's rolling eyes.

Theodor leaned back and glared at me.

I wanted to reach over and slap him. Hard. Wouldn't mind leaving matching handprints on both cheeks.

"David," Theodor kept his attention on David, but I knew he wanted me to pay extra close attention to the question. "You know Larry better than any of us." Fact my wolf disliked. No Royal Leader should have met my Keeper before me. David should not have rescued him. I should have.

"What do you think Larry will say?"

David's intense study of the ceiling had me squirming. The lifeless tone made my skin crawl worse than the little spike of wolf fur lacing my arms.

"He's open minded. Seems intrigued about what I am. His concern for Bryan has his upmost attention. The man has balls of steel. Only time I saw him affected by the events he faced was when his father's vultures were awaiting him. Other than that . . . He's accepted the overheard and witnessed slip up of my wolf."

"Not helpful."

Theodor was right. Another nail in my coffin from Theodor. David's answer hadn't been one.

"There'll be none of that now." Theodor pushed me back from David, who was snarling and being held back by Caleb.

Shit. What was . . . When had . . . What had pissed David off? Why was Franklin grinning like a cat who got into the cream?

"What happened?"

"Your wolf side took offense at David's generosity." Franklin said.

"Fuck. Sorry." I dropped to my knees and groaned at the pain shooting through my entire body.

"It's fine." David retook his seat. "I think it's clear he needs to present himself to his Keeper, but I fear Caleb is right. This entire situation is going to have to be handled different, which means adjusting the rule put into effect when I found Bryan."

"Right." Theodor put a seat in front of me. "Needs hashing out before he approaches Larry. Think you can keep your wolf in check while we discuss this and find a solution?"

"I'll do my best."

"All we can ask."

Chapter 7

Anthony

Idea after idea was thrown out. Stupid ones. Wanted to add my own opinion, but . . . Nothing truly registered. My wolf pushed at me like a raving mad man trying to escape a straitjacket. Each step I made across the light blue carpeted conference room came with a loud internal howl and a grunt of pain as lightening shook my entire body.

"Hey!" Caleb's shout had me stopping.

"What the fuck!" David's chair flew back from the table. "Stop the damn waterfall in my house. My mate will kick your ass if you destroy our home."

Ugh! I lifted my hand, staring at them as rain pelted against my shoulder. Shit. What was I to say? Sorry I caused a rainstorm on you, but if you'd hurry up and stop pissing on my wolf's parade it'd be pleased as the bowl of water you are drenched in.

"Don't even say it." Theodor groaned, pointing at David. "Tap into your power and make this shit stop."

"What?" That wasn't possible. Was it?

"Come here."

I walked towards him, tentatively. I tensed the moment he gripped my arm. Heat crept up my arm, over my chest, and down my other arm, stopping in the middle of my finger and thumb.

"Snap your fingers for me."

I did and the rain ceased. "Wow! How'd . . . Wow!"

"Extra ability of mine." David released my arm. "Don't make me do that often. It weakens me and I need my strength right now."

My arms still tingled, making me rub them. "I'm not keen on it either. Did you four work out a solution?"

"We have a good idea." Theodor snapped his finger three times and heat whipped around the room, drying them. "Can you hold it together for a little longer? We need to explain and sign the new order into effect."

Could I? Hoped so. Wouldn't promise. "Do my best." I shrugged, giving them the best reply, I could.

Theodor glanced Caleb's way, who tossed his head to David, who in returned groaned and slammed his head against the headrest of his chair. Franklin sniggered and leaned back, studying the three men.

What had I missed? Did it pertain to me? Why in the heck did Franklin find it funny? The man was a new Royal Leader, like me, why was he not standing at my side?

Because I wouldn't have been helping him. Fair game. Do to others what you want done to you.

Theodor and Caleb glared at David, which had my wolf snarling. Why wasn't they filling me in? I was one of them. They were always to be on the same page. I was out of the loop. Why? How? Each passing second kept me from my Keeper, which only drew my ire higher.

"Fine." David shouted, leaning forward. "If he kills me then you can explain to Bryan."

Kill him? Who would . . . Surely he wasn't referring to me. I would . . . Okay, my wolf was unstable. Didn't mean I'd attack another Royal Leader. Unless . . . Oh boy, they best not be . . . If they told me . . . Someone would have to explain to Bryan if David delivered horrible news. Then again . . . David wouldn't have allowed anyone to keep him from his Keeper. Nor would I. I'd eliminate any and all obstacles between me and Larry Wells.

"Here's what has to happen." David's dry tone made me stiffen. "This adjustment will be easier than the last one. There are no rules to be abolished. Only some rewording. Problem is . . . Theodor, Caleb, and I are a bit skittish. Rightfully so. Another vote behind closed doors . . . Unease doesn't fit."

Oh. Made sense. Last time all five Royal Leaders had been rewriting a rule it ended in an explosion and two dead Royal Leaders. Understandable. Admitting it was admirable. Still . . . Didn't explain what David wanted me to do about it. All of them knew the Ghoulians lost their leader. Most were killed in the resulting battle.

"We wanted Franklin to take the lead, but . . ."

"Stickler for rules." I really didn't give a crap about rules then. All I wanted was to be given permission to don the Red Hooded Guy costume.

I wasn't sure, but it felt like I was giving Franklin the same death glare I'd seen my Uncle give many times. "What rule would he be breaking if he took the lead. This bullshit needs to end so I can get thing moving with my Keeper."

"Theodor is the eldest. He leads every vote and meeting." Franklin's smirk pulled a deep snarl from me.

"That's the damn hold up." Could I get away with slicing Franklin's throat? "Since we've joined the Royal Leaders each and every meeting, has been more of less a free for all party. We joke. Fuss. Cuss. Come to a conclusion and vote. Who gives a flying fuck who starts, leads, or runs the damn meeting? Get to the point and be done with it."

Franklin snorted, earning another snarl.

Caleb's huff got him one as well.

Theodor made a kind of coughed and choking sound.

David was the only one who responded in a somewhat sensible matter. "Here, here."

"For peeks sake." Theodor shoved himself back from the table, snatching some tablets, tossing them on the table. "The previous rule added, basically stated . . . Hold up. The previous added rule dealt with the aspect of a Keeper or Protector requesting a Trial Run." If they stated the debate over again, which from the deep rubbing of

Theodor's chin they would be, I might just blow them all up. "Looks like this will be a simple add on."

Ugh! My chin hit my chest as I flopped into a chair.

"Okay. We can dive right into how we as Royal Leaders should handle one of us finding a Keeper or Protector, who requires special circumstances, because of their position among the human world." Caleb tapped a pen against the table. "Do we need to be specific as to what classifies as special circumstance?"

Bullshit. I force the scream rushing up my throat down. Didn't need a room full of Combatants. Strike that. Didn't need Bryan running in. From what David said Larry was pretty much stuck to Bryan's side.

"How about we word it, so it states that a meeting is required to gage the status of each Keeper or Protector found by a Royal Leader." David's voice sounded full of pain, which had all four of us whipping our heads toward him.

"You okay?" Theodor went to David's side.

David shook his head and jumped up, running into the hallway. Fear for Larry had me out the door first. What I found . . . Odd. David stood in between Bryan and a statue like Larry. I was about to jump to aid Larry, but strong hands gripped my shoulder. I spun around, slamming into Theodor's hard body.

"Let me go."

"Can't." Caleb said from my side where he had a tight grip on my upper arm.

Rain started pouring down around us. The area filled with smoke and wind.

"Stop it." Larry shouted as he dropped to his knees and huddled into himself.

My body jerked as the rain ceased. Wind whistled as it faded, leaving behind a heavy scent of lilacs. The change in the atmosphere had Larry uncurling and returning his gaze to Bryan, who was being cradled in David's arms.

"What happened to him?" Larry whispered, causing me to take a closer look at Bryan.

"Oh man. How . . . Is this another pregnancy thing?" I'd never seen such. Bryan's face had contorted until he had an elongated snout and pointed ears. My heart sank to my feet. If this new twist came from the pregnancy, I not only felt for Bryan, but my own Keeper. One thing we'd learned during our meeting with David's family was that there was no conception prevention. Could Larry, or any future Keepers, handle such? Larry more so. I mean he was getting a firsthand look at what his future might hold. Would that work in my favor, or doom me to a life in the confinement house?

"Not sure. Think David needs to check the led out while you explain what you need to." Theodor shot Franklin and Caleb a thin smile. "You two agree that the details can be ironed out while David is gone."

Perfect idea. Theodor and Caleb knew David well enough to know how he'd vote. Not that it would matter. We were a majority rules system. Right then all I could focus on was the state of my Keeper. And it was not good. I had no idea how to ease or help him cope with what he'd saw.

Franklin moved to David's side and knelt. "I do. Bryan," those fear ridden eyes, a look I'd never seen on Bryan before, and never wanted to see again. "You want me to call William?"

My hand went to my chest to ensure my heart had not fallen out as Bryan shook his head and buried his face in David's chest.

"How about Tommy?" David rubbed Bryan's back, but it did nothing. Wrong. It had Bryan shaking so hard he looked like he was having a seizure.

"Let me to him."

Franklin ended up on his ass as Larry shoved him aside and knelt beside Bryan.

I found myself closer to Larry, but my eyes were focused on Franklin and David. If they made one wrong move . . . Franklin picked up on my cues like a pro. He duck walked back, giving me more space. David's full attention was on Bryan. Every ounce of my mind screamed for me to yank Larry away from David and Bryan. Only thing that stopped me was the tears sliding over Larry's cheek and the choked-out words.

"Bryan . . . Please, please let David go and check on this lead. I can't stand seeing you . . ." Larry's sob tore at me, but what had me dropping to my knees was the way he curled into a little ball. I went to reach for him, but Theodor's grabbed my arm, shaking his head at me. I might have snarled at him, but knowing how distraught my Keeper was from the earlier rainstorm kept me quiet.

Bryan laid a hand on Larry's shoulder, giving it a lite squeeze. "He's going to. I think I'd like you and Anthony to keep me company."

"Sounds like a great idea." David ran a hand over Bryan's normal nose. "What do you think, Anthony?"

Sure did. I could use the time with my Keeper. It would calm my beast side. I must have given David some kind of signal, because he nodded back at me as he looked over my shoulder. I followed his action, hoping to find that my three other cousins were on the same page. Never in my life had three nods ease my mood so fast.

"Marvelous idea. David, you and Franklin go make the final arrangements you need and go take care of business."

Anthony followed Theodor to the office. Caleb trailed behind them.

"Does he cast the spell, or face him like he is?" Caleb asked as he came to stand at my side.

Theodor moved to his other side. "Like he is." He bumped my shoulder. "Don't think Larry can take facing the big bad boogieman."

Neither did I. It sucked that humans had taught their kids to fear the Red Hooded Guy. It degraded what was such a marvelous moment in a Bombardian's life. It debased the wonderful robe used as a sign of loyalty and devotion. Okay, the earth quaking and surrounding the young men in a cloud to disguise our self from others might be scary, but that could easily be explained away.

"He's on the edge of breaking."

I wasn't quite sure why. Was it because he cared so much for Bryan? Or . . . Did he have a thing for Bryan? David swore they were just friends. Larry's reaction was extremely strong for a newly formed friend. Was David oblivious to Larry's attraction to his Keeper? Was there one? Could Larry be that devoted to all his friends? Bryan and Tommy were that close. Even if Larry held deeper feelings for Bryan that would all change soon as . . .

"What if he refuses me?"

Caleb's deep snort had me throwing a punch, but Caleb's hand clamped around my balled-up hand.

"I'll ignore that and answer you." Caleb released his hand. "Doubt that will happen. Bryan's going to be in there. He'll make sure Larry understands if you fail to do so. You may not get a full relationship, but I don't think that man has a mean bone in his body."

"Anything . . ." No. Not anything would be better than nothing. Least not to all of me. Part wanted what David had with Bryan. A loyal, beyond fault Keeper, who loved and longed to care for me.

"Fuck. What if seeing Bryan like this makes him hate the idea of being my Keeper?" I flopped onto the small two-seater sofa in front of the desk. "I can't . . . There's too many unknowns. I don't go into things blind. It took me six weeks to work up the courage to ask Kevin out."

"Lord help us, Anthony is normal." Theodor yanked me to my feet, pushing me toward the door. "Go win your Keeper's heart. Royal Leaders go for what they want. Remember."

"Does he have the regular choices?"

"Can't."

"What . . . Theodor?"

"Not sure yet. Two of them seems okay to me." Theodor sighed. "Caleb what do you think?"

I let them discuss what lay ahead for Larry. While they did, I debated how much of Caleb's last comment was true. I'd never been normal. I'd been backwards from the time I gained the understanding of what my royal blood gene meant. Did me being a Royal Leader make me different? No. I was still the same man. My title might have changed, but I was still Anthony Samuel Lincoln. Being a Royal Leader did not make me normal. I was still far from it. Wasn't I? Didn't matter. I was paired with a man who was special among the human world, making our situation more compatible than I initially thought. None of that really mattered. I had a promise to live up to. I swore an official oath to Kevin. Kevin would want me to make my Keeper mine. Kevin told me many times that if I found my other half that I would pull my tight ass slacks up and claim what was mine in the proper manner. That I couldn't cheat myself, or my other half.

I took a deep breath and squared my shoulders, standing taller. "Where does David keep his herbs?"

"You're going to cast the spell?" Caleb rolled his eyes. "I don't think that is wise."

"I do."

All three of them spun and took step forward before it registered who spoke.

"Where's David?" Theodor took a chair over to Bryan, who had propped himself against the door frame.

"You don't want to know. I was on my way back to the living room when I overheard."

"You know you - -"

"Hey, you're in my home." Bryan was the only one who could get away with mouthing off to Theodor when he gave that don't mess with me glare. "I've been where Larry is about to be. I was taught the same as him. I do not think I would have believed David if he had approached me in his everyday clothes. The mark helped me comprehend magic existing."

"But Larry knows." Theodor helped Bryan take a seat.

"Yes. He's traveled by magic. Overheard lots of strange things, but never once has David's true nature been explained. It's way more than just magic with you guys."

"Babe," David ran hand over Bryan's head, making my wolf howl with need for its other half. He longed to have what his cousin had with his Keeper. "You were supposed to go back to Larry."

"I know."

"He eavesdropped." Theodor frowned at David.

"I thought I could help Anthony out." Bryan stood, taking David's hand.

"He's right." We are more. "Our second form will be hard for any human to grasp." If I hadn't known about humans, I would be weary of learning about their natural habits. "The humans pretty much brainwash their children. Some less than others. I bet . . ." More like could promise, "Larry's was harsher than most." How could it not have been, he was the son of a politician. One who held the highest-ranking spot among humans.

Theodor took hold of my arm and moved me over to the far wall of the office. He tilted a book halfway out, causing the wall to slid sideways, revealing four shelves stashed with all kinds of herbs. The smells mingled, but I could decipher each one, allowing my hands to move to the ones I needed.

"David, where you keep your mortar and pestle?" I carefully picked out the herbs I required, making sure that I did not drop one leave or twig. David was picky about how any earth item was handled and I was not going to disrespect his home. Looked like I'd be spending quite a bite of time there.

"Here." Franklin held it out to me.

"Caleb," Theodor rested his hand over mine, halting me from starting the spell. "David believes your wind might benefit him more than spirit will be able to."

My wolf snarled as fur erupted across my arms. More delays were not what I wanted. Although, I could see why David felt that way. Spirit was a great affinity, but it was limited on what it could do. If David found himself in some thicket of weeds, or grass, then Caleb could aid in separating those making their journey easier.

"Fine with me." Caleb patted my back. "Good luck. My fingers are crossed. I'm sure when we are back, we will be announcing another Pledging Ceremony."

I hoped. My mind wasn't sure. My Keeper suffered a lot recently. I was about to add to it. Might be the final straw. If so . . . My entire life might go more topsy-turvy than I dreamed possible.

"Hey, Caleb, what are my Keeper's choices?"

"I'll explain them as you prepare." Theodor took one of the twigs of thyme, dropping it into the mortar."

Chapter 8

Larry

"Larry," David's unusual tentative voice had my stomach swirling.

"Me and Caleb are going to check out the lead. Do you mind keeping Bryan company until Anthony can join him?"

As if. Not even my fear of being without my savior could make me leave Bryan's side. Nope. Not even my own self could tear me away from Bryan. David knew it. Knew why. Bryan explained the connection Larry felt towards him and why, when David grew concerned about my attachment to Bryan.

"Fine. Fine."

Wasn't sure what I looked like, but David held his hand up and backed out of the room. Bryan's huge, cocky grin told me I had most likely given David a major back off glare. Shawn always told me it made the strongest man fearful.

"Bye, honey." Bryan wiggled his fingers and blew David a kiss. "He's messing with you." Not something I'd seen much out of David since I arrived. He was a serious kind of guy with everyone but Bryan "Let's watch a movie. Comedy. No pregnant talking. No baby talking . . . Fuck. Make it a hardcore action flick. Lots of explosions and fist fights."

Sounded good to me, but wasn't sure if it was doable. "Not sure if that's possible." He picked up the remote and clicked a button.

"No. Go to - -"

Glasses rattled, sloshing dark brown and clear liquid over the rim. The flower tulip shaped light fixture swayed, clinking against one another.

"What in the world?"

I was on my feet and at the window. Nothing seemed off. Trees were still. Wind chimes made no noise. Okay. Not nothing. There was a little water raining down over the new tree sitting in the middle of the pathway. Bryan had accidently conjured it. It rested in the middle of the living room for a couple of days, before I woke up to find it in the middle of the walkway.

"Oh fuck."

My head lowered as I lifted my left arm as a blaze zipped across my forearm. Small sparks of current rippled under my tan skin.

"You okay?"

A greenish-blue haze blocked me from Bryan. I tried to move, but found my feet routed to the light brown, plush carpet. Might have been a good thing. I would have tripped over the glass coffee table or fell backwards over the sofa. Didn't cease my dire need to get to Bryan. Ensure he was okay. My vision blurred, but the last glimpse of Bryan was him sitting with his legs over the arm, watching me from the corner of his eyes.

Freaky. Had Bryan not noticed the shaking room? If the ground had been doing the same Larry would have thought an earthquake, but nope. Ground calm. Wind calm. No other weather seemed to be affecting the area. Only a haze. Bryan had to see it. Didn't he? I wasn't . . . Was I imagining things? Had I lost grasp of the world? My gut told me no. Something was off. Something came my way. What though? It wasn't like when David transported me here. Nope. That had caused the world to close in around me. Made me sick to my stomach. Left me dizzy. There'd been other . . . I'd heard lots over the last few weeks. Meant expecting the unexpected. What was going on though? Didn't matter. I had to get to Bryan. Had to protect him. Ensure he was safe until the others arrived. They'd come. Nothing happened in the house that David and his cousins didn't know about.

With all the strength I could gathered I tried to lift my foot, but . . . Shit. Where had . . . My fist flew across the air, but it went right through the figure that had magically appeared in front of me. I was about to throw a second punch when . . .

"Cr - - Crap. You're the . . ."

Red Hooded Guy. Why was he . . . "You can't have Bryan. I won't let you." Another friend would not be stolen from me. David wouldn't allow it. Shit. David's gone. Anthony. Where was he? He was to watch over Bryan.

I went to lunge left, praying my body moved. It did, but it slammed into something. I took a huge step back, once again hitting something invisible. Moving right and another barricade. What in the hell?

"Larry Wells, you've been marked as the Royal Keeper to Anthony Samuel Lincoln. Will you allow me to explain what this means?"

Me? Fuck. Nope. I . . . Okay, I was within the age group that the Red Hooded Guy came for, but . . . No way. I'd heard wrong. I wasn't associated with the Cult. Never had been. Father openly opposed the Cult but allowed its existence. The Cult was a curse. Bad omen. Cruel and unmerciful people.

What am I worried about? They won't come for me. My father would crush them if David . . . Oh, fuck. David left. Shit. Where was . . . Hold up. I knew . . . Yep.

I lowered myself, trying to gain sight under the lip of the red hood. All I saw was a pointed chin and plump lips.

Kissable lips. Like the ones I saw on . . . Yep. Saw them twice today. They'd distracted me both times. Made my body shiver with desire. It couldn't be though. Could it?

"Anthony?" Way to go. He done said his name. Still, I asked for more clarification. "David's cousin?"

"Yes, may I explain why you have been marked?"

Oh he would. And lots more than that. Starting with why the fuck my forearm . . . Ah, there it was. Plain as day. The one mark that I'd heard about growing up. It was the one thing my dad made sure I knew existed, but would never come my way. How wrong he'd been.

"Fuck."

"What is it." Anthony's eyes scanned the room and his knees softened. Ready to attack.

"This mark . . ." Larry listened as Anthony took in a long deep breath and spoke in a foreign language. One David used a couple of times. Ah crap. David was part of the Cult. Couldn't be. Dad wouldn't have enlisted the Cult to rescue me. Would he?

Ugh. My head hurt. I rubbed my temple, hoping to ease the throbbing. I'd missed something. What though? None of this made sense.

"May I explain."

"You have nothing to do with the Cult, do you?"

"May I explain?"

"Is that all you can say?"

"Until I explain, yes."

My finger ran over the newly marked skin. The burning faded, but it still stung a bit. Even that had lessened after Anthony spoke those unknown words. "Go on."

"It's not easy, or short. Bear with me."

Refraining from interrupting wasn't a skill of mine. I should have let Bryan fill me in the other day. David told him he could. Ugh. Being at a disadvantage sucked.

"Two hundred years ago, there was an experimenter named William Lincoln. Smartest man alive, maybe even to this day. Not sure. The higher ups took notice of him and decided they wanted . . ."

Gosh damn power trip. Hated people who flipped over power and prestige. Both sides of my family pretty much killed anyone viewed as a threat to their seat in office. Didn't mean I agreed with their actions. I hated people treating me different. I put clothes on one leg at a time like everyone else.

". . . Him to create the ultimate men. Men who could defeat anything and everything thrown at them. William Lincoln's experiment did way more than what the higher ups wanted. At first, everyone thought it was a flop. Years later one of the men told William his wife was expecting their first child. The child was born with a unique blood type."

Experiment worked. Anyone who took a psychology course knew what happened next. The test subject would be watched closer to find out what factor made the difference. Others would be called back in to ensure others had the same condition appearing.

"Come to find out any man who had been experimented on and married a woman with the blood type *A* bore sons with special blood. These children became the next set of subjects."

No life for a child. How could their parents let that happen? I would have fought like hell. Would have taken my family and ran as far as possible.

"What happened to those children?"

"They had long, healthy lives."

Right. "Tell someone else that BS."

"Not bull. They did. Thanks to their extra skills."

"Skills?"

My eyes followed the tanned skin of Anthony's neck as my mouth watered to lick up the narrow path as he tilted his head back, letting the red hood fall away. A pair of sapphire blue eyes with yellow pupils, instead of black ones, shined back at me. Frightening. Sexy. Sure had my dick waking up.

"Heightened sense of smell. Enhanced healing. Stronger eyesight." Anthony worried his bottom lip, making me want to reach out and tugged it free, before I sucked it between my teeth, "They have vast knowledge of herbs and how they worked when mixed together. As time went on children learned that requesting help from the five natural elements of the world worked in their favor."

I'd heard of such being possible in fairytales. Not in life. Some believed so. If he remembered right, some of those people where into Wicca . . . Or was it, Paganism? Whatever it was, I'd heard of it before. Just like I'd heard of some worshiping deities related to Fire, Water, Air, and Earth. What was the . . .

"Five?"

"Yes. Fire. Water. Air. Earth. Spirit."

Never heard of that being included with those groups, but it was possible. I'd never read up on the subject. Not in detail at least. I could see why people considered it a natural element, though. All life comes from a spirit and returns to a spirit in the end. Or so, I believed.

"Your baby browns say you've came to a conclusion. What would that be?"

Baby browns? Cool. Not the point. "Magic."

"My people call it spell casting."

"I knew it. Knew it. The day David transported me here. Maybe even the day he came in by himself and rescued me from the hellhole those damn fools took me to."

Heat seeped into my skin when Anthony moved closer to me. "I'm truly sorry you were taken. If I had known you then . . . They would never had gotten their grimy hands on you."

Even though Anthony's heat soothed me, his dark and determined tone had me flopping onto the sofa and pushing myself back as far as I could go. Wrong. That had desire rushing through me so fast it startled me. Okay, it wasn't so much the tone, but the bright red flares flickering across his Sapphire eyes that had my cock hardening. Not the time to focus on the reasoning behind that. Nope.

"What is a Royal Keeper?" I sat up taller, hoping to show a calm facade. Doubted it worked. The man in front of me was astute. All the men who hung around David were. Course they were. They are magical.

"These children," Anthony rocked backed on his heels, "had extreme lives. Some lived longer than one hundred years. Not odd since they were harder to kill. Extra healing abilities will do that."

Ah shit. The . . . "Old secret. This experiment was buried among the government for all these years. Why?"

"Last trait these children carried made most view the experiment as a failure." A long drawn out groan warned me of what was to come. "The main skill these children were blessed with was a wolf living inside them."

What? Nope. No way. I was up, marching Anthony back. "You are talking about supernatural. It doesn't exist."

"Does magic?"

Calm tone. Damn it. How did I dispute such an easy statement? I didn't. Damn. How in the . . . Pain shot up my knees as they hit the ground.

"Larry!"

Hands tugged me to my feet and sat me back on the soft sofa. I rubbed at my knees, taking in slow deep breaths.

"Th - - The ex - - experiment created another sp - - species. Fuck me."

I lowered my head into my hands, hoping the facts would shift, but I'd heard them. Saw the proof of such. Or some proof. I'd overlooked those things. There was no way I could dispute what Anthony said. Everything inside me wanted to, but . . . Large secrets weren't uncommon around me. Filled my life since before I was born. How could it not. I grew up with a father determined to be the president. Live in the White House. You didn't reach that goal without keeping secrets. That trait couldn't leave you once your reached it. Lots of the secrets I'd discovered over the years were huge. Why would another race existing be common knowledge?

It wouldn't be. People among the White House would work their assess off in order to keep it hidden, right down to . . . Ah shit!

"The Cult . . . It's not one." Its creation had been just another way to hide the truth in plain sight. A second lie to cover up the first one. Common tactic.

"It's a front for my race, Bombardians, who . . ."

"Finish it."

"Each Bombardians is blessed with either a Protector or Keeper."

Ah. Getting down to my earlier questions. Knew it would come around if I let Anthony fill in all the facts. "Which are what?"

"Do you know why your father agreed for the Cult to be created?"

Thought I had, but . . . "Know what I was told."

"Which was?"

"The House and Senate forced his hand."

Anthony shook his head, verifying what I already knew. Another lie.

"There are some of my kind who had children by humans. Never told them their secret, leaving many Bombardians unaware of their true side. Not all, but some over the years. Less of an issue these days thanks to the mandatory logging of blood types. The government isn't just logging your blood type, but checking for the gene that makes a person a Bombardian." Cleared up a point I'd asked my dad about three or four times. It's always seemed like a violation of rights to me. "We are told of any Bombardian child born. We try to find their fathers and have them raise the child. If that isn't an option . . . then we place them with a willing family. They are taught to control their other side. It's always a challenge to keep our other side in check." A hard breath had Anthony's broad shoulders lifting and falling. "There are humans who can calm our animals, preventing our natural wild side from running amuck, turning us into dangerous monsters."

What a secret to be kept. Everyone deserved to know all this. Dad had some explaining to do.

"We call the females Protectors. The males are . . . Keepers."

Anthony leaned forward, bracing his hands on his knees, but the gentle move had me jerking back. Wasn't sure why.

"Most Bombardians and their Keepers or Protectors are so intertwined with one another that they chose to become a mated pair. It's all but impossible for them not to."

Oh shit! I . . . He is . . . I can't . . . "You said chose. You don't force them into anything."

"We give them a choice. Three in fact."

Another deep sigh told me more than Anthony's watery eyes. Whatever I was about to hear would be . . . Different. He wasn't most humans. I was the son of the President of the United States. Theme of my fucking life. Every aspect of life revolved around my dad's decision to become President.

"What are my choices?"

"You are a bright one." The grin had me wiggling instead of openly adjusting my throbbing cock. "It pleases me that you are my Keeper. I do apologize that your choices will be limited to two, but because of - -"

"I understand." Did. Didn't like it, but at least Anthony had been up front about the difference. Most weren't. Believe it or not, the honesty meant a hell of a lot to me.

"You can accept me as your Bombaridan and live the rest of your life with me. If you don't agree with the way I live we can come to a compromise before we commit completely."

Anthony's sexy grin sent my heart fluttering. Appeared my heart made its decision. From the way my dick pressed into the zipper of my slacks, it had to. My mind . . . Not quite convinced.

"You can request a trial run. I'll court you and give you time to learn more about me and how I live. This is only for a period of time."

"How long?"

"Depends."

"On what?" I wouldn't make a decision without all the facts. No matter what my heart and body desired. I never went into a decision blind.

"We each give an acceptable time period, if we differ . . . we split the difference."

"Other words . . . I say five months and you say two the time frame would be . . . Three and half."

"Correct."

"After that time is up?"

"You have the right to refuse to pair with me and live in a Destroyer's Hermitage, seeing me every couple of days."

"Why see you?"

"Once a Bombardian runs into his Keeper or Protector they have to see them to prevent themselves from turning into a Mélange."

"What?"

"A Bombardian who is stuck in half human, half wolf form."

Ah . . . Dangerous monster Anthony mentioned. I couldn't imagine living in such a state. I wasn't sure if I could live another life without knowing exactly what it consisted of."

"You look deep in thought."

"Am." How could I not be. Everything I'd been told had been demolished. Bit over dramatic. Still, every detail I'd been taught about the Cult had changed. Dad's ability to lie and keep things from people had been reinforced. Not that surprising, but . . . Anthony asked me to choose him and his way of life, or confine myself to living in a Destroyer's Hermitage. Most of those who lived there were attacked when they went out by themselves. Few did. Life altering decision. That's what Anthony laid at my feet. No way I could decide without thinking things over.

"You can discuss your thoughts or hangups about this with me."

"I'll have to think on this. Can I do that? Can I talk to Bryan?"

"You can." Theodor appeared in the doorway. When had the fog disappeared?

"Theodor," Anthony's growl made my cock throb, but the frown he shot Theodor put an ache in my chest.

"Hold up, cousin." Theodor mocked Anthony's frown, but his downward lips did not bother me like Anthony's had. "You knew the entire situation was going to be different. Therefore . . ."

"Fine." Anthony crossed his arms. "I'll send him in."

"Already here." Bryan snorted from the chair he'd been silently sitting in the entire time.

A half snort, half laugh slipped from me. "Sorry, man."

"No worries. I'm sure Anthony forgot all about poor little ole me." Bryan tossed a balled up napkin at Anthony.

"No way I could do that. Feared you might douse me with a dose of David's Earth." Anthony's roll of the eyes had me snickering harder. "Don't give my Keeper no hard time, or I'll sick David on you the moment he gets back."

"You mean don't treat him like you did me." Bryan lobbed a pen at Anthony.

More laughter flowed from me, until I saw the sadness flow across Anthony's face. That look had me out of my seat and throwing my arms around him.

"Looks like we'll be having another ceremony soon." Theodor slipped back into the hallway.

Wasn't sure what that meant, but it if was related to accepting Anthony as my Bombardian then the man might be correct. The feelings racing through me was strong. Clarified why the Bombardians and Keepers or Protectors became couples.

Chapter 9

Anthony

One last look at Larry and I walked into the hallway, leaving him to discuss things with Bryan didn't set well with me. Yet . . . I understood why he requested it. Bryan experienced what he was, meaning Bryan could give him a clearer picture of what being a Keeper meant. Sort of. Each Bombardian, Royal Leader or not, had their own way of life. David and I wasn't that different . . . They might be. Anthony wasn't sure how David or his other cousins lived the main aspect of their lives. They'd not been around each other long enough to know those kind of details. One day, years from now, they'd be that close.

"See that scowl." Theodor pulled the door shut. "What did you expect me to do?"

"Let me listen. Let me protect what is mine." Wrong assumption on my part. Larry hadn't agreed to anything. He might have hugged me, but that's not a commitment.

"I see you done worked the issue out inside your own little head."

"Why can't I listen." Did I whine? Oh boy, I had. Didn't matter. Theodor had seen me at my worst. What was one more weakness visible to the eldest ranking Royal Leader.

"If you have to ask . . . You definitely need a Trial Run." Theodor's phone jingled. "What would Kevin have done if you listened in on what he thought was private?" Another buzz had Theodor sighing. "Think on that while I go make my apologizes to tonight's lover."

Not a hard one to think on. Kevin would have hung me up by my balls.

The rattling of my keys shocked me, then the hallway filled with the tune designated to Kevin. What was he calling for? What would he think of me finding my Keeper? Would he be happy? Pissed?

A second ring had me snatching it from my pocket. "Hello?"

"What, no wonderful greeting for your lover?"

Huh? Kevin left me. Why would I call him lover?

"Anthony, what's wrong?"

My heart did not skip a beat. No hardening cock. No image of me curled up with Kevin. My wolf didn't lift its head at the idea of talking to Kevin. In fact, the wolf whimpered and complained about not being able to hear Larry discuss what lay ahead for them. My mind was more focused on the brown door blocking my view. No desire rose up at all.

"Start talking or I'm calling Theodor."

"I'm fine." Was. Wasn't. I had my Keeper, but feared Larry refusing me a Trial Run. Small part of me feared that Larry would choose to only see me every two days. Chose no relationship between us. One good thing was that there was no chance of me becoming a Mélange.

"Don't sound like it. Start spilling."

"Swear. I'm fine." How did one tell their longtime lover that they'd found a Keeper? Why did it matter? Kevin had left when I became a Royal Leader.

"Phones in my hand."

"Well . . . I . . . Shit."

"Area code is dialed."

I heard the beeps. "Don't call him. Give me a minute to - -"

"Four numbers left."

"Fine. I found my Keeper." Words came out way louder than I meant.

Kevin's gasp made the phone creak. "When? How? I called . . ."

Why had Kevin called? He'd swore the two of them were done. It was the best option. He'd been given a job no one could turn down. He was doing what he loved. "You called because?"

Kevin cleared his throat and sniffed. "This is good. We knew this might happen."

They had. We'd agreed if the other found their Keeper or Protector that they'd be happy for the other.

"I'm glad. I'm sure you two are busy planning the ceremony. I'll just be going."

"No." I might not be drawn to Kevin, but I knew him well. The slight hiccup in the last word showed his internal struggle. "He's yet to accept me."

"Why? You are a great guy. Amazing lover. Will treat him like a king and half. Give him the phone. I'll make him understand."

"Thanks, but . . . He's got to make his own decision. You know the way it works as well as I do."

"He'd be stupid to turn you down."

"Thanks. Means a lot."

"We were good together. If he refuses you . . . Come find me. I'll keep your wolf grounded. Might not be able to keep you from turning, but I'll make sure you harm no one."

What? Why say such? He knew that wasn't how it worked. He knew a Royal Leader whose Keeper refused would be treated no different than any other Bombardian. I'd clued him in on the rule change. It'd been done to show him that we could have a wonderful life together.

"You okay?" I propped myself against the wall.

"Sure. Making sure you know where I stand. Things are different over here."

"I know. That's why I'm not allowed over there. It's why I couldn't come to you if he does refuse me."

"You could."

"Kevin, you know I couldn't. I'll be secluded if my Keeper refuses me." Not that, that could happen. It wasn't one of Larry's choices. Either one meant that I was safe from becoming a Mélange. That should ease my mind, but it didn't. "I don't think he will." No Larry wouldn't outright refuse me but seeing him every couple of days didn't set well with my wolf. Or me. Wasn't going to even think Larry would choose that. Nope. Going to keep my mind focused on the best option until I hear Larry choose the Destroyer Hermitage.

"How come?"

"Can't say. You know why."

"Stupid Royal Leader shit. Knew when you found your Keeper, he'd be all gooey over your power."

"Gooey?" My head ached from my brows furrowing. "In all the years we were lovers I never heard you use such words. What is going on? Has this upset you that much?"

"No. Threw me for a flip."

"Why? You left me for your job." All the anger that I'd suppressed since Kevin left bubbled to life. Rolled over me faster than a streak of lightening. I might have my Keeper, and not have any desire for Kevin, but I still ached over how Kevin left.

"I know I did. Never once said I didn't love you. Always will just like you will always have feelings for me. Right?"

Would I? Not in the same way. I'd met my Keeper. It changed everything. How could it not? Kevin knew it would. I knew it would.

"Right?"

"Kevin, you were a major part of my life, but . . ."

"You know we are best for each other."

"Kevin - -"

"Don't try to tell me one sight of this man destroyed everything you felt for me."

"Kevin, I . . . You were a major part - -"

"You know it did not."

Never expected Kevin to have such a hard time accepting how finding a Keeper affected one. We'd always said it would be an amicable split if that happened, but he was refusing to listen. Kevin had insisted that once they found the one that calmed them that all feelings for each other would cease. He'd been right. I doubted him, but . . .

"It didn't. Why are you trying to tell me it did?"

"Kevin, you are a Bombardian. You know what finding a Keeper means. You will always be a big part of my past, but . . ."

The living room door opened, and Larry's head appeared with a huge frown. Then slammed shut.

"Shit. I've got to go."

"He done got you by your - -"

I didn't hear the last part. My fingers pressed the end button. I reached for the doorknob, but it refused to turn. I slammed my shoulder into it, but it only opened an inch, revealing a strip of white that I knew belonged to the bookcase that usually sat beside the door. A faint chuckle had me blowing my breath out.

"Please, let me explain what you heard." I knocked. "Please, Larry. It's not what you think." Boy was it not. I'd been trying my hardest not to hurt a longtime friend, but once again I'd failed miserably and it led to upsetting the man I wanted in my life.

"Please, Larry, let me explain."

Chapter 10

Larry

I'd listened to Bryan's explanation about Bombardians. Helpful. Pinpointed some major issues. Bryan shared his and David's story. How David found him. How becoming his Keeper reunited him with his best friend, Tommy. How the truth about his birth father came to life as well. Bryan swore that becoming David's Keeper had released him from a hellish life. That had been the winning point.

Learning Anthony's way of life and accepting him meant my dad would be out of my life for good. First, Anthony and I had to come to an agreement. Either choice I'd been given meant I was out of dad's reach. Being away from dad kept me out of the press and gave me a better life. Win-win for me. Plain as day. All I had to do was talk to Anthony. I could do that. Couldn't I?

"You okay?" Bryan's gentle touch and warm grin had me nodding.

"I'm going ... Um ... It's time I ..."

"Spoke with Anthony."

"Yes. I'll get with you later."

"Sure you will." Bryan chuckled. "Enjoy your time with your Bombardian. They can be major fun." He waggled his eyes, laughing as he made his way back to the couch.

"I can see how much fun." I snorted which had Bryan turning back around. "You the one with the ... Oh, shit. Is that ... Can that be possible for all Keepers?"

A simple shrug made my heart plummeted to my stomach.

"We'll know soon enough if you come up that way."

"Don't you jinx my ass." Chills rippled up my arms. Still, I wasn't sure how much of a jinx it would be. If I knew more of what happened during a pregnancy, which thanks to Bryan being that way ... I might mind.

"You'd love it." Bryan winced. "Once you overcome the pregnancy issues."

Probably would. I'd always loved the idea of a big family. Then . . . Adoption would have been my only recourse. Wouldn't have been able to stand a stranger carrying my child.

With some excitement circling my stomach I made my way to the door. My hand was on the knob when I heard Anthony. No one else seemed to be talking to him. Phone call. I knew it was wrong to listen in on a one-sided call, but . . . Being his Keeper meant Anthony would have to share things. Sneaky way to gain knowledge. Old habit. Only method at hand growing up among politicians. A method I'd perfected. Most high influential children learned how to be devious.

Problem was . . . I forgot that at times you don't like what you learn. Or . . . What you hear pisses you off.

"Why? You left me for your job?" Anthony's words took my breath. More had to have been said between Anthony and the caller, but I missed it and came in on another section. "Kevin, you were a major part of my life . . ."

Why would Anthony want me if someone else had his heart? How could he give me a full life if he desired another? I might not have had a perfect role model, but I knew what I wanted from a relationship. A life partner who loved me for me. Not to benefit his way of life. I wasn't a pawn for a happy life. Wouldn't allow it. Even if I doomed Anthony to a life of visitation. Even if rejecting him had been an option I wouldn't have been able to doom him to a life in half wolf, half human form. I could prevent myself from falling further into Anthony's life. Right? Yep. But . . .

Did I misunderstand Anthony's conversation? I was only hearing one side. Should I give him a chance to explain? Maybe. Did it matter? Nope. Anthony had to learn who I was. I had to learn who he was. I'd have to understand his life. Bryan said it was different than what humans knew.

Television fell silent. The room closed in on me, stealing more of my breath. The dark brown door seamed to enlarge with each passing second, just like Anthony's voice had consumed my mind.

"Something wrong?"

I shook my head. "Nothing you can help me with." Took me and Anthony talking. A relationship of any kind, one that benefited each other, required communication. Even if one disliked talking. I turned the doorknob and pulled it open.

Antony was leaned against the wall, staring at me. Raw pain bled to life in his eyes. The thud of the door slamming was louder than the click of the lock.

"That won't keep him out."

I stuck my tongue out at the Bryan, who wore a huge grin.

"This will." I went to the other end of the bookcase and shoved as hard as I could until it blocked the door.

Bryan's chuckle radiated around the room. "Remember they teleport."

Shit. David moved me from the plane in a blink of the eye. I was sure Anthony and the other three cousins could do the same.

One thump. Two thumps. Both had me jerking back.

"Let me in." My hand covered my chest, holding the racing thudding heart in place. "Please. Please let me explain." The plea in his voice roared in my head and had me moving to the end of the bookcase, but I did not push it out of the way. Wasn't going to. Anthony could plead all he wanted. "Please, Larry, let me explain who I was talking to. Let me explain my words. Please."

The couch squeaked, making me glance at Bryan who was struggling to push himself up. "Don't get up. Tell me what you need. I'll get it."

"I have to let Anthony in. Don't know what you heard, but you need to hear him out." Bryan's grunt shot through me like lightening striking me. "You deserve happiness. Anthony can give you that. Give him a chance."

"Was going to." Shit. Did I snap at Bryan? "Sorry. I was going to until I saw the raw sadness in his eyes. Whoever he was speaking with is important to him. He can't be with him because of me. I won't be second fiddle to anyone. Not the man . . ."

Oh shit. I was . . . Ugh. When had I become so attached to Anthony? How had I? I'd only met him hours ago. The man hadn't even asked me on a date.

"Just what I thought." Bryan made two staggering steps. "Damn, don't make me have to make another step."

I was at Bryan's side and had him back on the couch before I could take three breaths. "Stay seated. David will kill me if you get hurt."

"That he will." Theodor's deep voice flowed around the room. "Why is the door blocked and Anthony sitting on the floor with his back to the door, hanging his head."

Fudge. Next thing I knew the soft couch cushions wrapped me in warmth. "I'll go talk to him." I glanced at Bryan. "Will you stay seated?"

"He will." Theodor sat in the recliner to the left of Bryan and grabbed up the remote. "I'll make sure. Go deal with my cousin before he has a freaking human style heart attack."

"Take him to your room. Let him see the feisty side." Bryan waved his hand at the screen. "Start my movie back."

Feisty side? Did I have one? Didn't think so. Shawn used to tell me I was a spitfire when I became ticked off at him and . . . Shawn loved for me to kiss him after we'd been apart for a couple of days. He swore the separation threw me into a maniac, gentle lover. There'd be no feisty loving of any kind going on between Anthony and me.

"Move back or fall on your back." I shoved the bookcase as hard as I could, but after the first push it moved on it's on.

"You're welcome." Theodor said as he faced the TV.

Chapter 11

Anthony

My feet hit the ground hard thanks to the force I jumped up with. I'd kiss Theodor's feet if he went in there and talked to my Keeper. He sure was saving my ass lately.

Larry's redden face ripped my insides in half. I even glanced down expecting to see my insides on the outsides.

"I'm - -" two steps forward had my Keeper's pointing down the hallway.

"Let's go."

No argument. I'd followed him halfway down the hallway, passing Franklin's grinning face. If Larry hadn't been in front of me, I might have snapped at Franklin. Larry needed to see my good side. Not my childish one. I was already on his shit list. He didn't need my stupidness in large doses. Small ones were inevitable.

"Don't even say it." Larry paused in front of Franklin, tossing his head to the door on his right. "I'll get Bryan on your ass."

Franklin lifted his hands and darted down the hallway.

"You've got to teach me that."

"What? Threatening someone. It's easy."

"No. Getting them to leave you alone."

"That's easy to."

"Not for me." My inability to do so was why I found myself in a fix with Larry.

"Come in."

Shit. Going in first wasn't high on my list. Picking your battles was the wisest. Carefulness was required or I'd run my Keeper right to a Destroyer Hermitage.

"Take a seat." Larry sat in the middle of king size bed with his legs crossed.

I'd love to be up there with him. See him stretched out and underneath me. Would in time. Hopefully. Until then . . . Relegated to the chair.

"I'm sorry you - -"

"Don't. Just answer a few questions."

"Anything."

"Who was you talking to?"

"An ex-lover." Not lying to my Keeper, but I made sure to stress the word ex.

"How ex?"

Shit. "Not long."

"How long is not long?"

"Right after you were taken."

"He the love of your life?"

"N - - I thought he was at the time, but we both knew what would happen when one of us found our other half."

"What's that?"

"We go to our Keeper or Protector. Kevin is a Bombardian. He knows the impact a person like that has on our lives."

Larry fiddled with the edge of the light blue blanket. I'd love to feel those fingers between mine. Love to know how soft and tender they would be exploring my body. One day. That was for sure. If I could wiggle my way out of the mess I got myself into. Shit. I was good at screwing up my life.

"I . . . I'm not sure . . ."

"Hang on. Don't dismiss us before we discuss what I was talking about."

"Then . . . Go on."

"I was telling him he was part of my past life. I feel nothing for him. None of the attraction that we once shared. The entire time I was talking to him I was thinking of you."

"You were not."

"I was."

"I saw the pain etched on your face."

"That's what made you lock me out." Unexpected.

"Course it was. It was clear you were heartbroken."

Misconception big time. Course he misunderstood. We know very little about one another. He only heard one side of the conversation and only a snippet of it then. "Not for the reason you think."

"I'm not stupid."

"Course not. That's me."

"Is not."

"Is."

"Not."

"Is."

"Lord have mercy, we sound like children."

Laughter, both of ours, rang through the room. Larry's rich smooth laugh sent shivers over my body, but what got my cock hard was the way his sweet, sexy eyes seemed to round as his amusement grew louder and louder.

"What?"

Before I could stop myself, my hand lifted and brushed across Larry's sexy lips, lowering across his light-brown stubbled chin.

"Something on my face?"

"You're perfect."

"Hardly."

"You are." I would have given anything to be sitting next to him. Holding him. Kissing him. Proving how perfect of a Keeper I'd been blessed with.

"You were going to enlighten me to why you were sporting heartbreak."

Right. Explanation. Time to ensure my Keeper stayed with me. "I was worried over Kevin's reaction. He was . . . Behaving irrational for him."

More than that. He'd been pushy. Not Kevin at all. Kevin didn't force anyone into anything. He lived a true and open life. That's why he'd left before I became a Royal Leader. It's what had spurred me into moving to California to be with him.

"You do still care for him."

"I will always care for him, but not the same way as before he chose his job over me."

"Fool."

"I can be a big one."

"Not you."

Larry would learn I could be pretty dunce and stubborn at times. "Who then?"

"Kevin."

"Oh." I leaned forward, bracing my elbows on my knees. Best option I had to be closer to Larry.

"I don't like it."

"What?"

"Your being concerned over him."

Crap. What was I to say to that? I dislike your concern for Bryan. Should I share that? Would it help or make things worse? Would it make Larry see a semblance to them? "Can I ask you something?"

"Sure?"

"How come you are so close to Bryan?"

"Jealous?"

"Yes."

"Good."

"Oh . . . I see. Fair play and all that."

"Something like that."

Dang it. Larry's luscious body was killing me. Each movement he made drew my attention but the long slim legs that slowly untucked and stretched down the middle of the bed had my cock thumping.

"I have few friends thanks to my dad's position. I had one . . . He was my best friend and lover."

A low growl slipped from me before I could squash it.

"What? You have Kevin in your past."

"Guess we have something to work on."

"Looks like it." Larry folded his hands in his lap, drawing my full attention to his zipper. Did he wear boxers or briefs? Silk? Cotton? Fleece? "Shawn, my best friend, the one who understood me and my situation, died suddenly. It tore me up for months. Bryan . . . He never treated me different. Welcomed me into his and David's home with open arms. Didn't hold me to some high standards. Didn't push me for answers about how it was to be the son of the President of the United States. He treated me like anyone else."

Never considered how hard it would have been for Larry to have a typical life. Bryan hadn't had one either. He would have in-depth knowledge of how hard Larry's life would have been. Not to mention Bryan seemed to care about anyone he met. He just had a way with people. He knew how to approach people and handle questions that were unwanted without being disrespectful. At the Pledging Ceremony he'd taken all the queries about his previous life with a grain of salt. And Bryan had reason to scream and shout to the world that his life had sucked. He never once did. He smiled and evaded the question without dimming the questioner's inquiry. Even told some people that his life had been decent compared to others. He swore that was the truth. In some ways, Bryan might have been right, but in other ways . . . Bryan hadn't even thrown a fit when David and his honeymoon was cut short because David needed to rescue Larry. Okay, a small one, but he had right to. Bryan was most likely just what Larry needed after his ordeal. Larry's state of mind had to be frayed after being kidnapped and held hostage. A friend . . . Was just what Larry needed and had gotten. I owed Bryan a huge thanks.

"I guess . . . I mean . . . Bryan helped me understand lots about what you are asking of me."

"He did?" Owed him, big time. I'd have to get him something nice. Not to nice or David would skin me alive, if Larry didn't. "Do you have any other questions I can answer for you?"

"How do you feel about being fated to me?"

"I love the idea."

"Don't lie."

"Not." I came to my feet. "Can I join you?"

"Sure."

I sat down, taking hold of Larry's arm. "This," my finger traced the mark that I prayed would hold my name soon. "Gives you my soul. My life is in your hands. I will understand if that is too much of a job for you. Being my Keeper won't be easy. Sure Bryan told you all about his experiences since he met David."

"Some. I'm used to my life being in danger. Constant thing for someone like me."

"I hate that." No one deserved such a life. "Hate that your father's guards let you be taken. Hate that I wasn't there to prevent it. Hate that I wasn't there to free you. It was my job. Not David's."

"You didn't know me then." Warmth zoomed over me as Larry rested his hand over mine. "I like you feeling that way, but don't beat yourself up. It still brought me here."

Thankfully. I would have rather met him any other way than for him to have suffered such an incident.

"I have an answer for you."

Oh boy. My fate was going to be given. My heat thumped so fast that I couldn't catch my breath. I knew it was as easy as inhaling and exhaling, but my body failed to do so. My mind seemed to be zooming down some invisible road. One that would either doom me to a life of visitation or a full life with the one who owned the other half of my soul.

"Breath."

Right. Easier said than done.

"You've got to breath for me to tell you."

Ugh. How was I . . . Okay. I could do this. Simple. Open mouth. Inhale. Let the air rush down my lungs and the come back out of them. That simple.

"Ready?"

Yes. No. Was my life doomed to a life of visits to the Destroyer's Hermitages? Would I be able to take Larry home and ravish him? Would I find myself flashing into Theodor's guest room again? One way to find out. "Ready."

"I want a three-month Trial Run."

Three months. Longer than I liked by about a month, but . . . If I said month, then Larry would have month and half to make up his mind. I'd have a month and half of having my life up in the air. Fearing every second that Larry would choose the Destroyer's Hermitage. Month and half of hearing Franklin and Theodor hounding me about having a Keeper in a hermitage instead of my home. What little good it did to store Bryan in one. They still attacked when he left the home. The Ghioulians might not be reformed, yet, but other enemies lurked. Like the terrorist that took Larry. The reason he was staying in David's . . . Ah . . . Larry wouldn't be going to the Destroyer's Hermitage until he felt safe. Until then he was under David's protection. Well . . . Under the guard of the Royal Leaders. Wasn't he? Was? Did this change things? Didn't see why, but . . . It might. I'd have to ask Theodor.

"Is that doable?"

"Month and half."

"That the difference?" I nodded at Larry. "I can do that."

"I'm not sure where you will be staying."

"Here." Larry squeaked. "I won't leave here. I can't. I'll do anything, just don't make me leave here."

"What is going on?" Theodor said as soon as I tugged Larry into my arms, rubbing his back. "Bryan heard him in the living room and tried to get up."

"Bryan . . . Shit is . . ."

"He's fine." Theodor held his hand up. "He'd like to know what is wrong with you?"

"I . . . Anthony, please . . . Don't . . ."

"Anthony?" Theodor drawing out my name didn't bode well. "Answer me now, before Bryan tries to come in here."

"He's not comfortable leaving here during the Trial Run."

"He won't." Theodor sighed. "David promised you sanctuary and that promise will remain intact."

"Not that I would have let you." Okay, that came out a bit more commanding than caring. Oops. Had to work on that. "I would not have let you leave safety. I promise." I ran my thumb across his cheek and around his lips. "I would never put you in harms way. Promise."

"You good, Larry."

"Yes, Theodor. Tell Bryan I'm sorry I bothered him."

"He'll be fine." Theodor nodded. "You two work out the basics." He tossed a phone at Anthony. "Take care of that damn thing. It's been ringing since you came in here. It's annoying Bryan and me."

I snatched the phone out of the air, shoving it in my pocket. Whoever it was could wait. I was holding my Keeper, who had agreed to a Trial Run. All I had to do was not screw up. How hard could that be?

My keys jingled as Kevin's ring tone filled the room.

"Let's see who this is." Larry slipped his hand into my pocket, tugging the phone free. "Who I thought it was. Your ex-lover is calling."

Chapter 12

Larry

Could anyone say bitchy? Hadn't meant to snap at Anthony. Thought of him talking to this Kevin guy sickened me. Anthony no longer belonged to him. He had a Keeper. I was his. It was my job to tend to him. My job to see to all his concerns. Or . . . That's how it seemed from what Bryan explained. My job to keep his wolf calm. Only achievable if I was involved with every aspect of his life. Every small detail, right down to the choice of clothes.

Hmm . . . What did Anthony wear under his nice black suit? Boxers? Briefs? Ugh! Where had that came from? Keeping someone calm did not pertain to knowing his underwear choice. Did it?

"What's wrong, honey?" Lord have mercy, Anthony's fingertip was so soft. Never had a touch been so sensual. So tender. "I don't like your lips turned down."

"Nothing." What a lie. I flinched when the same ring tone played through the room. "Answer it."

"No." Anthony reached for the phone, but I ran my finger over the screen, answering it.

"Hello, Kevin."

"Who the - -"

"Anthony will be right with you." I held the phone out. "Talk to him. Settle things. Then we can lay out the plan of attack for our Trial Run."

Anthony's preppy and sassy looking eyes dimmed as his plump lips lowered. "I don't . . . There's nothing left for me and him to say."

"There is. He thinks so. That's why he's calling." Much as I hated it. "Tend to your old business then your new."

"Like the sound of that." Anthony's arm slipped around my waist, tugging me forward.

I went with it, for a split second before I laid my hand against his chest. "Not that kind." Yet. Soon. Real soon. I wanted to taste every corner of Anthony's mouth. Find out if he was as delicious as he smelled.

"Hello . . . Anthony, Anthony, I can hear you. Answer me or . . . I'm calling Theodor."

"Won't do you any good." I scooted further away from Anthony, stretching out on the far side of the bed. "Take it to another room if you want. I trust you."

Did. Wasn't sure why. Might have been the reaction Anthony had after I slammed the door on him and locked him out. Rash actions rarely work. Seemed to have that time. Sucked that I hurt Anthony in the process. That hadn't been my goal. Okay, it had been. I wanted him to feel the pain I felt when I saw him hurting over an ex-lover.

"Won't be doing that." Anthony placed the phone to his ear. "I'm putting you on speaker."

Wow! Unexpected. Shocking. Didn't want to hear Kevin ask Anthony to give me up in order to rekindle their relationship. Nope. Wouldn't end well for Anthony or me.

"You sure about this?"

"I won't keep anything from you. I'm not that kind of man."

Good. Bad. Right then . . . Both.

"You best not do it."

"Kevin, you are on speaker." Anthony's tone held no ounce of remorse that I'd heard earlier. Why not?

"Take me off."

"I can't. Won't. Say what you have to. I have details to work out."

"I will not talk while he is listening." I was sort of there with Kevin. I mean . . . Hearing them discuss their past wasn't high on my list, but . . . Anthony being willing to talk to him while I listened eased the thudding in my heart. Or part of it. The rest was devoted to how much my body, mind, and soul was craving time with Anthony. Not just time, but alone time. Time to start our new life. "Take me off speaker. Now."

"Watch it." The words flew out of me before I could even think about what I was doing.

"Don't tell me what to do. You are nothing but a flea on my wolf."

"You best watch it." Anthony's snarl did little to ease the chest aching, racing blood in my heart. Revved it up. "You will not speak to him with disrespect. You will afford him the respect he is due being a Royal Keeper."

"He's yet to accept you."

"Doesn't change a thing."

Anthony's jumbled up words had me doing a double take. Okay, not the words, but the sharp canines that filled his mouth and the yellow wolf eyes that shined bright. Shit. Scary. Sexy as hell. I took hold of his hand, rubbing his inner palm. With each stroke his face shrunk back into a normal one and his eyes shifted back.

"It doesn't."

"Does." Anthony smiled at me, making my cock come to life, fast. What got it harder than ever before was when he mouthed thank you to me.

Anthony slipped his fingers between mine. Sort of liked Anthony paying more attention to me than his ex-lover. Showed me I had mistook what I heard earlier. Let me know that my Bombardian was indeed interested in me. Like that hadn't been evident from the hell of a boner Anthony sported. Not even slacks could hide it. Especially tight ones.

"You called for a reason?"

Anthony spoke in a clam tone, but the corner of his eyes had stretched and there was a stone aspect to him. Except . . . Anthony's attention wasn't on the conversation. Oh, he heard Kevin, responded to him, but . . . Every ounce of him was in-tuned with me. Weren't just the little squeezes he gave my hand as much as I could feel him seeping into my pores. Each breath he took was with mine. I shifted on the bed, he did.

"You the only reason I need to call."

"Not anymore." Anthony lifted my hand and kissed the top of it, grinning.

Instead of letting our hands rest back between us, I took one of his fingers and slipped it between my lips. Hadn't planned on taking him down that path, but . . . Hell. My body wanted the man in front of me. Bryan had been right about the attraction being stronger than anyone could describe.

My tongue swirled around his finger, drawing a deep breath from Anthony.

"You listening to me?"

Hoped not. I wanted Anthony's full attention. I had it. Anthony's shining eyes wrapped around me as he focused on my mouth. His silence said even more.

"Anthony . . . Hello."

"He's asking for you." I sat back, releasing Anthony's hand.

"So." Anthony mouthed.

"Take care of business with him. We have a long talk ahead of us." Wasn't sure how much talking we'd accomplished, but we needed to talk. Hoped it wouldn't take long. Sometimes getting on the same page with another can be difficult and time consuming. Still . . . The sooner we did that the sooner we could get to funnier parts.

"What did you call for, Kevin?"

"To make sure you are going to live up to our promise."

"What promise?"

I ran my hand back and forth across the bedspread, forcing my attention to remain anywhere but on Anthony. Wasn't easy. His attention was so intense that I felt it to my soul. It burned, not in a bad way. More like a reminder of just how much fun you had spending the entire day out in the pool under the scorching sun. My internal refusal to interfere in Anthony and Kevin's discussion had me picking at the edge of my shirt. Being in the room and the phone on speaker meant I heard the entire conversation, but . . . Okay, I was glad of that. Gave me an idea of what lay ahead of me with this Kevin dude. Sounded as if he was deeply attached to Anthony. Not a good thing. I wanted an uneventful life with Anthony.

"The one you and I made to each other when we began seeing one another."

"Not following." Anthony's fingers lifted my head. Our eyes locked onto one another, sending shivers over my body.

"You know very well what we agreed to if we met our Keeper or Protector."

"I do. We were not to interfere with the other, because it's our way of life."

"Wrong."

"I'm not wrong." Anthony laid back, scooted closer.

My heart skipped a couple of beats as heat arced between us as Anthony moved even closer. Kevin's voice faded into the distance with each passing second, I stared into Anthony's eyes. When Anthony's fingers began rubbing over the mark on my forearm, Kevin's voice disappeared.

I was less than an inch away from Anthony when his lips sealed over mine. Lightening had to have zapped us both. Only thing to explain the sharp shards of force drawing us deeper into the kiss. I slipped my hand around Anthony and up his back as Anthony gripped my waist. Our knees bumped each other as we closed the last few inches between us. Our chest was rubbing against each when someone grunted.

"Who dared . . ."

"Don't finish that, Anthony."

I buried my head in Anthony's neck as heat flooded my face from Theodor's voice.

"Why are you interrupting us, Theodor?"

"Kevin declared your Keeper had harmed you."

No he didn't. What the . . . "He what!" That was it. I'd viewed Kevin as a pest, but . . . More of a prick. I'd not stand for lies. "Give me that."

I snatched the phone off the bed.

"Listen here . . . You might have been the best thing in Anthony's life, but you chose your job over him. That much I do know. You were stupid to do that. He has me now. You won't be needed. Again. Keep your calls to yourself." I hit the end button and threw the phone across the room, shattering some glass vase that sat on the top of a dresser. Shit. Oh well. I'd pay David back. "That's that."

"Oh boy." Theodor laughter and huge smile had me snorting. "We have another Bryan on our hands it appears."

"Worse." I crossed my arms over my chest. "I grew up around assholes who thought they were better and deemed themselves laws unto their own self. I have many more ways of dealing with them than Bryan ever dreamed of."

"I bet so." Anthony tugged my arm until I was laying half across him. "I've got the best Keeper in the world."

"Better believe it."

"Does that mean . . . I get to plan another Pledging Ceremony?"

"Not yet." Anthony gave me a wink that had me melting closer to him. If that was even possible. I was already flush with is body. "Larry needs to be wooed a bit more before then."

"That I do."

"How are you going to do that when he can't leave David's house?"

Good question. Hadn't considered that.

"I'll work it out." Anthony kissed my cheek. "I'll work it out."

"I'm leaving." Theodor pulled the door too.

"How long before . . ." The ring tone from earlier filled the room. Vase broke, but not the phone. Damn. "Never mind."

"Let me cut that off." Anthony slipped from under me and picked up the phone, shaking some shards of glass from it.

"What if Theodor needs you?"

"He knows where I am."

That he did, but . . . I rolled onto my back, letting my arms rest beside me. "You should have answered that and cleared things up with him."

"I tried."

True, but . . . "I was on the phone." That would have pissed me off. Sure it did Kevin.

"So. You are my life now."

"Not yet."

"Yes. You. Are."

"I've not accepted you."

"Doesn't matter. You hold my life in your hands. Either choice you have makes you part of my life. One more deeply than the other. And Kevin knows this."

"He doesn't know that my choices are different than the other Keepers and Protectors."

"True. Doesn't matter though. He made me promise to live my life to the fullest. That's what I'm doing."

"He did?" Sounded like the man cared. Couldn't have been easy on Kevin to know that Anthony replaced him in such a short span of time. If I'd been Kevin . . . I couldn't say that. I wasn't him. In so many ways. Kevin was a Bombardian. He knew what a Keeper was. How special they were to one of his kind. I . . . Didn't quite understand that to its fullest. Yet.

"He did. Went as far as to make me promise my sacred oath."

"Wow. What's that?"

"Where I promised on my seat as a Royal Leader."

Major. "What exactly did he make you promise?"

"To take care of myself."

"Then not to leave him behind when you find your Keeper."

"It's one and the same."

"Huh?"

"If a Bombardian finds his Keeper then to ensure safety for themselves and all around they have to make things work with their Keeper, one way or the other."

"That why you are attracted to me?" Hoped not. I wanted more than that.

"No."

"Really?" I had to be sure for my own peace of mind. I wasn't getting that vibe from Anthony, but . . .

"No. I could hardly stand in the doorway when I first heard your voice. I freaked a bit." Anthony's shutter was sort of funny, but I made my chuckle stay silent. "Quite a bit, but . . . For many reasons."

"One of which was Kevin."

"Yes."

"Good answer." Truth. What I wanted.

"Truth."

"I know."

"That doesn't bother you?"

"Nope. Truth is truth."

"Then why'd you get so mad when you saw me talking to him?"

"Your face was full of sadness. I will not be second fiddle to someone."

"I," Anthony gripped my chin, "I would never do that to anyone. I was upset while on the phone, but because Kevin was acting weird. Majorly."

"How so?"

"He was wanting me to go back on our promise. I told him out right no. He flipped out and became irrational." His frown matched the one I saw on him earlier, but it did not . . . Bother me as bad. I knew the reason behind it. I'd overreacted earlier. Reacted to hearing a one-sided conversation. I know better than that. "I've never seen or heard him like that. Kind of worried me. Made me sad that I was hurting him, but we knew there was a chance we'd find our other half. Knew it since we met. It could have been him who found his Keeper. I would have lived up to our laws. Kevin knows that."

"Okay . . . Still think you need to call him and work things out. If you two had been in a relationship as deep as you seem to have been then there needs to be closure." I hated it, but truth was truth. "I'll go visit with Bryan. You join us when you are done. Then we can watch a movie, or something."

Chapter 13

Anthony

Perfect bubble but swayed as Larry left the room. Damn, it was made for gripping while thrusting in and out of what had to be a tight hole. There was nothing better than a firm ass to grip as my fingers spread round cheeks aside, revealing the perfect opening. I was sure Larry would handle me like a pro, even if he had little sexual experience. Wasn't sure about that, but . . . Didn't matter. I'd be glad to teach him all he needed to know.

"Damn."

I reached down and slid my cock to the left. Slacks had little to no room in them. My cock had been hard as a board since we entered the room. Watching Larry saunter out did little to ease my state of mind.

"What are you thinking about?"

I whipped around snarling, halting my advance as fast. "General Gobbler, what are you doing here?"

"Uh . . . Commander Anthony, you are here. That's why. You left the house without telling your guards where you were going. That is unlike you. I have called each Royal Leader, only getting an answer from Commander Franklin. He said you were here and fine, but . . ."

"You doubted him?" Not smart. Wasn't sure what I looked like, but my General fell to his knees and tilted his head.

"No, Commander Anthony."

"Then why come after you were told I was fine?"

"It is my job, Commander Anthony."

"He's right, Anthony."

Lord what was going on? A gathering of Royal Leaders and Generals?

"Franklin, General Regan, how are you? Did Bryan give in to call . . ." My words trailed off when Franklin ran his hand across his throat. I knew Bryan hadn't wanted his father called. Not even Tommy. Wasn't sure how David and Bryan expected to keep his state a secret. Tommy was General Thompson's Keeper and Bryan's best friend. Those two were tied at the hip ninety percent of the time.

"Why would . . ." General Regan's glare was as intense as my Uncle's had been. "If you . . ."

General Gobbler blocked my line of sight a second before General Regan made a step towards me.

"General Regan, stand down." Franklin snapped the command as two other Combatants appeared beside General Gobbler.

Shit. So not what I needed. If Bryan heard any commotion he'd come investigating. That would not only bring Theodor, but Larry. Neither of them would be pleased that Bryan was disturbed by something I could have prevented by keeping my mouth shut when I had not been told things had changed. Yep. My mouth got me in trouble, again. Would I ever learn?

"Stand down." I shoved the two newest Combatants back. "General Gobbler, I said stand down and you best not call any more Combatants. We clear?"

"Yes, Commander Anthony."

"Franklin," With one step I was back in eyesight of my cousin. "I'm truly sorry. I was not thinking clearly. Has there been a problem I should be aware of?"

Late questions. Should have been the first one out of my idiotic mouth. Wrong. First reaction should have been me running down the hallway to locate Larry.

"Is . . ." Two steps was all I got before Franklin held his hand up.

"General Regan came to investigate and gain permission to reply to your General's phone call. He was not aware that General Gobbler had reached out to me himself."

"He did what!"

Fudge. My General fell back to his knees before I could verbally rip him a new hole. He knew better than that kind of crap. There were procedures to follow if his concern was great. Did not involve him directly contacting another Royal Leader. What had my General been thinking. Did I even want to know? Not really. My Combatants knew how strict I was. Combatants were stronger and wiser than other Bombardians. It's why they held the job of protecting their leaders.

"No, cousin." Theodor stepped around Franklin grinning. "You can scold your General later. As misguided as his actions were, he did so out of concern for you." Theodor frowned at General Gobbler. "I hope that's why you reached out to four Generals."

Four? If all four Generals invaded David's home General Gobbler was dead. Least David would have clued General Thompson in on his whereabouts.

"How many is here?" My teeth clanked with each word.

"Three. Counting yours."

"How pissed is our young Bryan?"

"Lucky for you," General Regan crossed his arms, "my son is sleeping."

Doubted that. Wasn't about to contradict whatever Franklin, or Theodor, told General Regan.

"We would like to keep it that way." Theodor's tone shifted to one of pure authority, which had me standing up taller. "That's why all the Generals are returning to their previous location. David has enough Combatants to attend to each of us."

True. David insisted that the top ten and five reserves be called in for duty around his house. First clue of how bad Bryan felt was that he had not thrown a fit. Come to think of it . . . Where was General Thompson. Didn't recall seeing him, nor hearing him, around the house. Didn't matter. Wasn't my concern who David put guarding his house and Keeper. Then again . . . It was. My Keeper was there.

I'd have to have General Gobbler assign a few more Combatants. Normally, I'd coordinate with General Thompson, but . . . Theodor was here. He could . . . No. Wasn't going to be stepping over protocol to gain peace of mind.

"I do - -"

"General Gobbler, it is in your best interest to shut up and do as Commander Theodor has said. If I need you, I know how to call."

The room erupted into a fog of blue mist as the Generals and Combatants faded, leaving Franklin and Theodor shaking their heads.

"What?"

"You forgot to touch base with your Combatants."

"Give me some credit, Theodor." Wasn't that dumb. I . . . Hold up. Something wasn't adding up. "I told the ones at my house I was leaving for David's."

"Then why . . ."

What was going on? The Combatants would have enlightened their General. He should have asked them before jumping the gun. Man wasn't known for being rash. So . . . Nor was he one to break protocols. Nor was it like him to freak over something as trivial as not knowing my location. General Gobbler might be new to the General role, but he had been a Lieutenant before being promoted. What had . . ."

"Is Larry safe?"

"He's with Bryan."

"Where are they? I know Bryan is not sleeping."

Theodor grunted. "Barricaded in the living room. I shut the door when my General showed up. Why?"

"Something is . . ."

Wrong. Why did I think that? General Gobbler held his rank for two months. Still new. Yet . . . all the Combatants were on edge since the bombing.

"Something is wrong?" Franklin came over to my side. "Don't think so hard. Say what is lurking on the tip of your tongue. Sometimes the best thoughts come when we are free mouthing things."

Free mouthing things? What the heck did that mean?

"Don't think he knows what you mean." Theodor patted my shoulder. "What he means is you need to loosen up. Let your instincts lead."

Instincts? Did I have those? If so . . . Had I ever used them? Doubtful.

"Finish your statement and do not censor." Franklin took the antique chair in the corner.

"Was it something in particular? A word? Something said? A move? Unusual move? Out of the norm? What?" Theodor took a seat on the foot of the bed, tapping his foot.

"Not so much . . ." Had it been an action? It . . . Why though? People changed up routine all the time. I'd told the Combatants when they joined my ranks that I never stuck to a preset routine. "There was something . . . General Gobbler knows my feelings on protocols. He knows I'm not the type of man who sticks to a regimen. Why did me being out of touch for . . ." I glanced at my watch. Crap. Had I been at David's that long? Hadn't felt like it. Should have. I'd met my Keeper. Had a meeting with my cousins. Donned the Red Hooded Guy costume. Explained about my kind. About Keepers. Talked to Kevin. Twice. Solved a misunderstanding.

"Kevin . . ."

"Kevin what?" Theodor jumped to his feet.

"He recommended General Gobbler be promoted."

"Why?"

More importantly why had I listened to him? How had Kevin even known General Gobbler?

"Not sure."

"Think. This could be important."

"How? Kevin had nothing to do with the Royal Leaders or Combatants before I became one."

"Then how did he know a Lieutenant?" Franklin moved to Theodor's side. "There has to be a connection. What are you overlooking?"

"Nothing." Was I? Kevin and I knew each other for a long time. Been lovers for most of that time. We talked about every aspect of our lives.

"There has to be something. It ruffled your wolf's fur, even if you don't realize it." Franklin's huff pulled one from me. "Think on it. Figure it out."

"I have more important things to - -"

"Love life. We all know." Theodor wiped his hand across his leg. "You and David are going to be the death of me."

"I think it's sweet."

"Sweet? Franklin, man, you've lost it if you think what Bryan is suffering through is sweet."

"Not that, Theodor." Franklin's rolling eyes were more comical than when Caleb did so. Least Caleb's didn't go back into his head. "I meant them having the ones who calm their beast at their sides for the rest of their lives."

"Is that the case for you?" Theodor bounced on the bed, springing to his feet. "Has the President's son chosen you for the rest of his life?"

Wished. Wanted to shout from the rooftops that my Keeper chose me. Wanted to tell Theodor he had another Pledging Ceremony to plan, but . . . Not the case. Yet.

"Guess that frown means no."

"Looks like it. Least he can't tell him to confine his ass to a confinement house."

One part of the two options that Theodor and the other three cousins decided on that aided me greatly.

"He's going to." I muttered, only half sure that my Keeper would be mine completely.

"Good. Then you can devote your time to figuring out why your ex-lover would recommend you promote General Gobbler when you never heard him mention knowing any Combatants."

Theodor didn't wait around for my answer. He left, expecting me to take his last comment as the command it was. Even among the Royal Leaders there was a pecking order. Not adhered to as tightly as most, but there was one and Theodor was the top dog. Me and Franklin was at the bottom. Wasn't sure which of us held that bottom rank. Considering my lack of skills and knowledge about my affinity I'd say I was.

"He's right. You know it."

Sure did. Didn't need Franklin telling me it, though. Kevin requested the promotion for some reason. As much as I hated it, I'd have to take time away from wooing Larry to solve the issue at my feet. Least reaching out to Kevin wouldn't cost me my Keeper. Larry told me to solve the issue between us. Gave me the best reason to call Kevin back.

Chapter 14

Larry

Why in the world had I come back in the living room with a pep in my step? I'd given my . . . Bombardian, a man with a wolf lurking inside him and who could do magic and . . . An affinity . . . "Bryan, what did you say Anthony's affinity was?"

"Water." The weak smile had my excitement dying as I rushed to Bryan's side, lifting the glass of ginger-ale.

"Try some. Your throat is scratchy again."

The room filled with a greenish mist then a large bulky man appeared next to Theodor, who'd been sitting quietly in the far corner reading.

"What is going on General?"

"David?" Bryan made to push himself up, but I rested my hand on his arm.

"Stay seated. If this had to do with David, General Thompson would be here."

"He's right." Theodor's comment should have eased my mind, but I'd been guessing. My main objective had been not upsetting Bryan.

"You full of it." Bryan snorted. "But I know he's right."

"Good." Least I hadn't screwed up. Me getting a better grasp of the Bombardian world meant I needed to gain more. Bryan could aid me in that, while Theodor and his General whispered to one another. "Then fill me in on a few more things I can - -"

"Excuse me guys, but I need to shut you guys in here for awhile." Theodor pointed to the hallway behind him. "Nothing wrong, just a misunderstanding with General Gobbler."

Bryan's simple shrug and shut eyes should have eased me more than Theodor's assurance, but something . . . Didn't sit well in my heart. Didn't keep me from nodding at Theodor.

"I'll answer more of Larry's questions." Bryan cleared his throat. "Drink more ginger-ale if I can."

Theodor faded into nothingness, but second later I heard him talking loudly to someone.

"He's not happy." Bryan took another sip. "Now what are your questions?"

"Give me more information on what I can expect when I end this Trial Run."

"So, you chose a Trial Run, but done know what you are going to do."

I had. Didn't make much sense. I knew little about Anthony. Knew he'd been in a deep relationship with another of his kind, who was not one bit pleased about Anthony moving on. That alone should have had me running for a Destroyer's Hermitage. Being confined into a Hermitage did not set well with me. I might want to be away from the press and limelight, but I did not want to have to close myself off from everyone. Not all the time at least.

"Larry . . ."

"Yeah. But I . . . We just met. It . . ."

"Seems wrong." Bryan sat his glass down. "I know how you feel. It does. I went the Trial Run route knowing I was going to choose David. I used it to get to know David. Come to terms with the fact that the Cult wasn't a cult. That . . . What people named love at first sight, or soul mates, was true. It's a lot to take in. David and the other Bombardians are aware of having them from the time they are born. We don't have that option."

We should have. Every American should. The knowledge of another species shouldn't be hidden. Americans did not deserve to be fed lies about a Cult and Red Hooded Guy.

"My dad is a bastard."

"Huh?" Bryan opened one eye. "How'd we get to him?"

"He knows all about this and keeps it buried. He is supposed to be honest and do what is best for Americans. He's doing right the opposite."

"Like so many before him." Bryan sighed. "Any other questions about Bombardians or Anthony?"

Loads, but best if I asked Anthony. An interview gave as much information as actions. Not to mention it showed Anthony how serious I was. Better to get it from the source than Bryan. Bryan was a safer choice, but Bryan could not tell me the hardcore facts about who Anthony was. That came from Anthony alone.

"How much longer you think we'll be kept in here?"

"No telling." Bryan picked up the remote and cut the TV on. "Ready to watch the rest of the movie."

"Sure."

Chapter 15

Anthony

The phone rang and rang, going unanswered for a second time. Lord, I hoped Kevin didn't' decide to pout. Wasn't known for it, but when he did . . . He made a great job of it.

"What?"

A deep quick breath to squash my temper at the sharp tone and I dove right into the heart of the call to Kevin.

"Need to know how you knew General Gobbler."

"I need to know if he has you by your balls or if you are ready to talk about where this puny Keeper has you locked down to his side."

Puny? Oh boy. Larry wasn't as big as a Bombardian, but was far from small. Why in the world was Kevin bad mouthing Larry to begin with. He was a Royal Keeper. Demanded respect.

"Guess silence is my answer. Until you call to say I'm your main man and he's a stand-in to keep you calm we have nothing to discuss."

Cold day in hell. Kevin knew it, so why mention it. That wasn't their way of life. Once a Keeper or Protector was found others became off bounds. More like there was no feelings left. Me and my wolf would not be complete unless every aspect of our lives revolved around Larry. If Larry chose the Hermitage I'd feel as a major part of me was missing. I might see Larry every other day, but my wolf and me wanted him at our side. Wanted to lavish his entire body with love. Wanted to be mind-to-mind with him. Wanted the type of love that . . . He wanted what David had with Bryan. Larry could give me that. Kevin could never have.

"Do not hang up." Hadn't meant for it to be a command, but it was. Hated the idea of going Royal Leader mode on Kevin, but if he wanted to act like an ass I could. "I asked you a question as a friend. If you won't answer it that way, you will answer your Royal Leader."

"Do not go there with me."

"You best answer the question, or you will be recalled and face punishment."

"I am no longer a United States member."

"Did you properly request the right to leave the grounds of the United States?" One of my cousins would have told me if he had. They would not have allowed me to be blindsided by him leaving like I had been. And why hadn't . . . Shit. Why hadn't I thought of that months ago? I truly sucked at being a Royal Leader.

"Does not matter. I've been here long enough to be considered a member of their Bombardians."

"Does matter." Might not be the wisest about all laws, but I knew the leaving procedures. I'd hunted for loopholes to get myself off the grounds of the United States for years. There'd been no way without going in front of the Royal Leaders and asking permission. A fact most Bombardians avoided doing because Royal Leaders did not like to allow their members to leave for anything less than family in dire need of assistance.

"You did not mind when I left? Neither did your cousins."

Why hadn't Theodor jumped on the breech of rules? Did they think it would be easier on me? No. Theodor wasn't that way. Theodor would have nailed the proper paperwork to bring Kevin's ass home to my chest. Then again . . . might have been kept from me because I was struggling with losing my lover.

"Until the papers cross the Royal Leader's desk you are officially a member of the United States Bombardians and have to conform to our rules. Now answer my question."

Theodor could divulge the rest later. I was sure something had been done or said about Kevin's abrupt leaving. Even if I hadn't been privy to it. That would be a whole new issue for discussion. If I was going to be a Royal Leader then I had to be involved, even if the situation involved me.

"I answered you."

Damn determination. I'd gain nothing from Kevin. Not even a truthful response. Why though? Did he truly have something to hide? Was he that angry with me? Anger did not give cause for such rudeness, not from a person who . . . Had I overlooked something inside Kevin?

The doorknob turned and Larry's rich brown hair appeared before his slim body slid into the room. He leaned his back against the door, drawing my full attention to his blissful body. Larry stood there watching me as if he'd never seen me before. Did he like what he saw? Did he want what belonged to him?

"You going to ignore me, now?"

Shit. Kevin.

"Am I interrupting?" Larry mouthed and nodded at the phone.

I waved Larry over to the bed and tried to focus on what Kevin was going on about. Caught a word or two, both of which were unfriendly. Neither threatened, but the tone was clear. Kevin wanted his way, or there would be no answer.

Chapter 16

Larry

I tugged the door closed tightly behind me. Wasn't sure why. Theodor, Franklin, and Bryan couldn't hear my internal struggle. Wasn't even sure why I was having one. My decision had been made. I told Anthony a Trial Run. We'd set the deadline. I'd gone over and over these facts for twenty-minutes. When Theodor and Franklin returned, but Anthony did not, I became nervous. I'd given Anthony permission to call his ex-lover. To resolve lingering issues. Why? Had that been smart? No. Yes. Leaving him hadn't. i trusted . . . I did trust Anthony. Wasn't sure why. Yes, I was. Bryan told me a Bobmardians first purpose after finding their Keeper was taking care of them, loving them, protecting them, ensuring their happiness. All of which, included being truthful. All the time. Therefore, I trusted Anthony. I did not trust his ex-lover . . . Kevin.

What kind of name was that? The Vice President's name was Kevin. He was a bigot and skilled at lying his ass off. Nope. Didn't trust anyone named Kevin. Was not going to leave Anthony to the task of dealing with his ex-lover by himself. Nope. Anthony might desire to take care of me, but that was a two-way street. If I belonged to Anthony then Anthony belonged to me, even if he was dealing with his ex-lover like I told him to.

I slipped into the room, forgetting about my main reason of going in there when I caught sight of Anthony sitting on the edge of the bed with his legs stretched out in front of him. Man was sexy as hell. Took my breath away. Made me forget the main reason I came in here. Or . . . Brought the real reason to life. Whichever it was, I was there and would have Anthony's attention. I would show him who his Keeper could be.

I braced my back against the door, running my eye over every inch of Anthony's long body. Great sight. Long muscle torso with abs that all but popped the seams of the dress shirt. Shoulders strong enough to man handled me while fucking me senseless. Idea I hoped to explore sooner than later. Oh boy. Where had that came from? I'd only met Anthony a little while ago. My body didn't seem to care. Cock was throbbing in anticipation. Ass cheeks clinched, longing for the desire of a long, thick prick pushing between them. Was sure Anthony could handle that.

Anthony waved me over, never taking his eyes off me. Did Anthony like what he saw? Did he want to see more? Was he content with having the President's son as a Keeper? Did he still long for his ex-lover?

I took the empty spot next to Anthony, letting my hand grace Anthony's outer thigh, taking his breath.

"I'm waiting for an answer."

Tension radiated through Anthony's tone. The sound irritated me. The red creeping over Anthony's face . . . Sickened me. No one had the right to upset my man. My Bombardian. No one. What could I do . . . Ah . . . Just what my Bombardian needed.

My hand ran up his thigh and down the inner seam of his slacks, earning me another deep breath that ended in a bit of a hiss and glowing eyes. Anthony's lips curved up as he leaned closer to me.

"Answer your Royal Leader."

Anthony's tone was airy, but the command was strong. My dick twitched and my hand scooted higher, barely grazing Anthony's cock. I didn't stop there but kept moving up and over his abs and up to his chest, where my limber fingers unsnapped one of the shirt buttons. My hand slipped inside, tweaking Anthony's left nipple. Anthony arched forward. The second time I squeezed Anthony's nipple the phone hit the floor and Anthony's arms were around me, tugging me closer, sealing his lips over mine.

Just what I wanted. My Bombardian to forget all about his ex-lover and devour me. I longed to know I could make Anthony forget everything but me.

The harsh kiss had my mouth parting as Anthony's tongue slipped inside, tasting every corner of my mouth. Wasn't even sure how it happened, but we ended up with me on my back and Anthony hovering over me. Wasn't enough contact for me, so I slid my hand down and over his elongated dick, caressing tenderly.

"Shit." Anthony muttered as he licked my ear. "God that feels amazing."

Sure did. Would feel better once those slacks were out of the way. I reached for the zipper and button. Soon as I had them out of my way, I slipped my hand inside, gripping the hot, engorged cock.

"Nice." I squeezed, earning a deep groan. "Feel good, my Bombardian?"

"Uh . . ." Anthony licked a path down my cheek to my mouth, circling my lip, drawing a groan from me as a I pushed my hips up.

"Feels like a prize and half for me." Anthony pushed his mid-section into mine, giving me a heart-felt moan.

"Hope you enjoy it." In more ways than Anthony could think of. I wanted him to devour it every time we came together.

"Know I will." Anthony's hot lips pressed against my neck, sending warm ripples of pleasure over my body.

"When?"

"Do you know what you are asking?"

Didn't. Not completely, but I wanted to know. Soon. Wanted to . . . Skin to skin. Taste. Lick. Suck. Anything else I could get my Bombardian to give. Soon. Like . . . Then.

With my free hand I finished unbuttoned Anthony's shirt, following each new piece of skin with a chaste kiss all the way down to the edge of his slacks. Hands twined into my hair, tugging just enough to sting, letting me know how much Anthony enjoyed being lavished.

I released Anthony's dick, getting a whimper. "Miss that grip, do you?"

"Yes."

"Then you'll love this." I pushed Anthony's slacks down and over his hips. "Oh . . . Commando."

"Hate the pinch."

"Like the free access."

"Why?"

"This . . ." I took hold of the base of his cock and sucked the tip into my mouth.

"Shit!" Anthony's hips jerked, but he kept from pushing all the way into my mouth. "God . . . Wonderful . . . Hot . . . Moist . . . More."

Rambling was great, so I obliged and took Anthony further into my mouth, letting the tip of his cock rest against the back of my throat. Couple of seconds passed before I pulled back to the top of the underside of the bulbous mushroom head, loving the soft groans filling the room.

A faint knock, might have been loud, all I cared about was hearing more of that sweet music Anthony was making. Best music in the world. Wanted much more.

"What are you two doing?"

So going to kick a huge hole into Theodor's face the moment I had my fill of Anthony.

"You two can't be . . . Doing what it smells like."

Smells like? Did lust have a scent? If so . . .

Hands landed on my shoulder and Anthony pulled back. "He's right."

"Anthony, you know this."

"Go away." I snapped. "I'm taking what belongs to me."

Anthony tensed under me and his eyes bulged.

"Okay. Sorry, I interrupted."

"Larry, honey, do you know what you just did."

"Yes. Claimed you as mine." Hadn't meant to. Not then, but it had felt right. Felt perfect. Wanted everyone in the house to know Royal Leader Anthony had won his Keeper's heart. Was owned by his Keeper.

Fingers lifted my head until bright eyes met mine. "You can't take back what you just said to the eldest Royal Leader."

"Don't want to."

"Thought you wanted a Trial Run."

Damn it. Couldn't I go with the flow? "Thought you'd be happy about my stake of claim."

"Am. But . . . You've thrown me for a loop. You said - -"

"I know. I know. I changed my mind." Wasn't even sure when. Hadn't come in there with that in mind, but . . . Felt right. What I wanted. "No one else can have what is mine. Have you changed your mind? Do you no longer want me after you talked to the lying prick that is most likely still listening in on us?"

"Shit." Anthony glanced at the deserted phone. "Oh well, he knows I belong to my Keeper." I easily slid back into Anthony's arms when he held them out. "You are the only one I want. I do not want you to regret accepting me."

"Won't." I leaned my head into Anthony shoulder. "You belong to me. I'm not sure why my heart says so, but it does. I can't see my life without you at my side. Can't let your ex have any part of you. You belong to me. Do you not?"

"Every ounce of me is yours. You owned my heart the moment I heard your voice. You owned my heart the moment I saw you. The moment you . . ."

"Enough talk." I shoved Anthony back, straddling him. "Take what is yours."

Chapter 17

Anthony

A command I had no problem accepting. I snaked my hand around Larry's waist and shifted so he was under me. "If I start this . . ."

"Won't ask you to stop. Take what is yours."

"I am yours."

More than Larry knew. I had meant what I told him. Soon as I heard Larry's voice, I had belonged to him, even though my mind had been a bit confused and concerned. Didn't change how I felt. All feelings I had for Kevin had died the moment Larry came into my life. I knew it was for the best. Kevin did to if he thought about it hard enough.

"Then make sure that phone is cut off and come claim me."

With my full attention on Larry I felt until I found the phone. With one push of a button I ended the call and dropped it back on the floor.

"I'm going to enjoy this." I never broke eye contact with Larry as I untied his shoes, taking them off and massaging his feet for a second before running my hands up his legs until fingers rested over the button of his tight jeans. Jeans that showed how firm of an ass Larry was bound to have. With practice ease I used two fingers to unsnap them and tug the zipper down.

"Lift your hips." Larry complied and I gave the jeans one hard yank, taking them down to his feet. "Kick them off." I took a second to admire the way his cock protruded the top of his white boxers, before slowly revealing tanned skin. An outline of what had to be a speedo was the sight that greeted me. Each passing second filled the room with thick, musky lust. Musk would have chocked anyone else, but for me . . . Smelt amazing. "Take your shirt off."

Larry sat up tugging his shirt over his head.

"I like this." I licked an outline of the speedo swiping my tongue over the bare white skin. "This," I kissed the tip of the purpling head, "I knew would be wonderful." One fluent move and my mouth was full of Larry's cock as he gulped.

"Shit. . . More."

Was going to give him lots more. All he could stand. More than he could stand. Was going to feast on his entire body then slowly inch my ten-inch cock deep inside him, sealing us together for the rest of our lives.

"Dang . . . Where'd you learn . . ."

Knew Larry would love how I twisted the tip of my tongue into a scooper and dip inside his slit, feathering it back and forth. It had been a treat I'd given Kevin, who swore I used magic to do it. Never had. Pure natural talent that allowed me to pleasure my man in such a magical manner.

"I'm . . . Don't . . . Lord . . ." Larry gripped my shoulders and thrust his hips up, pushing further into my mouth. I gripped his hip and pressed him back into the mattress, pulling his plump cock from my mouth. Never once lost contact with my Keeper's smooth skin. Simply let my lips trail under Larry's balls and back to the treasure chest opening. I used one long swipe from front to back, following it up with my index finger. I dipped it inside his opening then replaced it with my tongue, getting my first glorious taste of my Keeper.

Larry. Man. Sweat. Lust. Keeper. That's what I got the taste of. There'd be no *only* one taste of such ambrosia. Nope. I'd have to feast on such luscious food each and every night and in between. Still wouldn't be enough.

"Shit . . . Anthony!"

I slid my hand up Larry's thigh and over his balls squeezing. Not hard, just enough to keep Larry from spilling before the main show. Then again . . . Might have been the simple fact that I wanted to hear more sweet music from my lust filled lover.

"I'm going to . . . Anthony . . . Please . . . Fuck me."

Three more swipes of that heavenly opening that would surround me until my life essences flowed from me. The mere thought all but made me shoot.

"Ready to become mine?"

"More than."

"You sure? There is no going back if we complete the bonding. You will be mine from now on."

"I want to."

"You sure?"

Larry's hand wrapped around his jutting cock and began stroking while his other hand pulled a bottle of lube from under the pillow. "Answer enough?"

More than. I took the bottle and flipped the lip open. "You done this before?"

"Yes."

My wolf rumbled his displeasure, but both parts of me knew that Larry had a life before us, just like I did.

"Get ready to become mine."

I pushed Larry's legs up and let the lube drip over his fluttering hole. I ran my dick back and forth through it and then shoved Larry's legs higher. Without one bit of wasted time I pushed forward, entering my Keeper an inch, stopping.

"Don't. Keep going. I can take it."

"Want to savor." I moved another inch in, soaking in the heat that surrounded me. "Every last second of this."

"Savor later." Larry thrust back, but I pulled back. "Hey!"

"Told you, going to savor my fun." I'd make him feel like a Prince being crowned a King.

"Need you deep in me. Now!"

I moved a bit deeper, earning a great impression of a wolf snarl. I was just about to move again when Larry wiggled and clamped his ass cheeks so tight that he stole my breath. It took all my strength to keep from losing my shit right then and there. It did have me thrusting forward in one fluent motion.

"Fuck!" My balls rested against his ass.

"Harder." Larry pushed up, forcing me in even further.

"Honey, stop. You're going to hurt yourself."

"I won't. Make me feel you for three days."

Damn. My wolf loved the idea of that as much as I did. Who was I to deny my lover something so simple? I pulled back and slammed home, filling the room with a loud clapping sound.

"Yeah . . . More." Larry gripped his dick, stroking up and running his thumb over the tip of his head. I became so engrossed in watching him jack himself that I forgot to move until Larry about clinched my dick off.

"More. Please. I'm close. Don't make me shoot by myself."

"Can't have that." I lifted his hips higher, going in fast and hard.

"Yes! That's it."

I kept the fast and hard pace going, nailing him on his prostrate with each stroke. Sweat clung to my back and dripped from my chin, landing on Larry's chest. Each thrust became harder and faster, more unsteady. I could feel the need bubbling up. My balls drew closer to my body. Larry's hands jerked his cock as fast as I entered and exited him. We were both nearing the tipping point and it would be . . . Magical. Mythical. Nope. Didn't describe what it would be.

Neon lights consumed my mind as hot spunk pumped against my chest and Larry shouted my name. Three more thrust and I bottomed out and held still as cum filled him. Before I was empty water began to gush over us.

"What the . . ."

"Are you laughing?"

"Yes." Larry snorted. "What is going on?"

"My affinity has accepted us."

"We are one now?"

"We are." Perfect. Larry would keep my wolf side calm. Soothe me when I needed it. Be at my side for the rest of my life. They'd share every aspect of life. Be happy together. In return, I would protect, care, and provide for him.

The water ceased, leaving behind a faint trace of a rainbow.

"Neat."

"Thanks." Wasn't sure how I managed it, but least it put a smile on Larry's face.

"It's peaceful."

"You are." More than Larry knew. My wolf was not shoving for control. No mental rattling around in my head. All that was left was contentment. Sort of felt like my wolf had fallen asleep. Might have. I sure was exhausted.

"That was . . ."

"Indescribable." I'd heard that each Keeper and Bombardian combining was unique, but . . . Beyond special. Something only shareable by two specially designated people.

"Man, I'm exhausted." Larry wiggled until he was on his side. "Come keep me warm. Please."

I stretched out behind him, tugging him against my body, encircling him in the safety of my arms.

A slight giggle slipped from Larry. "Bryan and David are going to kill us."

"Huh?"

"There bed is soaked."

Ah . . . Something I could take care of. I quickly muttered a spell for heat and rested my chin on Larry head. "Rest, honey. There's lots to discuss later."

Faint snore was answer enough. I took one more glance at Larry then shut my eyes, letting the wonderful peace settle deep in my bone.

Chapter 18

Larry

"What the . . ." I jerked up in the bed, taking in the room.

It was a large room. Had a king size bed and room for a decent size seated area, but it was full of people. Some held long swords, some slender and glistening with sharpness. Some like those blades people used to cut jungle veins with. Those killed in one strike.

"Stay still."

Any other time I might have taken offense to the command, but David wasn't home to protect me. Next best person was my Bombardian. Even if I didn't know him as well as . . . Lord have mercy. What had I done? Tied myself to a man without knowing much about him. I hadn't even learned how he lived his life. Could I still make compromises if I disliked his way of life? Shit. What a fuck up.

"What is he doing?" One of the sword wielding men said.

Eyes bored into me, but I remained motionless. I was unnerved but was not going to let any of these strangers know it. Showing one face while feeling a thousand other things wasn't new to me. Unfortunately, being around people who have no qualms about abducting was becoming the norm. Not that these invaders . . . Invaders? How? Who was stupid enough to try something? Not so stupid if they were in here. And they were. More than I wanted in my bedroom. Not that I allowed anyone with knives and blades near me. How had they gotten in here? David had at least ten guards stationed around the house. Where were they? David was going to be . . . "Bryan."

I was in mid-motion when strong arms gripped my waist. "Stay still, honey."

"Bryan?"

"He will be fine. Theodor and Franklin are with him. He's well taken care of."

Anthony's calm manner and neutral tone grated at my nerves, which had me wiggling until Anthony had no choice but to loosen his hold.

"Thanks." If Anthony wanted to play the calm and neutral game I could go along for the ride. "Who do we have visiting?"

Okay, maybe a bit of snark came to life in me as well. I'd come to David's to escape the world while I healed from my ordeal, only to find an entire new species existed and I was fated to one of them. A hot as hell one of them. I sure hadn't come expecting to have my room invaded by men baring knives after some amazing sex. I was beyond my limit on being a weakling and wasn't going to sit around and wait for information to be offered up. I wanted to know who the ten men where. What they wanted and how much of a threat they were to me. Not that I was too worried about being harmed. Anthony would protect me. David had taken out twelve men by himself, so I was more than sure in Anthony's ability to take out ten. Then again . . . Bryan said Anthony was new to the Royal Leader. What limits did that place on him? Any? Was his skills weaker? Same? Faster? Should have asked more questions instead of falling into the sack with Anthony.

"Not sure about all of them, but," Anthony pointed to the one standing on the right side of the door, "this one has lots to answer for. General Gobbler, what is the meaning of this."

There was that calm and neutral tone again. How could Anthony be so rational? Men with knifes circled them while they were naked.

"Answer your Commander."

His commander? Ah shit. General Gobbler was one of Anthony's . . . What were they called . . . Um . . . Combatants. Not just one, but the head one. Or that's what I'd gathered from what Bryan said about his best friend being the Keeper to David's General.

That meant that Gobbler had some serious explaining to do. Didn't explain who else, or how Anthony knew the other four. Since it appeared no answer was coming from Gobbler, I asked my own.

"The others?"

"He knows me all too well."

That voice . . . I knew it. Heard it earlier. Despised it. Wanted to rip it into shreds. He would not be taking my man from me. Nope. I'd eviscerate him before I allowed it.

"Kevin?"

Anthony nodded, but what had me grabbing his hand and pressing it between my knees was the five tight lines that stretched across his forehead and the fur that covered his arms. Bryan said a Keeper's job was to calm the beast side of the Bombardian. I hoped I could manage it, because even though I didn't want to face off with these goons, I didn't really want to see Anthony's beast. Yet.

"What's he doing here?"

"That's a good question."

I watched as Anthony locked his glowing eyes onto the man to the left of the door. He was tall. Bulky. Like most Bombardians I'd met. Was nice looking, but not my type. I sure didn't fit into the same class of guy as him, so what did Anthony see in me, other than I calmed his beast. Would I be able to please Anthony? Or would I always be compared to Kevin?

"He's not good enough for you. He's already doubting himself. I can see it in his eyes."

There was no way for me to dispute what Kevin said. I was doing exactly that. Most likely exactly what he wanted.

"He's perfect for me."

"He won't satisfy you."

"Done has."

Anthony scooted forward and in front of me, blocking my view of Kevin. I took the protective move as comfort and him silently trying to get me to ignore what Kevin was spilling. I knew the pure truth of what had taken place between us earlier and that was all the proof I needed. Or it should have been, but hearing Anthony zapped the doubt right from my mind.

"I believe," Anthony kissed my cheek, "it's time I called the others in."

"Others?" I snatched up the blanket and threw it over Anthony's lap. "No one else gets to see what belongs to me."

"Belonged to me for the last few years."

"Doesn't anymore." Never again. I crossed my arms, mocking Kevin's stance.

"Will again."

"Not hardly." I wrapped my arm around Anthony. "He's mine now and forever. That's all that matters. Now . . . I think . . . Anthony is right." Time David's guards came and did their job. Not that I didn't think Anthony could handle the situation in front of us, but . . . Knives verse . . . Fist . . . Not a good match up. I reached over and picked up my phone. Sent a quick text of three numbers. 911. Knew it would work. Wasn't expecting it quiet as fast as it came. I hadn't even lifted my finger off the send button before a dark rich green haze filled the room. When it faded Theodor and Franklin stood between Anthony and his General. William Regan landed a quick punch to the neck of the man in front of him.

"What the fuck in the meaning of this, Tanner?" William steadied the falling man by gripping his collar. "How dare you enter this house without permission."

"I don't need anyone permission."

"The fuck you don't." Franklin snapped. "You are a Combatant of mine. You do not have permission to enter another Royal Leaders home for any reason."

"I do not - -"

"Shut up, Pickler."

Appeared there was some kind of coo or something underhanded going on among the Royal Leaders. Not that shocking to me. I mean there was always someone trying to undermine or overthrow a politician. Just another part of my daily life. Shouldn't have surprised me that something similar could occur among the top dogs of another species. Power made people batty. All I could do when it occurred in my life was go with the flow, so that's what I chose to do. I sat back and listened and watched. Never knew where entertainment came from.

"Ah . . ." Theodor slammed his hand on Kevin's shoulder, "The one who chose a job over a lover of years. Nice to see you back in our region. You do know the punishment for leaving without permission do you not?"

"Don't consider you my anything. I do not live by your barbaric rules."

"Have all your life." Anthony's huff ruffled his bed hair. More like the hair that stood on its ends from my fingers running through it.

"He will get what is coming his way." Theodor moved to the man at the foot of the bed. "What do you think you are doing, Lieutenant?"

Just a blank stare. Theodor threw out a few more questions but got no answer. He moved onto another guy and received the same. The last guy he came to stand in front of lowered his head but did not answer Theodor when he asked what he was doing in another Royal Leaders home when he'd been told by Commander Caleb to guard his houseguest. I wasn't sure who the houseguest was, nor did I care. What I did care about is understanding how and why a group of Combatants ended up invading my bedroom with my man's ex-lover. Looked as if I wasn't going to get any answers either, but . . . Never think never.

"They will not give you what you wish." Kevin rolled his eyes, making me chuckle, which had him baring his teeth at me. "They will only respond if I give them permission to."

"You. If you think . . ." I shook my head. "What a joke. I can tell by looking at these guys that none of them consider you anything but a peon."

A snarl that vibrated my skin washed over me as Kevin made to step forward. Anthony's responded quicker than Theodor had to my text. He growled so deep and loud that three of the goons dropped their knives. Not that they had tried to use them. Wasn't even sure why they had brought them. Seemed pointless to come in with weapons and only hold them. Not that I wanted them to use them. Nope. Far as I cared they could all drop them.

"Larry, please . . ." Theodor waved at Anthony. "Help me out a bit."

Right. Me Keeper. Me calmer. I pressed my back into Anthony's and the growl subsided. Anthony looked back at me and I grinned. "It's alright babe. I'm not afraid of him."

"You are stupid then." Kevin snapped.

"No. I know your type."

I'd seen stronger people than Kevin try to pull a coo off in the White House. All failed. Many came close, but in the end . . . The current one had no reason, that I knew of, but I doubted it would come to full term. Kevin appeared to believe he was the leader, but he let his emotions run the show. Never boded well for anyone trying to take over.

"And what's that?"

"False Overthrower."

Anthony's eyes went wide and his mouth dropped open. I took my finger and shut it, shaking my head at him. His reaction was more comical than Theodor and Franklin's. They both released a snarl so deep that every wall in the room expanded and retracted as more Combatants filled the room.

Chapter 19

Anthony

What was going on? My life was . . . Not out of control, but . . . Confusing as hell. That was it. Larry had a valid point about what Kevin and the other nine guys were up to. Wasn't sure why Kevin would try to overthrow the Royal Leaders. Never thought he hated us so bad. There'd been no sign of such animosity. Oh, he'd bad mouth the rules we had about having to bed women to produce a child. Then . . . all the Combatants that had turned on their Commanders. Mine included. Gobbler . . . He'd been a great choice I thought. I mean I promoted him mainly because Kevin suggested him, but he'd been a solid leader for the Combatants under me. What had caused them all to go . . . Become a . . . Spy? Traitor. Lies from within had been discovered before Bryan and David's Pledging Ceremony. It left Bryan and General William Regan devastated. Looked as if all five Royal Leaders needed to do a deeper search into those working under them.

"What is the reason of the coo?

Anthony listened to Theodor and Franklin demand answers from the ten guys who invaded Larry's room, but all I could focus on was the unease and distressed feelings flowing through Larry. I couldn't hear him, but I could feel all the confusion deep inside him. It was distracting. If David felt all that Bryan was suffering through . . . I understood how grumpy he'd been. There had to be a way to lessen how much I felt, but . . . I couldn't remember how. Looked like I'd have to ask someone. I just hoped Larry wasn't struggling with feeling my own confusion and unease about Kevin and the . . . Attempted overthrow.

"Ha . . ." Kevin snorted and puffed out his chest, making my stomach churn at how easily he spoke. "Not the coo. Yet."

"Then why are we here?"

Hm . . . Pickler's question told more than I expected to get from any of them, considering how quiet they'd been.

"Good question."

Tanner's question only enlightened me more as to how much us Royal Leaders needed to research our Combatants more. I mean, how come Tanner and Gobbler came along with Kevin without knowing the real reason behind the invasion. Stupid plan to begin with. I mean popping into the room of a Royal Leader's house wasn't smart. No upper hand on taking me down. Four of the ten men were Combatants and should have known how ridiculous the idea was. They knew how the Royal Leaders would react. Okay, maybe we didn't react the way they thought. They might have expected me to attack and summon the other Combatants. I didn't. In fact . . . My reaction was very mild. Not like any Royal Leader should have done. Instead of a rash reaction I waited and attempted to take control of the entire situation. Gobbler should have known I would have tried to talk them down instead of attacking first. It wasn't my MO. I never went into a fight without all the information. They might have expected David's Combatants to storm the room, but they hadn't. They most likely were circling Bryan, making sure no one got within an five feet of him.

"Babe," Larry tapped my side, "Kevin told them what he needed to get them to do as he wished. Invade our room. Stop you from sealing your life to mine." The small huff and huge grin Larry gave Kevin had my cock hardening. "You were about an hour too late. Entire night was amazing."

Sure had been. I'd planned a second round, or two before we'd left the room. Might have kept Larry in the room for a day or three. Wrong. I would have, after I zapped me and Larry to our home. I wanted my keeper in my bed. Laying on 100% per silk sheets. Larry's beautiful tanned skin would look amazing against the navy comforter and mahogany bed frame.

Ah . . . Just what I needed. The confusion and distress Larry had been projecting shifted, lessened my headache. I could handle feeling his . . . Oh man. Lust Not only did desire rush through me, making my cock harden, but the room filled with a sweet musky smell. One quick scan, before my eyes stopped on Larry, showed me that everyone in the room stiffen, standing up taller and breathing in deep. All eyes shifted to Larry. I scooted a bit closer to him, making sure to hold the sheet over me, but it did little to hide my erection.

"Honey," I made sure to brush my lips across his ear as I whispered? "What do you want me to do?"

"Clear the room, please."

My sentiments exactly. "Theodor - -"

"I know, Royal Leader Anthony."

"Everyone knowns." Franklin winked at me.

"That's for me." Kevin sidestepped Theodor, but Lieutenant Ryan materialized in front of him. Instead of the room clearing it became engulfed in battle. The Bombardians who'd dropped their weapons snatched them up and charged.

General Gobbler darted in front of Kevin, nailing Ryan in the face, sending him flying back. Ryan landed on the bed. I barely had time to lift and scoot Larry out of the way. A snarl rippled up my throat and into the fray of the chaos around me. My hand lifted and a thick spray of water shot up from the floor, creating a clear, air bubbled wall of water. Ryan had been in mid-air when I managed to build the protection in front of Larry and me. My timing might have sucked, because Ryan slammed into it, bouncing back. Thankfully, he landed on his feet. Wasn't my goal to hurt my future General.

"Wow."

Couldn't have said it better myself. I might have impressed Larry, but I had no idea how I'd managed it.

"Thanks, babe."

"Anytime, honey. No one will harm you. Promise." Least I knew I could uphold that with my affinity as well as my body and limited magical talent.

"Uh . . . Commander, I need to get by the water."

Right. How did I . . . Did I just think it, or . . . Ask. Worth a try. "Water, please allow Ryan to pass."

A small section parted. Ryan slipped through and the water closed right behind him.

"That's neat as hell, babe."

Sure was. Made me want to learn more about my affinity.

"What's going to happen next?"

"The others will subdue these asswipes. We will be safe right here. None of this will get near you."

Least I knew I could keep my word. The wall would keep the fight away from my Keeper. Two or three of the guys had already bounced off it. Was neat as hell that I could watch what was going on while behind the wall of . . . Okay, my beast side wanted to be with Ryan as he slammed Gobbler into the dresser. Someone needed to watch his back, because Picker slammed his fist into the back of Ryan's head. Tanner made a move to lunge into the two on one battle, but General Regan shook his head and shoved his arm deeper into the man's chest. I was just about to shout at Ryan as a long fencing blade was raised by one of the men I didn't know, but a thick blue mist filled the room. The fight didn't cease, but I couldn't see anything. Swords clanked as the mist faded, leaving behind new Combatants. The room was huge, but not big enough for all that had gathered. As one moved another bumped into him. Made the fighting harder, but it didn't seem to bother the Combatants that had come to aid their Commanders.

A hard knock against my back had me spinning around to ensure no one had broken through my water wall, but no one had. Larry was scrambling up to the head of the bed with his hands over his face.

His sexy cheeks were as white as the material covering him. His body shook hard enough I feared him falling off the back of the bed. His eyes were closed so tight that his nose crinkled. Hands rested against his stomach.

I should have expected the chaos to affect my Keeper. It hadn't been long since he'd been taken by force and held against his will. I had no clue what had happened to him while he'd been held, but something about the violence had upset him passed the point he could handle.

"Get them out of here and clear the room, Combatants. Now!"

I lifted my hand and crooked my finger, drawing the water closer around me and Larry, who I had tugged onto my lap and wrapped him in my arms. I thought good vibes towards him, hoping to ease him. It didn't seem to be working. In fact, seemed to make him worse. He pinched and clawed my arm as he tried to shove them away. I released him and he scurried back to the headboard.

What did I . . . How did I get Larry to grasp that I had us protected? What would draw him back to the here and now. I hoped that he was just having a flashback. If it was more than that . . . I had no clue how to help him. Wasn't quite sure what I needed to do then. Ended up going with my gut. Always helped me in the past.

I grabbed his legs and straddled him, gripping his face between my hands so he had to focus on me. "Come on, honey. Relax. No one can get to you. I have us protected, even if I didn't, my Combatants would not allow a single soul to come within five feet of you." My words didn't cease any of the panic consuming my Keeper. The lines across his forehead tore at my heart. I brushed my thumb across his cheek then leaned down and caressed his cheek with mine, inhaling his scent. "Honey, open those beautiful eyes for me. Let me see them, please, honey."

"Anthony, you okay?"

Wasn't, but I couldn't take my eyes off Larry to ensure the room was clear of everyone but Theodor. I would not admit my own fear rode me hard enough that my beast howled and snarled for freedom. That it demanded to take out those who put our Keeper in such a state. Not one of the invaders deserved to know how much their actions pissed me off and put me in a state of fear.

"Do you wish me to get Bryan?"

Franklin's voice told me both of my cousins remained in the room, but the wavering tone ensured me that they remained on the other side of the water wall. Did them being in the room mean the Combatants remained. Wasn't going to take my attention from my lover to find out.

"Room cleared?"

"Yes, Royal Leader Anthony."

"You too, Lieutenant Ryan." No Combatants could be near my Keeper until I had time to fret out any other possible traitors.

"Yes, Sir."

"He's gone." Theodor voice was louder, but still distorted. Wasn't sure if it was the fact that he'd moved closer to us, or what, but a deep snarl flowed from me. "Fine. Franklin and I will stay back. You might want to drop the protective wall."

Why would I do something so stupid? I would not leave my keeper visible to others while he was so distraught. My man hadn't even opened his eyes. Shaking had slowed, but he'd began grunting.

"The room is safe. I have put up an outside wall of fire around the entire house. No one, not even Combatants can pop in."

"I'm fine, babe."

Thank God, Larry spoke. Not solid or steady, but it eased how much my wolf slammed against my internal barricade. "You are not." I placed a light kiss on Larry's dry lips. "You want something to drink?"

"Please." His eyelids fluttered a couple of times then his beautiful peepers appeared. They weren't bright like they'd been while we sealed ourselves together. They had a rich dullness to them, but what split my heart into was the blankness flowing from them. Thanks to our emotional connection I could feel the distress fading and his shaking had all but stopped. "Sorry, babe."

"Don't." I snapped my fingers and pressed the cool glass into Larry's hand. "Drink. Relax."

Wasn't sure how I managed to conjure up a glass of water so easily. Sure was better than water pouring over them. Last time I'd tried to do such I'd gotten soaked. Lost at least three couches over the years. Once I even got Kevin and I wet after a deep round of sex. Kevin hadn't been pleased. I found it funny.

"What has you grinning?"

Didn't know I was, but if it helped distract Larry then I'd do it the rest of the night. I filled Larry in about my mishaps.

"That should have enlightened you."

"Huh?" I tucked a stray piece of hair behind Larry's ear.

"If he got pissed over something so trivial . . . He didn't really care as much as he portrayed." Larry took a sip of water. "This is nice and cold. Thanks."

"Only the best for my man."

"Uh . . . Theodor isn't looking happy."

I glanced over my shoulder. Theodor stood an inch away from the water wall, snarling and hold a ball of fire.

"What does he think fire is going to do against water?"

I shrugged. "Not sure if I can drop the wall."

"Why?" Larry took a deeper drink of the water and pressed the glass to his forehead. "Can you conjure up some Aspirin?"

"That I can do." He reached over the bed and picked up his slack, tugging a single paper packet of pain reliever from the back pocket.

"I'm not going to ask why you have those."

"I'm prone to headaches."

"Thought you'd be above such."

"We don't get sick, but . . .Some human aspects still consume us from time to time." I tore the packet open and lifted Larry's hand, letting the two tablets fall into Larry's hand. "Take those and let your head ease off while I undo whatever I did."

"You seriously don't know how you did that?"

"No. My affinity skills are meager. I never applied myself to learning what I could do."

"Why not?" Larry's adam apple bobbed as he swallowed the two pills and scooted down into the bed, tugging the blanket up to his chest. "I would have loved to be able to create something so wonderful. Can you make a rainbow waterfall?"

Wasn't sure, but I sure would figure out how to give him what he wanted. In that moment, with the little bit of redness lingering on Larry's cheek, I knew I'd figure out how to eliminate the entire world if he requested. Not that he would. Larry was a good-hearted man. A man who loved furiously. Loved wholehearted. Cared with every ounce of his body weight.

"I'm waiting." Theodor tossed the fireball to his other hand. "Longer I wait the more likely it is that I will toss this your way the moment the wall is down."

"Put away your fire." I stood and walked over to the wall, pressing my hand into it. Coolness and wetness seeped into my palm. I studied it, looking for a small gap. No tears among the seam.

How had I created it? It was solid. Not even mist could seep through. "How do I undo this?"

"Think it." Franklin said from the doorway.

Was it that simple? I'd asked for Ryan to pass.

"Has to be, babe." Larry nodded at me when I looked back at him. "You said nothing before the wall appeared."

I hadn't. Wow. Neat. I sighed and let my mind clear before picturing the water fading away. Nothing happened.

"Thank your affinity." Theodor's fire had vanished and he had propped himself up beside Franklin. "Always let it know how much you appreciate its help."

Made sense. We had to do that when all four elements came to assist in a ceremony. Why would we not do the same when tapping into it.

"Water, I appreciate your help and time. You may go back and rest."

The water was gone as fast as it'd appeared. New for me. Most of the time when it showed up and left, I was faced with soaked clothes, or floors. Must have been my inapt knowledge of respecting my affinity.

"Neat." Larry yawned and turned onto his side. "I'm going to rest."

"You do that, honey." I moved to his side and tucked the blanket around him before kissing his cheek. I yanked on my slacks and shirt, leaving it unbuttoned. "Let's take our discussion to the conference room."

"Sounds wise." Franklin pushed off the wall and vanished down the hallway.

Theodor nodded out the window. "My fire wall will keep out all. I promise no one will zap their way in here again."

I pulled the door to. "So . . . we caught all of them?" Sort figured we'd miss one or two of them.

"Yes." Theodor pushed open the door to David's conference room.

Good. Did not need Kevin hell bent on getting back in here. He'd break every law there was just to achieve his ultimate goal. There would have been no stopping him.

"Good thing. He would have come back."

"What do you mean?" Franklin tossed me a bottle of water.

"He's relentless when it comes to getting his way." I gulped the water down. "It's one of the qualities I admired about him." If I'd known he was capable of such idiotic actions I wouldn't have gotten involved with him.

"We caught him. That's what counts. The others . . . well . . . those jerks thought they were coming to overthrow us." Theodor slammed his hand down onto the top of the table. "What the hell has gotten into our Combatants." Wished I knew. "Did Kevin come for a personal reason or business?"

Good questions. "We need to interrogate these traitors."

"Course we do."

"You're not getting me." I snapped, getting a harsh snarl from Theodor. "Sorry, but there are specific question we need to ask."

"What kind?"

"Not sure."

"Uh . . . Not much help." Franklin grunted. "If you don't know then we don't know how to come at these cretins."

How did we? Was it wise to lay out what we knew? Little that was. I didn't think so. I wasn't a good manipulator. Always went with the truth. Served me best over the years. Hadn't been truthful in all areas of my life. I'd kept my preference for men hidden. Not happening anymore. There would be no way I'd hide Larry. Family would be alerted to my truest desires when Larry and I had our Pledging Ceremony.

"That's it." I grabbed my phone. "That's it."

"What?" Theodor pulled a chair out and sat.

"Kevin's reason."

"You are making no sense." Franklin growled more than spoke. "I do not like the fact that Tanner turned on me."

"I will kill Pickler once he tells me what he was after."

I knew Theodor would. Out of all the Royal Leaders, Theodor ran the tightest shift among his Combatants. They knew to toe the line. Knew to stick to the rules that he laid out. Knew his feelings on going against the Combatant's oath. Theodor had caned and imprisoned former Combatants for simply calling in to lay around when they were needed to guard his ass.

"I'm not sure what those two were thinking." Weren't entirely sure what Kevin's motives were but I knew what pushed him into invading David's house. Question was . . .

"How did Kevin know where I was?"

"He's working with Pickler and Tanner." Franklin said.

"Yes, but . . . How did they know which room I was holed up in?"

"Gobbler." Franklin wiped his blood soaked hand on his shirt.

"What's that from?"

"My claws."

Should have expected Franklin to be close to shifting. Lucky none of us had.

"Stay on track." Theodor leaned back in his chair. "Kevin knew you two were together." Theodor sighed. "Calling him might not have been the best choice.

Might not have been. What wasn't, was me and Larry staring the sealing process while he listened. Hadn't been my finest moment, but what could I say. I was swept away by my Keeper.

The office door flew open, bringing all three of them to their feet. "Honey, what are you doing?" More like why had I not taken note of the anger surging through him before he stormed into the conference room.

"I'm fine." Larry ambled over to my side. "That asshole invaded a special moment for us. I will not stand on the sideline."

Theodor and Franklin snorted. I didn't find it funny. My man had endured a flashback, or something similar to a PTSD attack. He needed to rest. To recover. To let his man handle the hardcore shit storm at their feet. After all, it was my problem. Kevin came after me because of our past. Not because of Larry.

"That asshat knew what we were doing. I started the process while you were talking to him. He knew where we were." Larry staggered forward before I made a move, Theodor had slid a chair over to him and tucked Larry under the head of the table. "I may not be able to help take his ass out, but I can help unravel what his underlying plan is. I've watched and been involved, indirectly, in some of the most inhumane and underhanded attacks around the world."

Didn't mean he needed to be in the middle of a Bombardian mess.

"Do not go there." The rolling chair beside Larry flew across the room, stopping in front of me. "If you think you will keep me from this . . . You've got things all twisted. I might be the President's son. I might have had Secret Service around me for most of my life. I might have been kidnapped by foreigners, but I can take care of myself."

I was about to point out how he had just contradicted himself, but Theodor shook his head at me. Wasn't sure why, but I knew Theodor would not lead me astray. Or send me down a path that would cost me my Keeper.

Chapter 20

Larry

Who did Anthony think he was? Did he not know better than to keep his lover in the background? Would he have done the same to Kevin? Doubtful. Desire to protect me coursed down our mental link. I appreciated it, but I would not be a weakling. Never again. Felt that plenty when those jerks stole me from my limo. I'd known how to defend myself but froze when the Secret Service guys were murdered. Shock stole my reaction. All thoughts of escaping their grimy hands flew from my mind. Being a standby would never happen again. I would be strong. Would be the man Shawn loved and cherished. Would be strong enough to honor the name Royal Keeper. Support for my Bombardian was all that mattered. Being at Anthony's side was where I belonged. Not behind him. If Anthony could not accept that then . . .

Anthony came to my side, rubbing my cheek and leaning in. "We are tied together for life." Anger seeped from him, but I knew it wasn't because of me. "I'm confused. Not sure what I did wrong. What put the distress flowing from you?"

How to explain helplessness? Everything had been stripped from me when I'd been kidnapped. How did I get Anthony to understand that meeting him awakened a part of me that had been sleeping since Shawn died? I'd fallen into stasis after I lost the man I'd loved. The only one who saw my truest inner side. The one person who let me vent about being a son of a politician. Who didn't mind me being accompanied by security guards every minute of the day. Who didn't mind having to sneak out to hang with others. Who didn't make fun of me when I had never eaten french frys.

Anthony's hand cupped my chin, locking eyes with me. "You can tell me anything."

"I became stationary after Shawn died."

"You loved him?"

I nodded. "His life was ripped from this world. He let me be me. Didn't . . . There was no son of the President between us. No guards bothered him." I babbled the rest of how Shawn became the one person who owned my heart until Anthony came along.

Anthony's sigh spoke volumes. He wasn't mad at my honest response. Nope. But his beautiful eyes held a tint of the green monster. "I didn't mean to . . ."

"I know. I'm jealous he knew you so well. That you have such a deep admiration for him."

"No reason to be." I hated Shawn and his entire family had been killed in a bombing while on a safari in Africa. None of them, not even me, believed them going there would be an issue. They'd vacationed there for nineteen years with no incidents. Pure bad luck on their part. They had no way of knowing the owner had pissed off the wrong person two weeks before they traveled there.

"May not have, but I do."

"Then you know how I felt when I found out about Kevin."

Anthony's shoulders lifted and fell as he nodded.

"Least mine can't come back and attack us."

A rich chuckle filled the room, drawing the attention of Theodor and Franklin.

"What are you two discussing?" Theodor slid his chair across the linoleum, opening the min-fridge, grabbing a soda.

"Private discussion." Anthony winked at me.

I doubted it had been, then again . . . Anthony had whispered so low that I'd barely heard him. Still, they shouldn't have gotten sidetracked. There were more important issues to discuss. Way more.

I snatched a yellow notepad from the table. "Anthony's right about what he was thinking."

"And that was . . ."

"Franklin, don't be an ass." I snorted at him when he gaped at me. "Kevin came here for a personal reason, but he used what he had at hand."

"What's that mean?" Theodor sat back, tilting the can up.

"I'm assuming . . ." Hated doing that, but was all we had before we went the interrogation route. Having Anthony's feelings swarming me was neat as hell. Not only could I feel his love, but I could pretty much hear what he was thinking. Wasn't crystal clear, but it was as if he spoke to me. Was he? Or were we just that intune with one another. More likely the latter. "Well, Anthony's assumes Kevin came here because he's pissed."

"Why?"

"Don't interrupt me and you will find out." I snapped as I wrote Kevin's name down, drawing a vertical line before adding the nine other names. "Kevin had been ticked at him for basically hiding him away during their relationship." Added that thought under Kevin's name. "He had access to some kind of group with a motive for coming after the Royal Leaders." A huge question mark was added below the nine other names. "When Anthony found me, Kevin realized there would be no more living in the closet for Anthony."

"Shit!" Theodor slapped his head. "I can see why he would be ticked. Coming after the Royal Leaders with raging fire makes no sense."

"Death wish." Franklin said.

"More than." Anthony shook his head. "I never thought him stupid enough to act so rash."

I could see someone doing such. Years of being a hidden lover then . . . The man he spent years concealed for no longer kept his true life in the dark. Yep. I could see Kevin resorting to such. But that wasn't the only thing we needed to consider. "Did you think he'd be part of a group who would attack the Royal Leaders?"

"What? Honey, why do you think - -"

"He's right." Theodor laid his forehead on the table. "We thought we had all the traitors behind us once we took Tabor down."

Huh? Where had that came from? When had . . .There's been several incidents right after Bryan had became David's man. Which one . . . "Does this have to do with the bombing or - -"

"Looks like Bryan needs reminding to keep his trap shut."

Franklin snorted at Theodor's comment, sending his water flying from his nose and mouth. He wiped it off then locked eyes with Theodor. "I'd love to hear that. He'd wrap you in tree branches or bush."

Franklin had a point. Bryan hadn't been able to control his reactions lately. Bryan swore he kept tapping into David's affinity without meaning to. If Theodor tried telling him that I doubted the tapping would be an accident.

"Me to." Anthony pulled a chair up to my side, taking my hand after he sat. "If Bryan didn't take you down David would."

"I hate Keepers." Theodor grinned so big that his face had to hurt.

"You won't say that if you find yours." Franklin shifted his attention to the doorway, making me turn in my seat, but no one stood there. "Let's get back to business. William is missing his time with Bryan. Not sure how much longer Bryan will willingly stay in the living room."

"No longer."

Damn. Where had Bryan came from? He'd not been there a second ago. Didn't matter. He clung to the door frame. I was up and pushing my chair to him. "Sit. I'll scoot you to the table."

"I can walk."

"Didn't say you couldn't." Doubted he could take one more step. His dark brown eye bags had bags. Shoulder of his shirt hung three inches to the side. The legs of his jeans were baggy and those jeans were skinny jeans. Wished I knew how much longer David would be gone. Hopefully not much. Best not be, or I'll beat the shit out of him. Not that I could. Not that I'd have to. Anthony could though. Would he for me? Might try, but . . . Nope. Didn't want Anthony to fight his cousin. Wasn't sure he'd be able to beat David either. I knew David would be as fast as he could. There was no way he'd enjoy being away from his Keeper that long. David would beat himself up the entire time he was gone and even more when he got home and saw the state of Bryan. David deep emotions for Bryan had been clear since the moment I arrived. David would give his life for Bryan and Bryan would do the same for David.

"Update me." Bryan rested his head on the table, turning his head so he could see me. Looked as if Bryan trusted me to give him the hardcore facts. The others would try to keep him in the dark. Keep Bryan from worrying. Wouldn't work.

"Our room was invaded. My best guess were four Combatants, Kevin, and five other Bombardians. Kevin's reason was two-fold. Not clear on the other guys, but all have been safely secured." I tossed my hands at Theodor and Franklin. "They can interrogate them. These knuckleheads are pushing to get at that, but they do not have a full grasp on what they know at this point."

"We don't know shit." Theodor tossed his empty can into the trash, making a clinking sound that had me wincing.

"That's not where that goes." Bryan's wheezing cough had me running to the fridge to get him a can of ginger-ale.

"Don't get all green on me." Theodor stood, snatching the can up, taking it over to the blue container. "Happy?"

"Yes." Bryan winked at me when he took the soda from me. "What are they overlooking?"

"Not so much overlooking." I wished there was more info. Hardcore facts were limited. They'd have to go into the interrogation with possibilities. Better than completely blind. "We know Kevin came to gain revenge for Anthony coming out of the closest when he kept him there for years." Could see how that would sting, but . . . Gave Kevin no reason to invade like he did. "I believe . . ." Didn't want to state what my gut screamed at me. Anthony would catch onto it soon enough then he'd beat himself up over it. "Kevin's actions might have gone against his original assignment."

"What?" Anthony rested his arm behind me, rubbing my shoulder.

"I believe . . . And I'm sorry for what I'm about to say. I think Kevin might have come to you for a different reason than a relationship. I'm sure it developed into deep feeling." That was more than clear. Kevin's eyes held pure sadness and anger when he met mine. I wasn't a Bombardian, but his rage wrapped around me like a blanket. "I think it is also best for you guys to assume those four Combatants were traitors or plants."

"Aren't those the same?" Franklin slid back from the table, propping his legs up.

"Get those rank feet off my man's freshly stained table." Bryan threw his wadded-up paper towel at him, making me snort, which had Franklin glaring at me.

I shook my head and got up, picking it up after it fell on the floor.

"Hey!" Franklin gasped. "What you two doing? Teaming up?"

"Yes." Should have been obvious. Bombardians stuck together, so did Keepers.

"Back to the topic at hand." Theodor asked.

"Right. Traitors mean they were faithful to start with. Plants mean they came into the game for their own reason. Not one of loyalty, even if they claimed it." I'd seen many people try to pull those stunts in the government. All the ploys had been foiled at some point. The one or two that all but came to play were kept from the press. "I'm not sure of their motives, but they have one. One they are devoted to. One someone else started. These men are working for someone. Someone they admire. Someone they believe in."

"Kevin?" Anthony squeezed my shoulder. "Sorry, babe, but he's not . . ."

"Not leadership material. Too week, or he wouldn't have let himself fall for you so hard."

"Other words . . ." Theodor stood. "Whoever is running the show has a reason that motivates him far beyond anyone under him. He will be the hardest to weed out. He will be the hardest to take down."

"Harder than . . ." Who had done the bombing? Bryan had called them . . . What had it . . . Oh yeah. "This Tabor guy and his followers."

"Ghoulians." Anthony groaned.

"That's it."

"Where did . . ." Theodor glared at Bryan, who gave him a small shrug. "You know better."

"Okay, what do we need to know before we go in there?" Franklin stood.

"How well do you know these Combatants?"

"Every aspect of their life." Bryan replied. "David has detailed facts about every Bombaridan alive."

"Yes, but he's not here." Franklin's frown told me there was no way for them to get to those facts.

"I am." Bryan pushed the chair over to the door and rolled into the hallway.

"Where's he going?" I was in the hallway in time to see him disappear into a room I'd seen David go into several times.

"Office." Theodor sighed. "Leave it to him to have a way into David's private room."

"I bet he has access to every room in each place David has." Anthony wrapped his arms around my waist, resting his head on my shoulder. "My Keeper will."

"Good choice." I muttered. "Now if we can just work out the issue you feel about having to protect me all the time.

"Help if you could pull on my affinity."

"How do I do that?" I wouldn't mind being able to toss water around.

"Not sure. Don't know enough about my own power yet."

"Going to learn?"

"Theodor and the others are helping me."

"Good. Think you are way stronger than you think."

"Why?"

I pressed my butt into his mid-section, getting a faint groan from him. "You closed yourself off to what you could do, because you closed yourself off to your true desires."

"Not following."

"You kept your desires for men from your family. Did you not?" I knew the moment Anthony caught onto what I was getting at. Anthony's eyes went wide and his face reddened. "If you want to know your whole self it will come quickly. I'm sure, babe."

"Office is open. Make yourself at home, but stay out of his desk." Bryan didn't reenter the room, he kept rolling past the office and mumbled about hating being sick.

Bet he did. I sure would have. "You guys need to find out all you can about these four. Look between the lines. Find all those little things that will make them fear you. It might be - -"

"Family. Loved ones. Anything they hold dear to their lives."

"Right, babe." I pried his arms from my waist and gave him a chaste kiss. "Take care of business while I go tend to Bryan. If you need me, contact me."

Chapter 21

Anthony

"Never want to find my Keeper if he is like those two." Theodor slid around me, leaving Franklin and I laughing.

"He'll change his mind the moment he hears him." I followed Theodor into the hallway with Franklin trailing behind.

"We all do."

"All do?" Anthony paused and looked back at Franklin. "You done found yours and failed to tell us?"

"Nope." Franklin snorted. "I'd have him, or her, glued to my side if I had."

"Keep thinking that." Soon as Franklin found his and he or she requested space he'd give it. I would bend over backwards to ensure Larry had his deepest desires.

"We going to do this in here, or go back to the office." Theodor held up four folders as we walked into the door.

Right. David had three long rectangle tables, all filled with stacks of papers. Neater than anything I had in my office and I was an organizational freak. "Best use the conference room."

"Why?" Franklin pointed at the multiple file cabinets. "We might need more files."

"Yes, but . . . David appears to be more harmonized than me."

"So?"

"I'm telling you if someone invaded my office, I would have a shit fit if one little piece of paper was out of place." David didn't need to deal with straightening out a messy office, or what he'd view as one.

"Don't need David having that." Theodor slapped the folders against his leg as he passed by them.

* * *

I picked up one of the folders Theodor tossed on the office table, then took the yellow notebook Larry had abandoned. Best chance at discovering what lurked beneath the traitors was to dig through the folders and find what each of us overlooked. One way to do that, add my own questions to what Larry started.

Had Gobbler worked for Michael? He had. What position had he been promoted from? Had he worked for another Royal Leader before he joined Michael's team? What all had Kevin said to convince me to choose him as General? Had his only reason for choosing Gobbler been Kevin's word? What had happened in Gobbler's past? Did he have family that went Mélange? Was he close to them? Was he born into Bombardian family? Was he one of the Bombardian that lived among the human world until his Bombardian skills were discovered? What other items in his life made him turn on the Bombardian's way of life?

"What are you doing?" Theodor snatched the notepad.

"Hey! Work through things your way. Let me do mine."

"These are good questions." Theodor tossed the pad over to Franklin. "Can see why he's matched to Larry."

"Organized. Logical. Rational. Thinks things through."

"Course I am." I snatched my notepad from Franklin. "How else did you think I built five business from the floor up."

"You have?" Theodor's wide eyes were comical.

"Yes. Did you not know that?"

"No."

"Why not? Royal Leaders research every Bombardian."

"Not the higher ranked royal bloods."

Huh. Hadn't known that. Made no sense. "Don't you think that's dangerous?"

"Why? They are raised to come into their seat of power."

I had been. Cared less about my possible future position. "If you had done so on me . . . You would have known my feelings on becoming a Royal Leader. You would have known how little I knew Water. Do you not think that there might be others who disliked their future position as much, or more, than I did?"

"Why would . . . Okay." Theodor shook his head. "We might should have, but it felt like . . . I always saw it unnecessary. It is an honor among those who carry royal blood. Even a bigger one to become a Royal Leader. None in that position would turn on their heritage."

"Sure about that?" I wasn't. I had disliked the mere idea of being so close to the top of the royal blood list. I'd prayed nightly that nothing would happen to Michael. I would have done anything to prevent myself from having to become a Royal Leader.

"Yes."

"No."

Theodor and Franklin answered at the same time. Franklin had the right answer. I could see how someone who felt like I had would do whatever it took to keep from having his entire life uprooted.

"You two really think - -"

"Yes." Franklin and I said at the same time.

"Franklin, you and I have had many conversations about how I felt when Michael died. And why I verbally attacked Bryan when I arrived that first day."

"Let's say you are onto something. "Theodor laid his blue folder down. "Would such distaste be enough for a royal blood carrier to turn on the ones he was born to be part of?"

"Might." I hated the idea, but it was more than a big possibility.

"Did you ever think of doing such?"

Despised my answer. I'd dreamed of it. Many times. Acting on it . . . Never would have. Didn't like the idea at the time, but I would never had turned on my heritage. I had been told from the time I was able to talk and grasp the concept of what my future would be like.

"You know any other royal bloods who felt like you?" Franklin flipped a page, frowning at the sheet. "This might be the reason Tanner flipped sides."

"What?" Theodor lifted a photo and flipped it over, reading the writing on the back.

"Both of his brothers held royal blood, but only a trace. He was extremely close to them. Both were open about their desire to become a Royal Leader. Tried multiple times to get their royal blood status increased, but the last rejection pushed them both over the edge."

"What's that mean?" I pulled a sheet from my folder, trying to decipher some handwritten text beside a passage about Gobbler's father.

"They made a pack to kill the other one. In a duel like battle."

Shit. Not an easy way to go. Not a wise one either. It would have taken them both cutting the other's head off. Not a possibility for them to do at the same time. Someone had to have finished the job for the one whose head failed to fall.

"How did that go down?"

I listened to Theodor go on about how David should have brought that to their attention. I agreed. The fact that Gobbler's father spoke against royal blood carriers should have been brought to my attention. Gobbler's father voiced his concerns about how the Blood Testers chose those carrying royal blood. Gobbler's father believed that each Bombardian bore royal blood. He thought the ones charged with gaging how much royal blood a Bombardian bore were paid by families who wished to be a Royal Leader. Other words, if you had the cash, you got ranked higher.

"If David did this much research on them all why did we not come to him and ask for his results?" Franklin interjected. "I know I should have. I knew David had these files. Theodor knew he had them. You knew he had them. Did any of you come to him? Ask him questions?"

"David didn't have these files when I named my Combatants." Theodor sighed. "But . . . I should have come to him when he finished his project."

I should have approached him before I named my Combatants and General. It wasn't only David's fault. Was all of ours. None of them came to him. He didn't come to them. He would have known these facts when the Combatants were named.

"What have you found, Theodor?" I knew there had to be something he overlooked.

"You first." Theodor replied.

"Gobbler's father expressed his distrust of the Blood Testers."

"Pickler's grandfather held a large amount of royal blood. Right at the top of the list, but two days before the Awakening . . ."

The coverup that forced three Royal Leaders out of their seats of power. It's also what sent David in search of his Uncle for information about how a Keeper's pregnancy worked. A veil that should never had happened. Bigotry. Plain out bigotry. Sickening.

". . . He died of old age . . ."

Rarity among Bombardians. Most lived for two hundred years, or longer if they lived a safe life. Old age death meant the man had fought many battles among his life. Something that most high ranked royal blood carries avoided. It shortened their lives and most preferred to take their seat of power if possible.

". . . Pickler's father was only five when the man died and bore no royal blood whatsoever. Pickler's brother did, but only made the middle of the list, which he took as disgrace to his father. Pickler's brother found his Protector but before she accepted him, she was killed in one of the attacks on the Destroyer's Hermitages. He turned Mélange and confined himself. Still resides there according to this."

Why would that have affected a non-royal blood carrier. Knew one thing, it took a major offense to someone to set them off onto a tirade of destruction.

"We have the reason for most of these guys deception, but how about the ones we aren't acquainted with." Theodor glanced at the last folder, tugging it over to him. "Caleb's Combatant. The five Bombardians we don't have names for."

"Find out who they are. Let's take the ones we know first. Then we can go after the others if we need to." Franklin shut his folder, shaking his head.

"Right." Anthony followed Theodor out of the conference room.

"I'll go get William and we'll get this started."

Chapter 22

Anthony

I followed Franklin to the living room as he went to fetch William. What I saw had me pausing and my heart swelling to an explosion point. Sweet and sexy. Larry . . . Shit. I'd fallen head over feet for him. Not only the soft, tug worthy hair, but his devotion to his friends. As if that wasn't enough, there was how he had curled up holding a metal trashcan in front of the sofa Bryan slept on.

"You have a kind-hearted Keeper."

More than Theodor knew. I wasn't sure how, or why, I got so lucky, but I sure thanked all deities and my affinity. All of it, right down to what I've yet to learn.

"I'm glad he's not like I thought." Franklin and William joined me and Theodor in the hallway.

"What's that mean?"

"He's a politician's kid."

What did that have to do with anything? He was just another person. No, he wasn't. He was my Keeper. That's all that mattered.

"I don't think he gets what you mean?" Theodor's smile took away a bit of the sting that comment caused. There was lots I didn't know, and it was beginning to suck ass. "Have you not noticed how spoiled most children born with what the humans call a silver spoon in their mouth act?"

"F - -"

"Not quite what I was getting at." Franklin pushed my hand to my side. "No fighting. But . . . Theodor does make a good point."

"What was you getting at?"

"Don't be snapping at me."

Had I snapped? Yep. Might not should have, but the two of them was pissing me off. Larry was far from a spoiled rich kid. Theodor just said so. So . . . Where had Franklin pulled this shit from? He knew better than to talk about another Bombardian's Keeper. It wasn't done. Disrespectful.

"All I was saying . . . Larry is like us in many ways, but he's far from us as well."

Huh?

Franklin shook his head and rolled his eyes at me. Not sure what I looked like, but he picked up on me being confused.

"He was born to a man with money and with high goals. White House size goals. Would have taken Larry's father living a certain style of life. Just like it takes a certain lifestyle for us to keep the Royal Leaders seats. Means Larry's life was pretty much planned out for him before he was born."

"Like ours."

Franklin and Theodor made good points. I felt the resentment buried deep inside Larry about his false life. About how his parents married for the wrong reason and stayed together for them as well. Larry might not have been born with royal blood, like many Bombardians, but he held it none the less.

"I get that." What I didn't get was how come this conversation was taking place. Larry might have been born out of a man's plan, but he developed his own life. Stood up for himself. Managed to etch out a life of his choosing, for the most part. Larry was resourceful. Talented. Had a mind of his own. Knew how to gain what he wanted. Knew how to use his position to his advantage. All things it took to survive a preplanned life. Things I done each day of my life in order to appease my family. "Why does this matter?" I cursed the dirty dishes sitting on the bar. Spoke to how bad Bryan felt. The man loved pristine kitchen. I'd have to take care of them when I got a free minute.

"Because who he is." Theodor pulled the kitchen table chair out and sat.

"Because . . ." Larry's voice had me spinning around. "Theodor is like me in many ways. He uses what is at his doorsteps to gain any and all ultimate goals."

"He's smart." Franklin was behind the game if he just figured that out. I knew it from the moment I saw Larry.

"Explain it to me." I wrapped my arm around Larry when he came up to my side.

"Theodor knows me being your Keeper can either make, or break, whatever deal you guys have with the humans."

Ah fuck. Hadn't considered that.

"I knew it the moment you told me my choices were different."

Aggravation lurked down the mental link, but Larry did not express it in his tone or face. Man was truly a master at hiding his true emotions from people. Worse yet, I had not even picked up on how much this fact was bothering my Keeper. I would not let Theodor hound him about who he was. Would not.

"I will not - -"

"Babe, it's the way my life goes. Simple as that. I hate it. Love it at times, but I've known all my life that my life was based on my father's choices. How could it not be? He has an image to uphold. Goals to reach. He did it. It cost me, wasn't all bad." Larry squeezed my waist and grinned at me. "What is it that you'll be approaching my father about? How can I help?"

"You won't be." I said before I thought it out. I would not let anyone else plan my Keeper's life out because of who his father is. Nope. Not happening. My reaction must have shocked them more than me, because Theodor's eyes went wide. Franklin's mouth dropped open, and Larry chuckled.

"Babe, relax. It would be my honor to help in any way I can. I despise the humans believing such horrid and untrue stories about your kind. My kind." Larry kissed my cheek. "They deserve to know the truth. They need to see how great the Bombardians are. Also, so that you guys can find the ones that calm you. The world needs to know how wrong the government were wrong to hide your kind away."

"I don't like this." I huffed, knowing I was not going to change Larry's mind. He was determined to help. I loved him for that, but . . . "This is all useless right now." Boy was it. That being the case, it gave me time to find a way to talk Theodor out of using my Keeper for our own gain. "We've got people to interrogate and a kitchen to clean up."

"What?" Theodor looked behind him and frowned. "Crap. Bryan will have a fit."

"I promised to do them." Larry bumped his hip against mine. "It's why I came in here to start with."

"We'll let you take care of that then." Theodor huge grin had me chuckling.

"Since that's settled," Franklin stood, "Anthony's right." Franklin huffed and kicked his toe against the floor. "Everything can wait until we know who our enemies are and what they want."

Chapter 23

Anthony

Bathroom? Oh man. Franklin's General had a huge sense of humor. Every room in David's house had bulletproof windows. Still, William chosen to put the traitors in the bathrooms. Good idea in some sense. There were no windows in any of them, besides the main level one. Still, not like they could have busted through the windows anyway. He had hog-tied them and left them laying in the middle of the floor.

"Where did William put the unknown Bombardians?"

"Basement. No windows. No exit. And he put a magical wall that will prevent them from popping out." Franklin opened the bathroom, door revealing Tanner. "He did that to every room he stored someone in." He nudged Tanner with his foot. "Ready to tell us what we want to know?"

Wasn't going to be that easy. Tanner didn't go quite as far as I expected him to go, but he did stick his nose in the air like he was better than us. Man held no royal blood whatsoever. Barely ranked tenth spot among the guards according to Franklin. The man Tanner bumped to reserves was only one tenth weaker Tanner. Reserves Combatants were only called in when one of the top ten were hurt or went on vacations. Or worse, when an attack came. My Uncle referred to the reserves as people less than adequate. Not me. All the ones who could stand at my side to fight were equal. Some stronger than others, but when it came down to a fight, they all had one thing in common . . . They stood at my side. Protected me. Protected my Keeper. They all had benefits that aided them. Might not be strength, but other aspects could take down a threat just as easy.

"Would be in your best interest." Franklin flicked his wrist and a crystal style sword appeared in front of him.

What was that? Where'd it come from? Why was it see-through. Pointed end showed how deadly the mysterious weapon could be. From the way Tanner squirmed and scooted on his side he knew how dangerous the sword was.

"You know what my Spirit Sword can and will do."

Ah . . . Affinity. Cool. I'd never seen anyone use spirit in such a manner. Far as I knew the affinity came into play after death. Should have known better.

"Now, now, Royal Leader Franklin," Theodor clasped his hands behind his back, "I think we can get him to give us what we want without violence."

"We can?" One refusal was all the idiots got. Mr. Nice Guy did not exist. The asshats had invaded my Keeper's bedroom on the word of Kevin. Came in thinking . . . "What did you plan to do once you entered my Keeper's room?"

"Did not know he was your Keeper."

"Who did you think he was?"

Tanner's nose lifted higher as his eyes locked onto the Spirit Sword.

"Silence gets you know where." Franklin's sword moved closer.

"Kevin said it was Royal Leader Anthony's room."

"Then why invade it?" I braced my shoulder against the hallway, taking in the blue paper with yellow stars. Didn't suit the atmosphere of an always happy house and an exuberant mate. Bryan must not have started remodeling. Hoped he would work on the bathroom caging Tanner.

"Said you'd be alone and knew nothing about how to reach your Combatants."

What in the world was Kevin thinking? And why did any Combatant fall for such bullshit. Not to mention Gobbler was there and Tanner had to know he was my General.

"You believed such." Franklin snorted. "You know I can blink and have anyone of you at my side."

Theodor cleared his throat. "We all can."

"He can't." Tanner tossed his head my way, making me chuckle. Before I even thought about it, I'd reached out to Lieutenant Aidan. Aidan didn't appear beside me, or not like normal. He came through as a blazing red shape with orange flames circling his body.

"Uh . . . I told you I put a fire wall around the place."

"Sorry." Was and wasn't. I'd proved how competent I was. In some ways.

"Do you wish him to be present?" Theodor lifted his hand, ready to snap his finger, releasing the Bombardian from the wall of fire keeping him from materializing.

"No. My point was made."

"Do you still think your decision was wise?" Franklin closed in on Tanner, blocking my view.

Silence rang loud in the room.

"Do you wish to explain why you turned your back on your own oath?"

I made a small step to the left, giving me a better line of sight of Tanner, but I could not see Franklin's face. I was sure his eyes glowed bright with his wolf. I sure smelt wet fur and white ice like drops fell onto the baby blue tiles.

Tanner's eyes shifted into his beady wolf eyes as his body glowed from a pending shift. His teeth had shifted to wolf fangs and they snapped in Franklin's direction but pulled back when the sword moved closer.

"You fucking Royal Leaders took my brother's life." Tanner added something else, but I couldn't understand him thanks to the wolf surging forward. Kind of surprised the man hadn't tried to shift before . . .

"Why has he not shifted before now?"

"He won't shift now." Franklin shrugged. "William's little gifts come in handy when I need them."

Bet so. Not many Bombardians knew how to manipulate their magic to such an extent. Showed why William was Franklin's General.

"Don't count on that." Theodor pointed a finger at Tanner, who was snarling and salivating as he withered on the floor. "Damn it." Rays of fire shot from Theodor's finger, making Tanner's half shifted form squeal, or . . . Only way I knew how to describe the agonizing sound he made.

"What are you doing to him?"

"Keeping him mobilized." Franklin sighed. "My ex-Combatant just went Mélange"

Huh? "How?" When did Bombardian's start going Mélange without losing their mate? Was all turns that painful? If so . . . Thank the good Lords Larry could not refuse me. I never wanted to experience such. I'd seen many Mélange over the years, but never saw one turn.

"It's rare." Theodor said.

"Enlighten me."

"You really need to study up." Franklin shook his head. "Tells us that he is the one who killed the second brother?"

Shit. Murder, even if used as a weapon, destroyed a part of a person.

"Also tells us he sought revenge for being put in that situation to begin with." Theodor rolled his eyes as he lowered his head. "Waste of another Bombardian."

"Might be, Theodor, but Tanner did that to himself." Franklin tossed his hands up. "He had no right to blame the Royal Leaders. Had no reason to blame anyone. He could have told his brothers to go to hell when they brought that insane idea to him."

Tanner kept making noise, but the squealing had ceased and came across more like he was trying to talk, but his snout did not allow for it. Or so I thought. From Franklin's comment he understood what the Mélange said.

"You might have been young but knew right from wrong. Your parents were solid and strong Bombardians. They loved you. Taught you right from wrong. They taught their children to be devoted to the rules every Bombardian follows."

Huh. How did Franklin know all that? Was it in the records David kept? Had to have been. Man, looked like each of us needed to read up on our Combatants. Looked as if we needed to thank David as well as chew his ass out for not reporting such anomalies among their Combatants.

"None of this is helping." Theodor shouted, making me snarl at him.

"Hey," Larry's sleep filled voice made me spin.

"What's wrong, honey?"

"You guys woke me up. I'm sure Bryan is hearing you as well."

"Fuck." Theodor hung his head. "Franklin, transport him into a Confinement House while I go check on Bryan. We don't need David trying to pop in and not being able to. He will rip all of us into if he can't get to his pregnant Keeper."

He'd do more than that. I sure would have if someone blocked me from my own house, especially if the one who did so were there to keep my Keeper safe. I would have shredded them after letting my wolf toss them around for a couple of hours. Then I'd go and double reassure myself that my Keeper was safe and sound.

"I'm going to Gobbler." I placed a kiss on Larry's cheek and made my way up the next two level of steps.

* * *

Didn't even get the door opened before I heard Gobbler cursing the Blood Testers. Explained why he fell in line with Kevin. Didn't give me a solid reason as to why and who started the little revolt. Kevin sure hadn't. He wasn't smart enough. Oh, he had brains, but not the gusto to organize a coo of any kind. He'd stand by and take instructions. Every time Kevin tried to take the lead on any work event, he ended up falling flat on his face and seeking help. It is most likely why Kevin jumped into bringing a few people here under false pretense. Too bad, Kevin didn't give up information as easy as he screwed up leading people. Would have helped me and my cousins gain a better picture of the real reason behind the revolt if I could get the answers from him. Too damn bad we weren't allowed to use our affinity to bring the truth to life. Would save time.

I jerked the door open. "You going to keep spouting off?" I locked eyes with Gobbler, overlooking the fact that he reminded me of a roped calf. I'd have to ask William why he chose to tie the guys up like that. Comical as it was, looked like it would hurt them. Not that I minded that. "If so . . . Give me something useful."

"You wouldn't know useful if it slapped you upside your stupid head."

"Don't play games with me. Don't like them and won't play. I know what got you involved with Kevin and whoever is leading you guys around."

"You don't know shit. Never did. Never will."

"I know your father openly, and you secretly, spoke against the royal bloods. Believed the Blood Testers chose the ones they wanted to lead. You believe that each Bombardian carries royal blood. You believe the man in charge of testing the blood is paid off, putting who gave him the most in the line for Royal Leader."

Gobbler's eyes faded from a blue to a solid black ball. His normally tanned skin paled and his mouth hung open.

"Not as stupid as you thought." I didn't give my words time to sink in. "It is clear that whoever is leading you has chosen people who detest the Royal Leaders in some form and shape. What is unclear is the reason behind his decision to do so. You and the other Combatants, who joined in, have solid reason to join whoever this is, but did he tell you the truth, or did he lie to you like Kevin did to get you here."

"Lord Tangler would not dare lie to any Bombardian."

Lord Tangler? Bombaridans didn't have Lords. Who did?

"Did you say Lord?"

I looked over my shoulder at Theodor as he stopped behind me. "You have heard of Lords before?"

"Folklore story my Uncle told me."

"Same Uncle that was sent into hiding?"

"Yep."

"Looks like you'll be going on a hunt as well."

"Looks as if my Uncle wanted me to know what he feared would be kept from me."

"Uh . . . What did I miss?" Franklin walked up to Theodor's side.

"You ever heard of Lords?" I hoped I wasn't the only one in the dark.

"Only in human history books." Franklin leaned forward and nailed Theodor with a look that demanded explanation. "What's he going on about?"

"See . . . None of you know what you are facing." Gobbler's chuckle, setting my arm hairs to prickling. "I can't wait for him to come for us."

"Come for you?" Theodor snorted. "He will not get into this house."

"He can get wherever he desires."

"You think?" I hoped Theodor and Franklin kept their questions short and vague. The less we let onto how much in the dark we were about Lords the better.

"Know so. He's had our blood. He can get to us no matter what affinity you use to block him."

"Glad you think so." Theodor waved his hand at Gobbler. "Lock him in a wall of water."

Might have frowned at Theodor if Gobbler hadn't been watching me. Gobbler knew the instability of my Water affinity. I didn't need to retract the little bit of power I showed when Gobbler and them invaded Larry's room. I needed Gobbler to continue to think I'd gained knowledge of my affinity. How did I mange that? Protecting Larry had come naturally. I simply thought it. It appeared. Thought about it vanishing and it did so. Was that all I had to do? No. Had to be more to it. I had to thank water for releasing the wall. Did I need to request her help to gain more?

My forehead lifted as I glanced at Theodor, who simply shook his head at me. It was the best I was going to get without vocalizing my need for help. I just hoped Theodor understood why I looked his way. If not . . . I'd embarrass myself and lose all footing I'd gained earlier. What the heck! I tossed my hands up.

"Water, I beg your pardon, but I require your assistance in restraining Gobbler from leaving the wall of water I am putting around him."

Before the last word left my mouth a tsunami high wall of water circled Gobbler. There was little to no space between Gobbler and the tub and commode. I could not have sat down if I needed to.

"Great job." Theodor patted my shoulder. "Now, let's go pay Pickler a visit."

Chapter 24

Anthony

Pickler was stored in the second bathroom at the other end of the hallway, but I wasn't going there. Pickler wouldn't give them more than Gobbler had. Nope. No sense in talking to him, or the other two Combatants. One person would give them what they needed to know. If not all, definitely more than what Gobbler gave us.

Soon as the steps to the top level of the house came up, I made my way up them.

"Hey." Theodor's sharp tone didn't faze me. "Where are you going?"

"To get to the core of things." My cousin might like wasting time, but I did not. Pickler came with Kevin. Came at Kevin's orders, or request. Which was it? Did it matter? Kevin rushed to stop me from sealing myself to Larry . . . Why would he do that? He gave me up for a job. Ah . . . Shit.

"There was no job."

"What?" Franklin's grip would leave a bruise on my fair skin. "What have you put together?"

"There was no job." Stupid's, my second name. Trusted the wrong person, third name. Brought trouble right to the Royal Leaders. Or had I? "Who else is against us? How many enemies do we have?" Only one I knew of was the Ghioulians. They were out of commission. Right? Unless . . . "What is a Lord?"

"Pretty much what you read about in paranormal romance fiction."

"Vampires?" Franklin snorted. "Theodor, you've lost your mind."

"Has he?" People didn't know about Bombardians. "Some would consider us werewolves. We have a wolf inside. Does that make us fictional?"

"No, but . . . Okay. Let's say Vampires are real. Why would one attack us?"

Good question. One I had no answer for. Did have more questions for Theodor. That man had been tense and tight lipped since he heard that name. Why?

I spun, putting my arm in front of Theodor, stopping his advancement. Time he coughed up some answers. "Do you know what they are capable of?"

Theodor shook his head.

"What all did your Uncle tell you about them?"

"They survive off blood. Few left. The ones left are old and dangerous."

"Dangerous." Franklin's huff was comical thanks to him rolling his eyes. "Course they are. They drink blood."

Doubted that was what Theodor's Uncle meant. More like . . . "He meant to us as well."

"Yep." Theodor sighed and shrugged. "We were . . . Interrupted before he could tell me more. The Awakening."

Former Royal Leaders were fucking twisted. They'd messed up lots of stuff with their bigotry. Why couldn't people get over their hatred and live peacefully.

Theodor knocked my hand down. "You know what is going on, don't you?"

Did I? Sort of. "Not really. More jumbled up thoughts. No proof."

"Don't care about that."

"Me neither."

My insides twisted as my shoulders went to my ears. David's calm and deadly tone filled the hallway.

"I want to know why the fuck I had to come into my own home through the front door. Who the hell is stashed in my house when I'm not home?"

He deserved answers. He wasn't going to be pleased. His ire would be directed right at me thanks to Kevin's foolhardy attack.

"Well . . . Long - -"

"Don't finish that comment, Theodor." Caleb came up to my side. "Last few hours have been hard as hell on us."

Damn. Not good.

"What happened?" A faint squeak flowed up the staircase.

"Honey, what are you doing up here?" I held my hand out as Larry topped the last step.

"I saw David come in. Came to find out if he found anything to help Bryan."

David nodded at Larry. "My Uncle is with him. He had some medication that would ease his upset stomach."

A huge smile filled Larry's face, but it faded as quick as it came on.

"There's more, isn't there."

"You are too wise. "David winked at Larry, getting a faint snarl from me, which he ignored and faced Theodor, who was staring at me.

My ex-lover caused the stink, so it was my place to fill David in. I did so quickly. Needless to say, he wasn't pleased with me. Nor did he like the idea that his house had been breached while he was not there to protect his pregnant Keeper. Worse was how he felt about Theodor, Franklin and me. We were there to take care of Bryan, and we'd failed. Sort of. No harm came to Bryan, but that wasn't the point. Danger had entered David's house where Bryan was supposed to be far from stress and worry. Least David refrained from shouting or throwing a tantrum or attacking. Was sure none of that came our way because Bryan was downstairs. Otherwise, I bet David would have opened up the Earth and let it swallow us three.

"Fine." David spun and walked back down the stairs. He made it to the second level before he shouted for us to follow.

A huge belly laugh slipped from me when Theodor growled and muttered, "I'm the eldest."

"Don't give a fuck." David kept on making his way to the stairs. "This is my home."

Comradeship between all of us was amazing, but at times it became scary. Not because we fought, but because we laughed, joked, and worked so cohesively, even in the midst of chaos.

"David," Larry dropped my hand and moved to my cousin's side. "What did you find out from your Uncle?"

"He has medication that will help Bryan's sickness, but he's concerned about how intense it is."

"What's that mean?" I wrapped my arm around Larry when his shoulder dropped.

"Means . . . Not sure exactly. His Keeper never experienced extreme sickness. He does not think there is a chance of Bryan dying, or losing our child."

"Why not?" If Bryan did not get where he could hold down food, then . . . I would not be able to standby and watch Larry go through what Bryan was.

"Gut. Instincts. Mine agrees with him."

"You know more than you have told us." My gut told me that was the case.

"Not really."

"What's that mean? "Theodor blocked David's path, making me tug Larry to the other side of the landing where Franklin and Caleb stood.

"Means . . . Something special between me and my Keeper."

"Can't hold out on us." Franklin said but stood motionless. "Bryan's state could affect us all at some point."

"I don't want Larry to go into this blind, if there is any way around it." I kissed my Keeper's cheek. "If you know something then please, please don't keep it from us. Or at least tell Larry what to expect."

Begging wasn't high on my list of things I did often, but I'd do anything to ensure Larry was safe. Was my job, but . . . Three was no way I could watch him suffer knowing information was nearby.

"Please, I know you and I didn't start off - -"

"Don't." David ran a hand over his face. "I will not keep things from any of you. You know that." His shoulders lifted and fell so hard that mine ached. "It's just . . . It's private. Intimate."

"Huh?" Theodor stepped back from David, giving me the ability to loosen my hold on Larry. Hadn't taken such a tight grip out of meanness, but in case I had to rush us away from a fight.

"I can . . . It's like I'm connected to my child."

"What?" Larry stood taller. "You mean . . . Like a mother says she can tell what she's having?"

"More." David shifted his eyes to me. "It's like I can feel my child. My child is fine. Safe. Healthy, but . . . Confused."

Huh? Sounded like a garbled mess. How could anyone feel what an unborn child felt? "What did your Uncle say about this?"

"I," a man resembling David topped the last step. "Experienced the same. In the sixth month. I could tell my Keeper carried a son. I could communicate to him, mentally."

"Mentally?" Right. Never heard of such. Why was . . . "Is that because of our blood?"

"We don't know." David said. "What I do know is that my Keeper is suffering and I can't take it away from him. That . . . Tears me up."

Bet so. I would hate being in David's shoes. A Bombardian's first job was to keep their Keeper safe. David had to feel like he failed and that he caused the trouble to begin with. In a sense he did.

"I think I have figured out the issue." David's Uncle grinned way too big for someone who just delivered medication to a man who'd been horribly sick. "Bryan agrees with me."

"He does?" David crossed his arms. "Then enlighten me."

"He's carrying twins."

Next few minutes blurred together. David fell backwards. Theodor shouted, "Yes." Franklin busted into a huge round of laughter. Caleb dropped his bottle of water, and forgot to pick it up. I went into some kind of trance. Only one that seemed to function, other than David's Uncle, was Larry, who slipped free and made his way to David's side. He tapped his face a couple of times.

"Wake up you big goon."

Goon? Lord have mercy, Larry had a death wish.

"I do not." Larry shot me a frown. "He won't hurt me. He'd be breaking his own word. David's not a man to do that."

Sure wasn't, but I disliked the idea of Larry purposely putting himself in danger.

"Give it a rest." Larry hit David's face harder. "Wake up before Bryan comes up here."

Right comment to make. David shot to his feet and brushed his shirt off, facing his Uncle. "You sure?"

"Your Keeper is."

"Why?" I interjected, even though it wasn't my place.

"It's like what David was explaining. Bryan has a deeper connection to their children. My mate did. He described it as a . . . Dream come true, because he could tell if our son was happy or angry."

Nice. I would have loved to be that close to a child before he or she was born.

"Excuse me." David darted down the last flight of steps.

"Okay." Theodor's tone shifted from thrilled to serious. "We have to speak with Pickler."

"No." I turned, snagged Larry's hand and headed back up the stairs, going all the way to the top level.

Theodor groaned. "There he goes again. Have all of you forgot who the eldest is? Where are you going Anthony?"

"Kevin will give us what we need." I hoped.

Chapter 25

Larry

I tried to tug my hand free, but Anthony tightened his hold. Not painful tight, just enough I knew he wanted to maintain it. Kind of nice. Spooky. Confusing. Why did my lover want me at his side when he spoke to his ex-lover, who invaded my bedroom and a special moment between us? One I had hoped to extend for at least twelve hours. It'd been amazing to feel Anthony slamming into me. Hadn't felt so thoroughly loved since Shawn.

"What are you hoping to gain from him?" Theodor came up to our side, matching us step for step. "I'm sure your Keeper does not need to be here."

Doubted it either. Didn't want to see the prick who came with the sole purpose of keeping me from sealing myself to Anthony.

"Why am I here, babe?" I hoped whispering kept it between us. Doing so before had worked. Or I hoped it had.

"You are my ace in the hole."

"Huh?"

"Kevin thinks he can manipulate me.

"Not on my watch."

"Mine either."

Simple conversation that said more than words could. Deep guilt flowed through my man. He wasn't pleased about bringing such a revolt to David's house. Not that it was his fault. Anyone who knew how manipulators worked knew that the underlying reason for the revolt had been planned for months. Maybe the invasion wasn't supposed to take place then, but it would have. Kevin just sped it along so he could gain what he wanted. Anthony. Like most overthrowing attempt it was overlooked.

"How can I help?"

Anthony ran his tongue over his bottom plump lip. "Do what you do best."

"What? Drive you up the wall?"

"N - - Yes."

Had Anthony lost his mind? There was no way I would . . . "Ah . . . See where you are going."

"I don't." Theodor grunted.

Damn. Thought we'd spoken low enough, but . . . Bombardian hearing.

"I don't want to see him groping you." Franklin came up to our side as we stopped in front of what I assumed was the bathroom.

Finally, a job I could sink my entire mouth around. "I'm following you, babe. Let's get to work."

Anthony nodded at me and opened the door. My arm slid around his waist, letting my fingers rest an inch from his cock. The mere jester worked like a charm.

Kevin lunged upwards, but a wall of water slammed him back onto the hardwood floor. Not that he could have gotten far. A funky knot . . . no, not a knot. Someone had hogged tied him. Wasn't sure how he managed to lunge any, but he had, only to be sent back to his side.

"Nice." Theodor crossed his arm and winked at Anthony. I had to admit it was an amazing show of power. I knew Anthony wasn't strong at using his power, but it looked as if that was changing, fast.

"Very." Franklin propped himself against the other side of the door. "Think he's learned his lesson."

"Doubt it." People like Kevin never learned their lessons. "The prick is too smart to know when he's outsmarted."

"You're the stealing prick." Kevin's words were muffled, but I caught the gist of what he was after. Didn't need Anthony to tell me not to rise to his bait, but he did. There were congressmen with more bite than Kevin.

Anthony's body stiffened under my hand. Didn't last long, but it reminded me that Kevin was a Bombardian. A man who had been in Anthony's life for years. A man Anthony had loved. A man Anthony had been ready to spend his entire life with. There would always be some lingering feelings deep in Anthony. Entire situation Kevin laid at Anthony's feet hurt my man. I did not need to add to my man's distress with mere words.

"You said nothing wrong." Anthony tugged me closer to him, kissing my cheek.

"I know, babe, but . . ." I would not have liked anyone else talking about Shawn in such a manner no matter how big of a screwup he'd made. Not that Shawn was anything like Kevin. Shawn was loyal to a fault. Oh, I'm sure Shawn had secrets lurking in his life. Everyone did, but I was sure whatever Shawn buried was nothing like Kevin's.

"He could best you with a wink of his eye." Theodor titled his head at the water barricade. "Cousin, you got some mad skills."

"Thanks." Anthony's *I think* went unsaid, but I could feel his unease at his eldest cousin's praise. I knew Anthony saw himself as ignorant about the basics, but I bet my man was more than suitable. He just needed a bit of confidence.

"He's right." Franklin tossed his head so fast it made my neck pop. "I saw Michael practice many times. He never conjured up something so solid."

"He's always been talented." Kevin's voice was distorted but it was still easy to decipher his words. "He just needed me at his side to enhance him."

"Fuck you." Those words flew from me before I thought them, which had me biting my tongue when Anthony pinched my ass. Wasn't reprimanding me, but letting me know there was no reason for me to feel threatened.

"You know it's true, fucking human."

Breath in. Breath out. No reason to rise to Kevin's bait. I knew who Anthony belonged to. Kevin was the one behind the water wall. Not me. I was only here to help Anthony out. Easy. Enjoyable. Also showed Kevin who Anthony truly belonged to.

My hand slid forward, covering Anthony dick. From the way it elongated my man was keen on display of affection. With a small move onto my tiptoes I placed a kiss against his ear then whispered, "Like that, babe?"

"Love your touch." Anthony's hand squeezed my ass, making my own dick thicken. "You okay with this?"

Boy was I. No qualms about touching Anthony at any time, but I preferred us to be alone so I could go down on him and drink him dry.

"Would love for you to do that?"

Shit! "How did . . . Ah, our link."

"You were wide open right then." Anthony nosed my cheek, then licked a path down to the crook of my shoulder.

"Good. You know where I stand. Want me to take care of that . . ." I squeezed his package again. It had the result I desired. A full and erratic cock and he thrust his hips.

"Shit, cousin." Franklin waved his hand in front of his nose. "What is your Keeper trying to do, chock us on pheromones?"

"Smells like it." Theodor glanced down at my hand, nodding in approval, which almost had me chuckling. "Looks like he's trying to make him bust in front of his ex-lover."

"He could." Anthony's tone showed how serious he was about my capabilities.

I hoped Franklin and Theodor was playing along with us. Still, I'd go down on Anthony then. Not so keen on doing so in front of his cousins, but . . . I'd do so in front of Kevin in a matter of seconds. I wanted that prick to know he no longer owned any part of Anthony's heart. I hated I was jealous, but I was. It didn't matter that

Anthony's mark stretched across my forearm waiting for Anthony's name to be tattooed there as well. That last part of the mark proclaimed who I belonged to. It would not come soon enough. Before it could . . . There were some major issues to work out. Like the way Anthony and I would live. What we would tell my father. That wasn't going to be fun. Theodor was going to . . . What did Theodor expect of me? Would he ask me to work on my father until he believed the way the Royal Leaders desired? Surely not. I was sure Anthony would tell them no. He would never put me in such a spot. Then again . . . The world's eyes needed to be opened. Still . . . Anthony would let it be my choice. Not Theodor's. Not Franklin's. Not Caleb's. Not David's. Not Bryan's. Mine. Mine only. Knowing that made it easier for me to see how much of a benefit I would be. I knew my father the best. Knew how he worked. Knew the best way to gain what I wanted from him.

Anthony's hand slid down the back of my sweats, reminding me what we were there to do. I knew better than to get sidetracked with other problems.

"Don't know what you two think, but that bulge is because of me."

"Wrong." Anthony and I said at the same time. Anthony moved close to Kevin, but I refused to release my hold. When we stopped, I rubbed my hand up and down his bulge, making it more prominent before I squeezed it a couple of times, drawing a deep moan from Anthony. It worked just like I'd hoped.

Kevin tried to lunge again. Didn't work. Kevin snarled and growled instead. What little he did manage to move was erased by the water wall closing in on him. That wasn't the most shocking part. Nope. Kevin howled loud enough I winced, but what got Anthony's mouth hanging open was the blood gushing from Kevin's nose.

"What in the world did you do?" Franklin moved to my side, making sure he did not touch me.

"Nothing." Anthony's bewilderment made my stomach spin until I had to cover it with my free hand. Better yet, I had already started moving behind Anthony when he pushed me towards his back. Wasn't sure who had bloodied Kevin's nose, but no one was in the room.

"Theodor?"

"Not me." He held his hand up and shook his head at Anthony, who moved us two steps back.

"He's sniffing." I said into Anthony's back.

"What is it, Theodor?"

"Not sure."

"Then take the fire wall down." Anthony snarled. "I won't subject my Keeper to danger."

Wouldn't taking it down make it easier for people to attack? Then again . . . You couldn't fight what you couldn't see.

"It's down."

Before a breath could be taken, thirty puffs of blue haze consumed the room. It faded away leaving thirty-one men. One of which the other thirty surrounded. The hall was so full that none of them could have moved to defend the man. Not like we could have worked our way through the massive crowd to attack. As if that chaos wasn't enough, David could be heard shouting for an explanation from the bottom floor. Shoot. Bryan didn't need this. He was suffering already. Extra stress wouldn't be good for him while he carried twins. Not that I wouldn't have minded one of the Royal Leaders answering him. I was clueless and I hated being that way.

"I see you are catching onto this being more than you can handle." Someone from deep within the group of men spoke.

"Fuck you, prick." I smarted off as I leaned around Anthony.

"Mere human. Flea to me." The voice from the crowd said.

"You are in bed with someone you have no control over. That is clear." Baiting an unknown threat never worked out. I knew better than to do so. Didn't keep my mouth shut though.

"What you mean, honey?"

"Did you guys not knock him on his ass? I sure didn't, although I would have loved to. Had to be either the man hidden buy his own crowd, or whoever Kevin is in league with." Could have been the one and the same. Wasn't sure on that.

"Lord Tangler." Theodor whispered, but it was still loud enough for all four of us to look his way. The deep frown and red face detoured me from asking him questions, so I directed them at Anthony.

"Who's that, babe?"

"Not sure."

"Sounds like royalty."

"From what I know . . . Which is little, it is more than that."

Footsteps filled the air behind us as men came to stand, and battle for position, among the stairs. Combatants couldn't get to their leaders to defend them, so they were getting as close as possible. I shoved all the racket to the background and focused on Anthony's comment.

"Little you know?"

Anthony quickly filled me in on what Theodor enlightened them to after Gobbler let that name slip. Mere idea of another supernatural being existing was more than I could handle. I gripped the back of Anthony's shirt, keeping myself upright.

"You okay, honey?"

"No."

"Let me get a Combatant to take you downstairs."

"No."

"Please, honey."

"No. Not letting Kevin see me as a weak human." No Bombardian needed to see weakness from me. Anthony required a solid and steady Keeper. One that others could follow as example. One as strong as Bryan.

"You are not weak."

I knew it, but wasn't going to let anyone think different. "I'm fine. Just shocked." Understatement, but I'd go with that until I was alone with Anthony, or by myself. Then I'd freak.

"You know about . . . Which rat squealed?"

The voice from earlier pulled a faint snort from me. Anthony on the other hand took the lead since Theodor stood there like a shell-shocked man.

"Which one didn't." The words were kind of hard to hear thanks to Anthony speaking through gritted teeth.

Franklin on the other hand knew how to go with the flow. "They all had no problem telling us how Lord Tangler manipulated their ass to get what he wanted. How he kept an eye on his pawns, ensuring they did not go off half-cocked."

"They didn't do their job." Theodor stood up taller and sounded stronger than I believed him to be. Least he was talking and steady sounding. Whatever had shocked him, he'd made peace with it. To some extent, at least.

"That's why they were so freaked about Lord Tangler coming."

"Sure was, Franklin. They knew we could protect them best from the monster they got into bed with."

I stood there gripping the back of Anthony's shirt as him, Franklin, and Theodor spun their tale. Not sure what I could add to their little ploy, I did what was best. Stayed quiet and watched.

A small growl flowed through the hallway as Theodor moved up to Anthony's side, but a moment later he took a huge step back. Not something I ever thought Theodor would do. Something . . . What caused it? Did he smell something off? Was it another ploy? Wasn't sure, but I was sure Theodor knew more than he'd told Anthony and his other cousins.

"They fear," Kevin's words where still muffled from the wall of water, but it didn't keep him quiet. "My reaction when Lord Tangler releases me."

"You sure he will?" I doubted it. Once again, the frown marring Theodor's face bothered me. I pressed my head into Anthony's back and whispered, "He knows more than he told you."

"Sure does, honey."

"Do you know what's up with him?"

"No. He's not acting like himself. That's for sure.

"My task," The newcomer's words ruffled through the air as it evaporated into a blue haze that trickled into nothingness, "has been accomplished."

Theodor cursed under his breath while he waved his hand through the mist. When the hallway cleared out, the other invaders were gone. I stood there waiting for the next move, but all I got was Theodor pointing at the wall of water.

"You know he's not coming to release any of you." Theodor spun and headed for the stairs. "Leave him locked in by water."

What the . . . I was sure my face matched the wide eyes of Franklin.

"Tell your Combatants they can leave."

Like that was going to happen. David would never have his guards leave his house after he came home to invaders being held in his bathrooms. Not to mention the ones that just vanished. Nope. Doubtful that Caleb would give such an order either. Not once he found out how strange Theodor was acting.

"What was that about?"

"Not sure." Anthony faced Theodor who was halfway down the stairs. "I'm not sending my Combatants home until I know what is wrong with your ass."

I liked that idea. Not that I was … Okay, I was a bit scared. Those new invaders had been huge and bulky like Bombardians. I might know how to fight, but I had limits to what I could take down. Worse those guys brought up all kind of flashback. I'd had one earlier and never wanted another to incapacitate me.

"Thanks, babe."

"You are not going to be alone until this shit-storm is resolved."

"No back-talking from me."

Anthony snapped his fingers and a brown-haired man knelt in front of him. "Yes, Commander."

"Lieutenant, this is my Keeper, Larry. I want you to assign three people to watch him. They are to stay with him at all times, unless David's Combatants are in the room. We clear?"

"Yes, Commander Anthony."

Three might be excessive, but I wasn't going to argue. I hugged Anthony tight and kissed his cheek. "Figure this out and let's get to work on how to deal with my father so we can celebrate our combining."

Chapter 26

Anthony

Soon as Larry and his guards were out of eyesight I spun to Franklin. "You know what that shit was bout?"

"No."

"That all your got to say."

"Yep."

"Fuck!"

"Sums it up."

"What is going on?" David stood on the top step. "Why did Theodor tell me and Caleb to keep a watch over your two assess until he got back?"

"Got back?" Where would he go? Why?

"Watch us?"

Why did that bother Franklin more than Theodor leaving us while we had no clue as to what this Lord Tangler wanted?

"Yeah." Caleb halted at the step behind David. "I can see us watching the newest member inducted into the *I've got a Keeper* but not you."

"Me either. I'm the sanest of all of us."

"Hey," Caleb shot Franklin a finger. "I take offense at that."

I took offense to the entire conversation. None of them seemed to care about the situation at hand. "You two quit fucking around." Oops. Didn't mean to shout.

"Wow!" David winked at me. "Finding your Keeper has given you a set of balls."

"That it has." Caleb smiled at me. "Bout time."

If they wanted me to . . . Whatever I did, stand up for myself, or take charge I would. "Stop fucking around. Did you guy not find that unusual? Did Theodor tell you where he was going? What happened up here? Anything?"

"Nope. Not unusual for him, though." David's wide-open arms ripped a snarl from me. "What? He's usually leaves it up to us to unravel the mystery that is him. Care to explain why my hallway was full of strangers?" Okay, he'd known what had taken place up here, but chose to stay downstairs. That made sense. He needed to be there to protect his family. I sure wouldn't have left Larry. "And why there is three Combatants trailing Larry. Why he said they were to stay attached to him unless he was around me and my Combatants?"

"Someone, or something knocked Anthony's ex-lover on his ass."

Franklin nailed it. Sort of. Someone had managed to breach Theodor's fire wall. Then I'd told him to take it down. Not my finest moment. Should have just told him to let my Combatants in. Then again . . . That required the fire wall to be lowered, meaning whoever tried to enter the house would have gotten in. Including the invasion of thirty-one men. Then again . . . Might not have been safe for me to have done that. Although . . . David probably knew it already. What did . . .

"You guys ever heard of a Lord?"

"No." David and Caleb replied.

"Has your Uncle?"

"Why do you think he would have?" David waved at Cain, who had come up behind Franklin. "Fetch my Uncle."

"Theodor mentioned his Uncle telling him stories about them."

"More fucking secrets?"

"What now?" David's Uncle stopped three steps behind David.

"Previous Royal Leaders secrets." I sighed, shaking my head. Not been a Royal Leader for half a year and another secret came to life, as well as another attack on us. Okay, the first attack might have led to me becoming a Royal Leader, but . . . I could imagine how aggravated David and Caleb was.

"I know of no - -" David's Uncle stopped himself from spouting a lie

"Lords? Tell us what you know."

"Leaders of blood drinkers. They created the fictional stories of Vampires to cover their tracks. Keep themselves hidden. Unlike the stories they don't feed from humans. They obtain their substance from others like them, or their fated partners."

"Why was none of this passed down?"

Franklin asked a great question. How did the other Royal Leaders expect the newer ones to protect the Bombardians without all the information?

"Not sure why the other two did not enlighten the ones who replaced us. Sounds like Theodor's Uncles thought they would keep loads from Theodor."

"Good thing." Sure was. If someone had jotted it down in a Royal Blood's textbook then I would have known. "Do you know why one might team up with some of ours to attempt a coo?"

"They wouldn't."

Sure looked like they had. "Why not?"

"There's a truce between our race."

"Truce? Why would the others keep that from us?" David groaned. "Is this going to bring more danger to my home?"

"Doubt it." Theodor said from behind them.

"Thought you left." It's what Caleb and David led me and Franklin to believe.

"Not yet. I know who this one is. Not sure what he wants, but . . . I do not believe his appearance is meant as an attack." Looked like one. Felt like one. "He wants something. Not sure what, but . . . going to find out."

"This has nothing to do with me?" That should make me feel better, but it didn't. It effected one of my cousins. Which one? Theodor. Why else would he take off. Then again . . . Theodor always took charge of the situation.

"Lord's interference doesn't. Kevin may have chosen his own fate when he turned on the Vampire."

Fact I no longer cared about. All I wanted was for Larry and I to sit down and work through the small details. Then the major ones.

"I'm leaving right after I gather some clothes. Not sure how long I'll be out of touch. If a situation comes up that needs addressing right then, take a vote."

"Hey," I got Theodor's attention before he could depart. "You okay?"

"Will be."

"Can I help in anyway?"

"Just listen to David and settle things with your Keeper. We need to know what approach he is going to want to take with his father."

Something I could do. Something I wanted to know as well. "I'll keep it as simple as I can, and I'll try not to destroy the agreement we have with the President."

"Make it better." Theodor winked and grinned at me. "I know you two can accomplish that. Your Keeper is wise and you are smart." Theodor turned to David. "Congrats man. Take care of your Keeper and children. Get these traitors locked up."

Theodor's tone sounded more like one who knew he was going to his death. Was he? How would he find out what Lord Tangler wanted? "You sure you okay, Theodor?"

"Will be."

"Take your Combatants with you."

"I can contact them if I need them."

Not good enough but knew it would be the best I'd get from him. Theodor was more than stubborn when he got a bur under his ass.

"Call if you need us."

"Will do." Theodor faded into nothingness.

"Anyone want to tell me what he meant by traitors?"

Oh boy. Fun time. "You've got one on the first floor."

"I what!"

"Only one who didn't have one turn on him was David."

"My guys know better than to turn on my ass." David chuckled. "I can see why Caleb's guys would turn."

"Really?"

"Yeah, after a few days of sharing a motel room with your farting ass."

Lord have mercy. All of my cousins needed help. "I'm going to get my Keeper and take him to his room."

"Don't be doing anything funky in my bedroom."

"Too late." Franklin huffed. "You should have heard the bed pounding the wall."

"Best not be a hole in it."

"There will be." I darted around David as he reached for me, thinking God David put in extra wide steps. All of them followed me down and stopped in front of the doorway as I did.

"Looks like your planned fun will have to wait."

Sure did. Larry was curled up on his side, sleeping. He looked so peaceful. A huge smile and tussled hair. There was no way he could be comfortable, so I walked up to him and scooped him into my arms, praying I did not disturb him. Prayers wasn't answered. Larry wiggled and opened one eye.

"It's me. Rest."

Chapter 27

Anthony

I tucked a stray piece of hair behind Larry's ear, snuggling closer to him. Larry's warmth warmed my body, giving me enough calmness that I could debate every little detail in my life. What would Larry disagree with? I wasn't delusional. I knew my life wasn't perfect. Knew I was a bit of a control freak. Had a bit of OCD when it came to certain aspects in my home. Like the dishes being color and shaped coordinating. If one was in the wrong place it drove me up the wall. Oh, I was picky about how the towels were folded. I could be adjustable on the small things, but the bigger ones . . . We'd work through them. When it came down to making love that was an easy one. I didn't mind bottoming, but I preferred to top. Loved to give blow-jobs as well as receive them. When it came down to it, compromise could be formed on almost anything, besides Larry's safety. Pretty much all Larry had to do was ask for something. I'd get him whatever he desired.

"What if I want you to have all your desire?"

"Sleepiness is sexy on you."

"Is it?"

"Yep." I nuzzled the back of his neck. "Thought you were sleeping."

"Was, but your emotions crept down our link. Your thoughts are becoming clearer and easier to read. How deep will our link go?"

"Sorry, honey." The deepness of the link varies from one pair to the next, so I skipped over that question.

"No problem."

I wrapped my leg over Larry's as he stretched.

"Did you guys solve the issue?"

"Sort of." I quickly recapped what he'd missed and about Theodor's parting order.

"Guess we have our assignment." Larry twisted around until he buried his nose in my neck. "You smell amazing, babe."

"It's all you, honey."

"Doubtful, but I'll let you get by with that." Larry wrapped his arms around me. "Where do we start?"

"Right here." I gave Larry a playful push back, straddling him in one smooth move, ensuring my bulging cock rested right against Larry's. "Time for you to see how your game to drive Kevin off his rockers worked on me."

"Knew . . ." Larry kissed my chin, "it . . ." He bit my lower lip, "did."

"You left me with a massive hard-on and having to deal with my cousin's craziness."

"What you going to do about it?" Larry thrust up. "Punish me?"

"Lavish you." I slid my hand under the back of Larry's shirt, pushing it up as he arched. "Strip you naked." The shirt flew over our heads as I leaned forward, clamping my teeth onto Larry's dark brown nipple.

"Damn, lover."

That Larry was. "You are my everything."

"You are . . . Agh . . . Do that again."

I hoped to always be. Hoped that making an agreement would be easy. That Larry's father did not view Larry's decision as a method to deconstruct what he'd worked for. Personal threat. Royal Leaders did not need the President hell bent on destroying them because his son belonged to me. Nope. We needed the President of the United States to accept his son's place among the Bombardian world. Needed Larry's father to love his son enough to listen to him. To assist him in his new life. Not take offense and punish the entire Bombardian race.

"Babe?"

"I'm fine." I gave his nipple a softer bite then licked a path up to his sexy lips. My hand slid from his back to his ass, squeezing and pulling him closer to me. "Ready for some of my Keeper. Can I have him?"

"Whenever you want, babe. Whenever you want."

All I needed to hear. My tongue followed the path I'd made earlier, but instead of stopping at his nipple I stopped at the top of his sweats. I took my teeth and tugged the band down. With a tap to the hip, Larry lifted, and I was able to push them down his legs.

"Amazing."

"Sure is." I pressed my nose into his pubes, inhaling deeply, reveling in the sweet musk that belonged to my Keeper. "Wonderful." I trailed my nose up to the top of Larry's cock, then licked a path to the mushroom head before I engulfed it. Larry sucked in a deep breath then groaned as he released it.

I pulled off his cock, grinning up at him. "Something wrong, honey?"

"No." Larry thrust up. "Want more."

"Going to give you all you need."

"Now."

"Patients my love."

"Have little of that."

"You will grow to."

"Don't want to. I'm starving for you."

"Like you that way."

"Then feed me. I promise to be hungry a minute or two after you have the fill of me."

"Never will have enough of you." I swirled the tip of my tongue around the head twice before I ran the tip of it thru his slit, getting a shout from him.

"More. Please."

Something I could do. I went down to the base of his cock, letting my tongue dart a bit further until it touched Larry's balls.

"Suck them."

Didn't have to ask me twice. I came off his cock and scooted down further onto the bed, taking one of his balls into my mouth.

"Fuck yeah."

I sucked on the one, then tugged the second one into my mouth, getting an ear-piercing scream from Larry. I ended up having to pinch the base of my cock, which had me snapping my finger until the bottle of lube appeared in my hands. I squeezed some on my fingers and pressed one in until I was knuckle deep.

"More, babe. More."

A second finger slid in beside the first then a third.

"Yes . . . Oh babe . . ."

"You want more?"

"Dick. Now. Hard and fast. Rough."

"You sure, honey?"

"Yes!"

My fingers slipped free and I lined my cock up with his puckering hole. "I'll give you all you want for the rest of my life."

With one hard and fast thrust I was balls deep in my man, with my cock resting against his prostrate.

"Oh . . . Fuck. Do that again."

I pulled all the way out, slamming back in.

"More, babe. More. Please."

Again I exited and reentered, ensuring I hit his prostrate. With more speed than I meant to use, I pulled from Larry's sexy hole and slammed back in. Twice. Three times. Four times.

"So close . . . More. Don't stop."

As if I could. Larry reached for his dick, but I knocked his hand away and gripped it. Began stroking him with the speed I busted through his pucker.

"Anthony . . . You will always remember that I am your equal."

Shit. How could Larry be thinking about anything other than me fucking him. I had to work harder.

"I want us to do this while we are connected. Don't you dare stop making love to me."

Okay. In a twisted way I understood what Larry desired. What a better chance to make a partnership agreement than while making love to one another. Kind of hurt my ego a bit, but . . . If this was when Larry wanted to do it . . . Fine with me.

"Never will forget it."

No way I could. I knew how my Keeper felt about being kept in the loop and being told the truth about what was taking place around him. How could he not. His father lied to him most of his life. Those lies and manipulation of his entire life resulted in Larry being kidnapped.

"Ah shit . . . Prefect." Larry panted and took a couple of deep breaths. "I do not care what all your way of life entails as long as you keep that in mind and run things by me before you make a final decision.

Larry's hole tightened around me, making me tighten my fist around his dick.

"Understand."

Right. Discussion. I shook my head, not completely dissolving the lust rushing through me. "You are going to be easy to please."

"Try to be."

Great, but I would ensure that Larry's deepest desires were met.

"I knew we'd work great together." Larry grunted and thrust up, making my cock hit his prostate a bit harder. "Tell Theodor we have a partnership agreement."

My balls slammed into Larry's ass, but what I heard from him was way better than anything.

"Oh . . . hell yeah. Do that again."

"That what my honey wants?"

"Please. Harder."

"Can do nothing but abide." I leaned over, bending Larry double as I claimed his lips and dueled with Larry's tongue until neither of us could breathe unless we parted. Faster we went, the further we became one. It was right where I wanted us to be. Always.

"Now!" I didn't need to hear Larry's response. I knew his explosion was ready to free itself. No reason to stop it.

"Now." Larry's hole gripped my dick so hard I could not pull back. He held me as deep in his body as he could. Spunk splashed on my stomach and chest. My own release rushed from me. We both shouted each other's name. I collapsed on Larry, knowing exactly what David meant earlier when he talked about feeling a connection with his children. I could also see how he might have missed what he was feeling when he knocked up his Keeper.

"You know, don't you?" Larry's smile warmed me all the way through.

"You to?"

"I can feel him."

"It's a him?"

"Yes."

"You pissed?"

"Hell no."

I was so excited. I was going to be a father. Going to have a son. Going to have to keep both my Keeper and my son safe. Okay, a bit of fear lurked inside me, but it could not out do my excitement. Thankfully, David had found his Uncle and they had an idea of what to expect.

I shifted to the side, wrapping my legs and arms around him as my hand rested against Larry's stomach. "Let's get some sleep. Then we'll deal with . . ."

"My father issues."

"Hah. But yes."

"I love you, Anthony Lincoln."

"I love you, Larry. Rest for our son."

Chapter 28

Larry

I wasn't sure how I managed it, but we both slept until eight the next morning. We might have slept longer if someone hadn't banged on the door. Not someone, but Bryan shouted for me to uncurl my ass from my lover. His strong word had me jumping out of the bed and yanking the door open.

"I didn't mean show me your goods." Bryan's chuckle let me know I had overreacted at his tone and words, then again it didn't.

"You are up. You have color. You re joking. Shit. I'm naked."

"Yeah, honey." Anthony growled and snapped his fingers. "Better."

"Thanks, babe."

"Nice, but not his color." Bryan shook his head. "These Royal Leaders have no sense of fashion."

"Tell me about it." I loved hearing Bryan having fun. So much better than the past several weeks. "You look . . . Wow. That medicine worked miracles."

"Sure did."

"That it did." David came up behind Bryan, wrapping his arms around him. I no longer felt the desire to have a love as deep as theirs. Had no reason to. Had it myself. "You are still supposed to be taking it easy."

"I am." Bryan stuck his lower lip out. "Had to show my second closest friend that I was better."

"Right. You just wanted him downstairs when Tommy and Cain show up."

"True."

"I'm going to get to meet the legendary Tommy?"

"If you want."

"I want, but . . ." I looked back at Anthony.

"Go on, honey. I need to talk with the others for a bit. Get us a solid starting place before we try to tackle an attack path for you father."

"Shit." Bryan coughed. "Major advancement in your relationship."

"You sure, babe?" I didn't want him to deal with my father issues by himself. It was too much of a headache.

"Yes. Go enjoy Bryan being well and make another friend. Tommy is a great guy. Fits in well with Bryan and you."

"Means he has no qualms about putting his big bad . . .General Combatant in place."

That made three of us. Not like it took much to put them in their place. They'd do about anything for us, long as we were safe. "Come on, Bryan." I slid around David and Bryan.

"Take it easy, honey." David called as Bryan and I made our way down the hallway.

"Don't worry, David. I won't let him overdo."

"You don't overdo either, honey."

"I won't." My hand covered my stomach as I realized there was no way I would endanger my precious cargo.

"You too?" Bryan froze and spun back around to face Anthony. "You hound dog. Wasted no time."

"What's you going on about?" Anthony asked from the doorway as he gave me a huge wide smile.

"You know damn well what." Bryan's chuckle was more than music to my ears. "Honey, you need to have a talk with your cousin about protection."

"About . . . Ah fuck. Anthony, you knock him up. Already?"

"How did we get on this topic?" Anthony snorted.

"I rested my hand on my belly."

"I saw it. Loved it."

"You not upset I let it slip?"

"Not hardly. I want to shout it from the rooftop.

"Wouldn't go that far."

"Me either, but I'd love to."

Totally understood the jester but knew how dangerous it would be. Certain ones knowing would put me in more danger than being the President's son. The Royal Leaders already had one Keeper expected twins. A second one carrying a child would put them all on edge.

"Don't worry, honey." Anthony stood in the doorway, fully dressed. "I've got three guards downstairs. I'm sure David has the outside very well guarded."

"I do." David replied. "No one will come into my home without my consent."

"Not even popping in?" I despised how weak I sounded, but I'd witnessed two good Secret Service guys killed in order to get to me. Being held in a stinky, dank place did little to ease my mind when it came to me being in danger. Just thinking about bad guys getting their grimy hands on me made me skittish.

"Earth has all, but my cousins, blocked out. Promise."

Was all I needed to hear. "Let's go. I want some food before this elusive Tommy arrives."

"Food sounds great."

Best words I'd heard from Bryan since the second day I arrived.

"Take it easy, Bryan."

"I will, worry wort."

"I won't let him overdo." I gave a finger wave to David and Anthony. "Faster we approach my father the better off we will be. He's still stewing over me requesting David guard me."

Chapter 29

Anthony

"He's right, you know."

Sure did. A stewing father was one thing, but a man who demanded everything go his way was . . . Disastrous.

"That's why I gave for him to go visit while I find out how and what you three want from him."

"Nothing but happiness." David patted my shoulder.

"Not the time to joke."

"He's not joking." Caleb appeared beside David in a haze of blue mist.

"Right." I pulled the bedroom door shut as I stepped into the hallway. "I know Theodor wants Larry to convince his father to come clean about our kind."

"Don't we all." David motioned them to the conference room."

"Why not the kitchen?" Caleb rubbed his stomach.

"You are always hungry." David shook his head but did not supply Caleb with an answer, so I did.

"Bryan and Larry are fixing their food." No way was I going to discuss this around them. Neither needed the extra stress. Not that their conditions would keep them from trying to snoop. Thankfully, Tommy was on the way. That would occupy them for a bit. I hoped. Sometimes Tommy aided in Bryan's stunts, other times he came up with the craziest stunts to pull.

"Plus," David smiled at Caleb, making me shake my head. "Franklin's in the conference room with fresh coffee from Jabber Coffee House."

"Say no more." Caleb sprinted through the conference room door with David and I following a bit behind. Not much.

"Best coffee in town." Caleb sighed as he picked up his own brown thick paper cup.

I doubted that, but I took the cup Franklin handed me and sat down. "It's not Fran's Coco Coffee, but it's decent enough."

"No one can match Fran's Coco Coffee." I took a sip.

"True, but . . ." Franklin took a small taste of his coffee. "There's not one around here." He tugged the chair beside me out and sat. "How was your night?"

"Amazing."

"He had a bit too much fun." David grinned. "He's put a bun in his Keeper's stomach."

"He what!" Franklin glanced at me and I nodded. "Fast tracking things, aren't you?"

Might have been, but it hadn't been done on purpose. Just happened. Not something I minded though.

"I don't think I'd be telling my father-in-law, Mr. President of the United States, that I knocked his son up before I met him." Caleb snorted. "Can you imagine what you would do if a daughter came to you and introduced you to the man who knocked her up?"

The man would be dead in a blink. Nope. I would not be telling the President that his son was expecting.

"Can't tell him anyway." David added.

"Then he won't be enlightening the man into every one of our secrets if he agrees to tell the world about our kind?" Caleb sighed and swallowed a deep gulp of his coffee.

"I personally do not think it is wise to bring that part to the President's attention." David sat his cup down as if he'd not just dropped the bomb that all knew was coming.

"What?"

Wasn't surprised to hear a double response alongside mine. David knew how important it was for us to bring the truth to life. We had a solid way to force the issue, but David did not want us to. Made no sense. Yet . . . it did. Was sure Theodor would not have agreed with David.

"I'm serious." David shrugged. "It's a lot to put onto one person's shoulder. I would kill anyone who put that kind of pressure on Bryan. Anyone of you would do the same for your Keeper."

True. It was the whole point I wanted to discuss with my cousins before we approached Larry with an attack plan. It was even more important to me since he was carrying our child.

"Why would you think that is pressure?" Franklin sat his cup down and clasped his hands across his flat stomach. Man had to work out at least seven days a week. Even I couldn't get the six-pack that Franklin had.

"How could it not be." David leaned his arms on the table. "The President is Larry's father. He might not believe the man could protect or keep him out of the limelight long enough for him to heal, but the man created him. There has to be feelings there."

Caleb's eyes shifted to me. "Doesn't your Keeper know the seriousness of the situation?" He tilted his cup back.

"He does. Dead set on helping get his father to tell the truth."

"For you, or himself?" David asked.

"Both." Larry said from the doorway.

"Why does these Keepers think it's fine to invade our conference room when we are in a meeting?" Caleb eyes rolled, making me throw my hand over my mouth to keep the chuckle silent. Still my wolf took offense to the tone Caleb used.

"Watch it." A deep snarl rippled free from my throat. "Honey, is something wrong?"

"No." He held a plate of food out. "Thought you might be hungry. Bryan said David and Franklin ate already and that I didn't need to worry about Caleb."

"What?" Caleb glared at David who gave a nonchalant shrug. "Your Keeper is mean. Pure out mean."

"Seems right to me." Franklin glittering eyes were as comical as Caleb's rolling eyes. "Breakfast was great. Remind me to return the favor at lunch."

Lord have mercy. So much playfulness took place during our meetings that I wasn't sure if we truly had meetings. Laughter, wasn't common in board meetings, but . . . Interruption . . . They always arose during financial meetings.

"Here you go, babe." Larry sat a plate in front of me.

"This smells amazing."

"Hope so."

"Did you eat?"

"Some toast."

"That all?"

"All I could."

"What's that mean?"

"His stomach is already rebelling." David tossed a small plastic bottle of pills at me. "He takes one each time he gets sick."

No label. "This what your Uncle gave you?"

"Yep."

"Fine." I lifted Larry's hand palm up after I opened the bottle. With a tilt of my hand, one small white round pill fell into Larry's palm, but Larry picked it up and dropped it into the bottle. "What's wrong?"

"Nothing. Bryan gave me one already."

"Oh." I closed the bottle and laid it in Larry's hand. "Keep them with you."

"Okay." Larry tucked the bottle into his pants pocket. "I have no problem beating my father at his own game. I want the humans aware of the truth. Your kind, and mine, deserves everyone to see us for what we are. Not for what one group of people deemed necessary." Wasn't sure if necessary was the right description, there might have been better words, but . . . it fit. "Make a plan. If I can pull it off . . . I will."

"That's what we'll do, honey."

"I know." Larry laid a fork on the table. "I'm going to go meet Tommy."

"They are in the living room filtering through the movies." Cain said from the doorway.

"Too many people walking in here." Franklin frowned. "Caleb's right about that."

"I'm always right."

"Lord, honey, you best be going before the room fills up with shit that keeps you rooted in place."

I nabbed the napkin, that Caleb through at me, from the air.

"I was called in here." Cain said as he laid a sheet of paper in front of David. "There's what you asked for."

"Thanks." David said, but Cain had already faded away. "Hate when he does that."

"It's Franklin's fault." Caleb snatched the paper from in front of David. "What's this."

"I thought . . ." David took a huge sip of his coffee. "That Franklin and Anthony would like to see the original draft of the agreement with the President."

I leaned across the table, taking the sheet from Caleb. "Thanks." I scanned it as I ate the eggs and bacon Larry had brought me. "This is detailed, but not either."

"Right." David said. "They wanted it vague, but . . . nailed down as well."

"Why?"

"We thought it was so we could advance the agreement, but . . ."

Hadn't been the case. From what Theodor, Caleb, and David told me the President had detoured them each time they approached the government about changes. Couple of times the President threatened to revoke the agreement. Not that I thought he would have done so, but the mere idea was enough to bring the Royal Leaders to a halt.

"How come you guys did not push back harder?" I passed the paper to Franklin.

"Hard to find the true details about people in charge of the humans."

Other words . . . The Royal Leaders chose not to start a battle they could not gain the upper hand in. Never go into a fight you can't . . . Win properly. Or . . . through underhanded methods. We preferred to go the straight path, but we never did anything that would come back to bite us in the ass. Although . . . the agreement with the humans had done so. An oversight of how underhanded the President of the United States could be. We'd learn from that mistake and would not made it again.

"I don't want my Keeper used as a bargaining chip." I was going to make sure that my cousins knew it up front.

"Me either." David nodded at me. "Neither would Theodor."

"I wouldn't do that. "Caleb said.

"Neither would I." Franklin slid the paper back to David. "Thanks. That helps."

"How so?" I saw the wiggle room, but if humans kept refusing to meet then what could we do. Minus using Larry as a bargaining chip to get his dad to meet with one, or two, of us.

"David has the president's agreement to discuss renegotiating thanks to rescuing Larry and guarding his son.

Right. Forgot about that. We did have a way in, but still it left a major opening for my cousins to try and use Larry as a pawn.

"I say . . . And I mean with Larry's and Anthony's agreement, that we all go with them to tell the President that his son is a Keeper."

"That might not be wise." I knew it wouldn't be if I was the President. There was nothing more personal than a son.

"Why not? This man has proved that he cares more about his status among the world than his own son." David frowned. "He brought a damn storm of people to the airport when I brought Larry home. He wanted his son to meet with the press before he'd even had time to digest what happened to him."

David made good points, but still it seemed . . . "Counterproductive."

"Huh?" Caleb tossed his empty coffee cup into the wastebasket.

"Not sure, but it is." One thing I never done was ignore my gut when it came to business and from the sound of it, Larry's father was a straight-up businessman who was after an ultimate goal. He'd do whatever it took, even disown his son. Doing so . . . "Larry's going to be a threat."

"What?" David and Franklin's voice blended together.

"Who?" Caleb tossed in.

"How?" Franklin took a huge swig of his drink.

"I'm . . ." Answering meant bringing up some personal issues Larry trusted me with. I would not do so without permission. Not even for my cousins."

A light knock at the door had me up and on my feet in less than a second. I yanked the door open before I asked who it was. Didn't need to. I could feel Larry's unease. Not so much his, but how much he was feeling my distress about answering my cousin.

"It's fine, babe. They are friends. I trust them to keep it to themselves."

"You sure, honey?" Anthony looked behind him. "I can tell them they have to trust me."

"They also have to know I trust them. I do." Larry leaned in and kissed my cheek and whispered. "It's fine. I mean it."

"Okay." I spun him around and gave him a nudge forward. "Go back to your friends."

I shut the door once Larry disappeared from my sight. "This does not leave the room."

"Course not." David said.

I sat back down and took in a deep breath. "Since Larry's father was a teenage, he has not made a move unless it moved him towards his ultimate goal."

"Presidency?"

"Right." I couldn't believe someone could be so obsessed. "Even his marriage and his son were a part of the game to move him into the highest-ranking seat among the world."

Sickened me. I'd seen many humans play such games with their lives. Saw them bring innocent people into the middle of something they set in motion long before they even met.

"That might . . ."

"Stop us in our tracks." David supplied.

"Yeah." As much as I despised it, David was correct. Yet he'd not covered all my thought. "Wrong thinking."

"Huh?" Franklin banged his head on the table. "I'm lost. Hate being that way."

"Don't we all." David added.

"Larry's father will try to use that to get his son to do what he wants. Keep the humans in the dark." I'd been told, firmly, that was not an option. Larry believed humans deserved the truth about what their leaders hid. "Larry wants everyone to know the truth and he will refuse to keep his mark hidden." In fact, I could all but hear my Keeper going toe-to-toe with his father and ordering him to either tell the world, or he would go to a national TV news station and reveal his mark. Wouldn't surprise me if Larry took along a Red Hooded Guy and let him tell the truth. "Larry will put his father in a such a position that his father has to choose between us revealing the truth and making his father look like a fool, or his father would spin the truth so that it made him look like a golden man."

"How would he do that?" Franklin tossed his empty cup into the waste bin.

"Reveal his Mark to the world on national air."

"Shit." David sprang to his feet and paced. "That might work."

"How could it?" Caleb leaned back in his chair. "We are forbidden from going to the public."

"Yes, but . . ." I snatched the agreement and pointed to the last line. "This is our loophole."

David, Caleb, and Franklin moved so they hovered over the paper. Knew the line wasn't long enough to take five minutes to read, so they must have been going over and over it. None appeared to be grasping it, so I enlightened them.

"It states that unless another high-ranking person is with us the secret can't be revealed."

"We don't have . . . Fuck. You are brilliant." Franklin slapped me on the back. "Will that work? He's not a member of the government, is he?"

"Not officially, but unofficially he's right at the top. His father left the opening for us."

"How?" Franklin asked.

"Fuck. You are smart." David slapped the table. "The President wants Larry to give an interview about what happened. He will expect his son to spin the tale he gives him, but Larry will be truthful. Right down to the part where his father sent a man who took out twelve people to save him. No one would dare dismiss the President's son as spinning a lie. They will jump on the fact faster than a dog gnawing on his thorn ridden paw. When he brings it to life, we will be able to prove what he says."

"You want him to give away some of the secrets he promised to keep?"

"That's hanging you up, Caleb?"

"Yes, Anthony. Larry gave his word to David. If he breaks it for this what's to keep him from doing it for - -"

"If you finish that I'm going to bite your nose off your perfect face."

"Shit." Franklin moved to my side and placed a hand on my shoulder. "Calm down. He did not mean that . . ."

"You can't even finish it. You don't know how he meant it."

"I'm sure he didn't mean it like it came across." David said. "Caleb's a prick in lots of ways, but he would never think the worst of a Keeper."

"I did . . . Shit. That came out the wrong way." Caleb hung his head. "Sorry man. It's just the entire subject is iffy and dangerous for everyone we lead."

Caleb was right. I knew it. Still . . . Shit. I should have expected our tempers to flare but hearing someone think my Keeper would turn on us . . . Set my wolf off.

"Think," David retook his seat. "it is best that we all take a few hours and think this option over. Then we can reconvene and nail down the details."

Sounded wise. I wanted to run it by Larry and ensure myself he was on board with the way things were headed.

Chapter 30

Larry

I tucked my legs between Anthony's, letting the tip of my keen rest against his balls. I'd feel my Bombardian for the next few days. Anthony achieved his goal, if exhausting me was it. The interview with Susan Tinker, the biggest political newscaster among the world, was mere hours away. Anthony spent hours questioning me about my true feelings about having the interview without my dad's knowledge. Wasn't the option I dreamed up, but . . . Life didn't go the way one wanted. A fact I knew well. My family destroyed my view of a loving and devoted one the moment I discovered the real reason they stayed together and had me. Then my life turned upside down as I became secluded because of who my father was. My dad's political life kept me from having friends. Shawn was my only true one and my first love. Until . . . I met Anthony . . . My Bombardian. My savior in many ways. I owed him and I had no qualms about going along with the interview. After reading the agreement between the Royal Leaders and my dad, I agreed with Anthony. It was the only loophole in the contract. David and Caleb spent a few hours cursing themselves for believing the President of the United States left the agreement vague to allow advancement. I would have done the same, if I didn't know my dad so well. Was a stupid mistake, but one the Royal Leaders could learn from. Least they had me to make sure there was no repeat, which was how I found myself in a different spot than I expected. After a couple of hours of deep internalization Franklin, Caleb and David came to the same conclusion. Going to my father first wasn't wise. I agreed. He'd try to beat us to the punch and put out a warning of lies coming from possible terrorist. The idea had not crossed my mind until David reminded me of how they tricked them to leaving only one loophole. Still, it hadn't been what I was hoping for.

When Anthony explained the plan to me, I expected them to let my dad setup the interview and take the lead with me standing at his side. Like most of the press visits went. Right the opposite. Instead of my dad enlightening the world to a race that had been hidden for two-hundred years, I would be. Instead of my dad telling the world the truth about the Destroyer's, aka Marked Ones. Explaining how connected to a Bombardian they were, I would. How some Bombardian's chose to live a full life with their Bombardian and others choose to live in the Destroyers Hermitages, I would be. Instead of my dad revealing the back story about the Red Hooded Guy, I would be. Weight of the truth hung on my shoulders. I'd hope to have the backup of all five Royal Leaders, but not happening. First Theodor was still away. Anthony and the others came up with another track. Wasn't too keen on less mental support, but I would be fine. Sitting in front of a camera wasn't new. Taking the lead of an interview was. Opening up about what my father, and previous government, covered up was hard to cope with. Not to mention I'd never liked the press conferences.

There could be no messing up. There could be no lingering doubts about . . . Was it betrayal to tell the truth? Felt like it. Was that because I was going behind my father's back?

"Honey, you aren't."

"You are supposed to be asleep." I wiggled when Anthony licked the side of my ears.

"You are too."

"Can't sleep."

"I felt that."

"Huh?"

"I can feel your unease." Anthony rested a hand over my stomach. "Need me to get you something to settle your stomach?"

"Nah." Wasn't our son making me sick. "Nerves."

"Then . . ." His hand slid down and closed around my cock. "Let me take your mind off of tomorrow."

"Babe, you've wore me out." I looked down at Anthony's deflated cock, grinning. "Yours too."

"Best way to be. Sated by my man so good that I can't even get it up with a single touch of his luscious body."

I snorted, shaking my head. "You are crazy, babe. Crazy."

"I know it." Anthony leaned back, locking his eyes on me. "I'm serious, if you need to cancel this, we can go about this another way."

"I'm fine."

I was. Nerves didn't mean I would back out. Too much rode on my interview. Not only for me, but every Keeper and Protector, Bombardian, and human. The world deserved to know what their government had done two centuries ago. It might have been my father's place to educate them, but I had no qualms about stepping up and taking over for my dad. I might not be a politician, but the government viewed me as a high priority because of my dad. Many times my dad had told them that I would be following in their footsteps. Major lie, but it helped him in the polls. If he wanted them to think so then . . . I'd used it to gain results. Never done such before, but nothing had been as major as what the government had hid.

"You know," Anthony kissed my cheek, "you can't lie to me."

"Didn't mean to."

"It's your go to phrase, isn't it?"

Never thought that, but those two words left my mouth many times over the years.

"Mine to."

"Why?"

"Kept me from revealing how much I disliked the idea of having to date women. Having to make my family believe marriage was in my future. Children in my future."

I snorted when Anthony paused, grinning. "Guess they won't have to worry about that last one."

"I love that idea." I did to. "Shawn and I talked about adopting a dozen kids when we were settled. I thought dreams, all my dreams, died right along with Shawn."

"I'm glad you had him." Anthony tugged me closer. "I can feel how much you cared for him. How much he cared for you. He saw you for who you were. That is special."

"I'm thrilled it doesn't bother you."

"I hate it, but . . . Understand it."

"Hate it?"

"Jealous thing, but it's fine."

"Why?" I wasn't sure if I asked why he hated it, or why it was fine.

"You were mine from the time you were born. It should have been me. I should have been protecting and taking care of all your needs." Anthony sighed pushed me back, and his inhale pulled me forward. "I know we didn't know each other then. If I had I wouldn't have known you were my Keeper until you turned eighteen, but to my wolf . . . It doesn't matter."

In a twisted kind of way, I understood. In fact, I felt the same way when I thought about Kevin being with Anthony. Anthony was mine. Had been for as long as there had been breath in me and would be until I took my last. Still . . . We hadn't known each other but for a few days.

"I'm pleased you had Shawn to take care of you in the way you needed. He was the best friend you needed. The lover you wanted. The one to listen and let you vent about your life. Things I was not there to do."

"You are here now." I closed my lips over his mouth, giving him a tender kiss that I hoped melted him.

Soon as our mouth parted, Anthony said, "That I am."

"You will be for the rest of my life."

"That I will."

"Then you know I can accomplish the goal of my upcoming interview. That I can get through it because I have you."

"Then let's get some sleep, because David will be waking us up in a few hours."

I didn't need to see a clock to know what time it was. Since I arrived at David, when he was home, he was up at the crack of dawn. Wasn't sure if that was his norm, or if it was because Bryan had been so sick. Whatever the case, he was up early and they all needed to be.

Chapter 31

Larry

Sweat bubbled across my forehead. Heat from the overhead light in any studio made me feel icky. Susan Tinker's backdrop bore a photo of me standing next to my dad. We bore bright smiles, both fake, but I suspected no one could tell. My entire family had perfected the facade of happiness. Had to. It kept voters on our side. Constituents desired stability in their presidential family.

Jean wearing, t-shirt camera man held up five fingers, lowering them with each passing second. Time had come. It not only brought the truth to Americans, but . . . Peace to me. I was finally going to get to help others in my own way. Yet, another dream Anthony made possible.

"Welcome, welcome." Susan Tinker gave her traditional Miss America wave to the camera. "Today we have Larry Wells. We've all heard how he was taking time to heal after foreign mercenaries attacked his limo, killing his Secret Service detail."

Hadn't known how much of the story dad released to the press. I'd purposely refused to watch the news. I had not wanted to hear the press speculation or the story dad's press team spun. I might should have taken time to catch up. Susan was known for doing her research, but I'd given her little to work with. She'd tried demanding her pre-show questions be answered but the main man told her she would not blow the chance at the ratings they would achieve from such an interview. I tried to settle her down by telling her that my interview would take her to top of the networks.

"This is the first face-to-face interview since he was rescued during a silent mission by the amazing Seals Team."

Seals. Team. My ass. David was one man. Powerful. Dangerous. Deadly.

"How are you holding up, Mr. Wells?"

"I'm doing great, Mrs. Tinker," I sat up taller. "Please call me Larry."

"Then you must call me Susan." She grinned, making me think of a vulture right before it swooped in for its meal. "You requested this interview can you tell me why."

"I believe it is time to set things right."

Susan hadn't been expecting that, so she glanced towards the suit wearing man just off stage. I'd never seen her with wide eyes and a blank stare. She never turned away from one of the monitors, but . . . . My open ended response shocked her more than I expected. Pretty sure no President's son made such a strong statement.

"By all means." She waved her hand at me.

Her shock and uncomfortable state faded as quick as it came. The TV viewers probably never caught it. Her ability to go with the flow was why I chose Susan. As much as she hated not having her pre-shows questions answered, she knew how to run with the flow. She wasn't blind to when she had something major handed to her on a silver platter. She also knew it would be yanked away from her if she dove in with a barge of questions. She was known for giving her guest more freedom of speech than most. The woman had a teleprompter with possible questions she worked up from her pre-show ones, but that day . . . No use for one, so the screen was black.

"There was no Seal team sent to bring me home." I shoved my hands under my legs. "One man came at my father's request. He took out twelve men and brought me home. He has been keeping me in a secure location since, at my request."

I paused, giving Susan time to form the most important question. Didn't have to wait long. Another reason I chose her. Smart and logical minds react faster than others.

"You are telling me that one man came in and took out twelve mercenaries."

"Yes, Susan."

"Then . . . You did not choose the story about a Seal team?"

"When my plane landed dad had a team of reporters for me to speak to. I was in no mental shape to do so. I wanted time to heal, mentally. I was not harmed physically, but watching good men die while trying to protect me was hard. Being bound and blindfolded messed with my head. I needed time, not invasion of my privacy."

"Then you have not been at a retreat?"

Of course, that's what dad's press team would come up with. Typical. "No. I have been with my rescuer and his family."

"Who rescued you?"

Question I wanted her to come to. Quicker than I expected. "David Lincoln, Royal Leader of the Bombardians."

"Who? What" Susan's stumbling and constant glancing at her boss warned me that they were fading to a commercial. Susan needed time. She'd been giving more than she could comprehend. Not to mention her boss would have to ensure the station remained live. If my father was watching, and I knew he would be, I'd made sure he knew what was about to be broadcasted. To some extent.

"Larry . . . Are you . . . I need to know if . . ."

"Susan, we run with this. Sit back and let him tell his story. Uninterrupted." Susan's boss shifted his body so we were face-to-face."

I nodded. "Thanks for the airtime."

"No, thank you."

"Don't say that until you've heard the entire story."

The boss man walked off stage, muttering about no matter which way this turn of events went their rating would be through the roof. Man was right. Some would think I'd lost my mind while being held captive. Others would believe me. Others would be searching for the truth just from what I'd already said.

The silent count down began. Susan once again gave a smile and wave, but I saw her lower lip quivering as she told me to tell my story.

"There will be some people who think I've lost my mind, but I have visual proof."

"You do?" Susan winced at her interruption but gave him a small wave jester to continue.

"Let me tell the entire story and the proof will be given as I go." I sat up taller and made sure to keep my eyes on the camera in front of me. "A special race of people have lived among us for two hundred years." I kept my voice strong and solid, even though my insides twisted and swirled. Warmth flooded me as it flowed into my mind. Anthony was taking care of me. He always would. "These people were created by a great man with extreme amounts of knowledge and skills for his time period. He did so at the behest of the commander of the War of 1812. That leader desired stronger and powerful men. Ones able to fight anything that came his way. He got his wish, but not at that particular time."

Anthony had asked me to refrain from going into the exact details of how they came about. Some of their story had to or it held no credibility. It had little anyway until David popped in wearing the Red Hooded Guy garb. I'd wanted all five of them there, but that was off the table since Theodor was still on some secret trip. David was also timid about all four of them showing up. So, I'd gone for David and whoever he brought along. If anyone. I hoped for more than one to show that the Red Hooded Guy was more than one person.

"The Bombardians have worked hard to keep themselves hidden from us. Not at their wish, but at the Presidents. Each one since they were created knew about them. Refused to let them make themselves known, until . . . My father made a compromise with them during his first term."

Susan and all the crew members full attention was on me. The crew members had leaned as far as they could without coming into view. All the sounds accompanied with equipment had gone quiet, except the faint hum of the lights. All the eyes increased my internal swirling. I was going to be sick if it didn't fade.

"The agreement gave the Bombardian some semblance among us. Wasn't a good one. My father deemed them a cult. One he and others have worked hard to make us fear. Fear the Red Hooded Guy. Fear the mark that comes before he does. It became so horrible that the Destroyers and their homes were violently attacked for being who and what they are. Even then, the Bombardians did nothing to retaliate. They could have. They are stronger than any other person alive. They have skills that help them. That saves lives. It saved mine. That is why I think it is time the world knows what this group my father deemed as a cult is. It is time that all us of learned what the Destroyers are. What the Destroyer's Hermitage are there for."

Way past time. Lies never bode well. Anthony and the other Royal Leaders kept a tight leash on their people, but there are enemies among all races. Like all enemies they make themselves known when they think they have the upper hand. That is why there had already been one deadly attack on the Royal Leaders and another spoiled one. The Royal Leaders needed to be known to all before there is a mishap that cannot be covered up.

"The Red Hooded Guy is not what we are taught. He is not the leader, or not always, of the Bombardian. The Red Hooded Guy is not one person. It is a Bombardian whose half of his soul belongs to the one they have graced with their mark." I nodded at the camera, letting Anthony know it was time for David and whoever else was coming forth at the time to materialize. I knew Anthony would be at David's side, because he was scared for me.

Three blue puffs of smoke appeared in front of Susan and me. Several gasps filled the air as the smoke disappeared leaving behind three people wearing the Red Hooded Guy costume. Didn't need to see who had come. Each Bombardian was a different height. David was the tallest of the five. Anthony was on the shorter side. Franklin was only an inch of two shorter than David and Theodor. David and the others made a great choice of who came. Leaving Caleb in the background was a wise decision. The man was a huge jouster and did not know how to control his mouth and tone. Not bad in all situations, but this . . . Tack and smarts was required. Not that he wasn't smart, just . . . Man had no tack whatever so ever.

Poor Susan shoved herself so far back in her chair it all but toppled over. Even the camera men jerked back, but never moved their huge piece of equipment. Well, besides the zoom in on the Red Hooded Guy.

"I would like to introduce you all to," I stood and took hold of one side of David's and Anthony's red hood and pulled them backwards. "David Lincoln and Anthony Lincoln." I moved behind Franklin and pulled his hood down. "And this is Franklin Lincoln. They are three of five Royal Leaders of the Bombardians." I squeezed myself between Anthony and David and wrapped my arm around Anthony. "This one is my Bombaridan." I rose on my tip-toes and kissed his cheek."

I hadn't planned on doing that, but I needed to feel Anthony. I'd made it through telling the truth. Rest was up to David, Anthony, and Franklin.

Chapter 32

Anthony

I let my hand rest on Larry's back, hoping to ease his nerves. Larry swore he was fine with their plan of attack, but my man hated having to out his father. My touch did little to settle the distress spinning inside him. Then again all, or part of, it could be coming from our son. Either way by being in the middle of this major task I was not able to give him a pill, nor was he able to rush to the side and snatch a sip of water.

Soft lips pressed against my cheek. It brought a huge sigh from me, which earned me a glare from David. He'd have done the same if Bryan was here. Still, they'd came to do a job and it was time for him to do his part.

It'd be quick, so I could get Larry away from what distressed him. "As you can see," I waved my hand to David and Franklin, "All three of us are wearing the Red Hooded Guy costume that was forced upon us to join our lives with our other half. There is no one Red Hooded Guy. They are cloaks passed down from generation to generation. If no one is available to pass one down then the Bombardian comes to the Royal Leaders, myself and my four cousins, to gain one. It is a cloak to tell the man, or woman, who owns the other half of their souls. The man, or woman, in question is protected by our kind. It is our upmost cherished job to keep our other half safe from harm of any kind. The mark is placed by a mixture of herbs and the pull of the five elements among the world." I stretched my back, giving that time to soak in before I gave the newscaster the chance to ask questions. I took a short glance at David, who nodded his agreement about it being time to bring things to a close. We wanted to make ourselves know to the world, but not open our entire world to them. It would be too much for any of them to grasp and some facts might turn others further against us.

"Mrs. Susan Tinker you can ask us a total of five questions then we must take our leave."

"Five, that's all? An that's not a question."

"It is, but . . . It does not count. And yes. Five is all at this time."

"Do you really expect us to believe the Cult Leader has not sent you three in the Red Hooded Guys robes to trick us about his existence?"

"No." David and Franklin moved closer to Larry and me. "We expect you to do what you do best, uncover the truth for yourselves. Provide the proof the world needs to believe what has taken place."

I was kind of glad that all four of us studied Susan Tinker and came up with a list of fifteen questions she would mostly ask. Each of us went over and over to find the best response that would give the world the truth without giving away more than we could. The goal, David thought, was to get the humans to force the head of the government into doing so or aid them in doing so. We wanted the humans' curiosity to come alive. Wanted them to find enough information to form their own opinion and find ways to bring forth the truth. First step had been having Larry tell his story. Larry wasn't the President, but thanks to his father's status he was a man the humans listened to.

"Is there any physical proof that you took out twelve men like Larry Wells stated?"

"No. I can give you an example if you would like." David motioned towards the television crew. "I can gather all eight of these camera men and bring them in front of the main camera."

Susan Tinker looked at the man in the suit and mouthed what do I say.

The man gave a small nod. David took the man's cue. He faded away and a reappeared with all eight men. Great show of his talent. What wasn't so good was how pale the eight men where, even the two African Americans and one Latino. Not a good look for them.

A few staggered back, falling over the abandoned stage chairs. Two of them ran off the stage and out the door. Susan Tinker stood there gaping.

"You have three questions." Anthony doubted she could even form one word, let alone sentence. I'd been right. Susan Tinker stood there with a wide-open mouth for half a minute before she shook her head and sat down on the remaining upright chair. "Does anyone else have one?"

The suit wearing man came to stand in front of Susan Tinker and held his hand out. "I run this station and I'd like time for my crew to take a deeper look into what you claim. Then I'd like to request another interview."

Not a response we considered, so I glanced at David, who stood stone faced and with his arms crossed. Thankfully, David did step up.

"I will give you this . . ." David offered his hand, "When and if we give more interviews, of any kind, you will be the one we come to. Good enough?"

"Yes." The man all but bounced into Susan Tinker's chair.

"That settled we'll take our leave." I took a tighter hold on Larry and left David standing where he was. I zapped us right into Larry's bed, helping him into the bed. I took off his shoes and tucked his feet under the sheets.

"Thought you'd take me to your home."

I longed to, but until we knew if any threats would come to life it was best if all of the Royal Leaders stayed close. Taking Larry to my home and watching him redesign it would be the best day of my life. Wrong. The day Larry pledged himself to me would take that spot.

"Soon, honey. Soon."

Chapter 33

Larry

"Ouch!" My hand flew to the back of my head, rubbing the sting away from knocking it against the headboard as I scooted higher in the bed. "Stupid."

"You okay, honey?"

How did I answer that? Was, yet . . . Wasn't. We'd accomplished what we set out to, but I'd openly told the world my father lied. Backlash would be major. Not at first, but soon as the proof began showing up my father would be drowned in a public nightmare. Hatred loomed in the future. Not at me, but at my father. He might disown me. He sure would. He'd try to do more than that, if he could find the time to take his anger out on me. Then again . . . The situation would keep him at bay until his ire calmed down. If it did. I hoped it did. Then again . . . Would my father reach out to me? Hoped so. It's what Anthony, David, Franklin, and Caleb wanted. It would be then that the real test would be upon him.

"Honey?"

"As I can be."

"What's that mean?"

I scooted into his wide-open arms as he climbed onto the bed. "It's time I turn my phone on."

"You can wait a bit."

Delaying it would have made things worse. My father would be pissed enough. Making him wait . . . Helped no one.

"Okay. Let's go to the conference room." Anthony pulled me into his arms as he scooted to the edge of the bed, then maneuvered me so I was on his lap. He stood and headed for the door. It opened wide for them.

"You'll regret doing this."

"Not one bit, honey. Not one bit."

* * *

The phone rested in front of me on the huge square light brown conference table. Why did David have such huge rooms? Was Anthony's house this big? I'd get lost in it, if it was.

What was I doing? A major call would come in any second and I was thinking about my new home. In a twisted sense it made perfect sense. The table was as huge as the one dad had in his office at home. The one before he became President. People thought my life changed drastically when dad announced his intention to run for presidency. It hadn't. My entire life had been spent among the political world. My father tried grooming me to follow in his footsteps, but I outright refused. Ticked him off, but that would be nothing compared to his reaction to my earlier action.

Phone remained silent longer than I expected. Thought my dad would be holding his finger on the redial button until I answered. Guess not.

"Ah ha . . ." The phone beeped again and again as text after text flowed into my phone. Dad's fingers had been flying across the keyboard of his phone. Not normal for him, he only done it when he was too irked to speak.

"Lord." Anthony picked up the phone after the beeping stopped. "How many?"

"Fifteen."

I took the black phone from Anthony as he held it out. It felt like a rattler being passed to me. Would it sting me? If it did . . . What would I do? If only it had been a rattler stinging me. That would be easier than reading my dad's . . . "Not all of these are from my dad."

"Who then?"

"Two from his Public Relation's guy. Three from Senator Graves, my Godfather. He's not as harsh as my dad. He supported my decision to forgo being a politician. Rest my dad." I laid the phone on the table, not bothering to read any of them.

"You going to . . ." Anthony's question was cut off by the shrill of my phone.

"Show time." I reached for the phone, but Anthony grabbed my wrist.

"You aren't going to read them before talking to him?"

I shook my head. "Can't."

"Can't what, honey?"

What a good question. Read the text? Answer the phone? Let it go to voicemail? Text seemed smarter. My dad was known for his tongue lashing through text. Probably why there were so many at one time. Most swore they heard the President in every word of his texts.

"Need me to take the call for you, honey?"

"Can't." Was that my new answer. Seemed to be saying it a lot.

"Larry . . ."

David's questioning tone came from my right side, which meant he'd left his seat at the end of the table. Wasn't sure when he'd gotten up, but I knew he was asking me something without doing so. The wavering tone that came with many questions. No fear showed on his face, but I knew he feared me backing out. I wouldn't do that to them. To me. To my kind. I was not human. I was a Keeper. I was the only one that could show the world what a Keeper or Protector truly was. It was time.

I squared my shoulder and sat up taller and rejected the phone call. Then I opened the first text message. No sense in going in completely blind.

What the F you thinking?

I expected that. Second message held pretty much the same tone, if a text could hold a tone, but there were a few more choice words. Last message shocked me the most.

Call me. Now. Longer you take the worse your jail time will be.

A snarled had me crunching my shoulders and scooting down in my seat, drawing my knees to my chest. I focused on the floating leaf photo in front of me.

"What is it?" David's hand, or I thought it was him at first. But the large signet ring Anthony wore on his right index finger told me different. Anthony snatched the phone from my hand, making me jerked back so hard I rolled about a foot away from the table. As the phone flew into the photo I'd been staring at.

"I will kill him if he thinks . . ."

The rest of Anthony's comment was a . . . Distortion, but I didn't need to ask him to repeat it. Anthony's wolf side had come forward. The President of the United States had made the biggest mistake.

There was no attack coming my way, so I uncurled myself and scooted the chair closer to Anthony and let my hand rest against his thigh. "It's fine, babe. Look at me." I waited until Anthony's sexy wolf eyes and half wolf shaped face were trained on me.

Should have scared me, but it humbled me to know that the wolf side of Anthony would kill anyone who tried, or threatened, to harm me. Not that I wanted him going around attacking people who ticked me off or hurt my feelings. That was part of life, but a dad being so cruel was another thing. In my opinion. "I'm right here. You won't let anyone get near me. I know it."

"Okay. Minor twist in our plan." David passed the phone, which survived the toss across the room, to Franklin. Caleb came up behind Franklin and read the text over Franklin's shoulder.

"Major twist." Franklin sighed. "We should have thought of that."

"He will not come near my Keeper." Anthony leaned across the table, nailing David with a glare worthy of my dad's outraged expression. Right down to the narrowed eyes and straight-lined lips. Kind of freaky to see, but it pleased me.

"No. He won't." David pulled his phone from his pocket and flicked the screen a couple of times. Two seconds later he laid it down on the table as a ringing filled the room until Theodor's voice rang clear.

"Saw it." Theodor said. "Went good. You did great, Larry."

Had I? My father seemed to think I betrayed the country. Oh, dad didn't say it right out, but . . . He made his point clear. Had I betrayed . . . Might have but threatening me with jail . . . Was more than a valid response. I hadn't thought about how people would view my actions. Should have. Some would call me a traitor. Scream for me to be taken down for treason. Others would be on my side, but none of those opinions mattered. When it came to it . . . I had given top secret information to the world.

"Am I correct in thinking there is an unexpected problem?" Theodor's tone became tight and stern.

"Yes." David quickly explained what happened.

Anthony snarled, saying something that even I couldn't grasp. I slid my hand up and let it rest over his chest. "I'm fine, babe."

"You will stay that way." Theodor said. "Your father knows how we feel about our Keepers and Protectors."

"It won't matter to him."

My dad would send in the military to capture me after he listed me on the American's Most Wanted. The crime my father threatened me with was the next too biggest one I could have committed. Then again . . . Dad could have, and might have, considered me a terrorist.

"It will." Anthony said. "I'll kill the bastard before he lays a hand on you."

"No need in that." David said.

"If he sends one person after my Keeper there will be."

Shit. Not an idea I liked. My Bombardian did not need to be going after the President of the United States. I might not have liked my father's threat, but he was right in what he said. Still, the

Americans had a right to know, but I had done what my dad threatened to accuse me of.

"I'm serious." David laid an envelope in front of us. "Read it again if you have to."

I couldn't see clear enough to read anything. My head throbbed. My stomach spun and my legs were numb. Not a good thing either, because I needed a bathroom.

"Anthony."

Next few minutes were a bit of blur of craziness. I found myself in the air then leaning over a toilet. My eyes fluttered opened and a dull white ceiling loomed over me as warm arms clung to me, pressing me against a hard body. Musk and a scent that belonged only to Anthony cocooned me.

"What happened?"

"You passed out on me."

"Sorry."

"You are fine, but there is to be no more worrying over any shit storm. We clear, honey?"

"I have to speak to my dad."

"No, my Keeper."

"Yes."

"No. I won't endanger our son. We clear?"

Shit. Had my stress harmed our son? I'd kill myself if it had. "Is he alright?"

"Yes, but . . ."

"What?" I wiggled until Anthony loosened his hold and I could lean back to stare at him. "What happened? Tell me. Now."

"Calm down." Anthony ran a hand over my face. "Your blood pressure spiked to high."

How did he know that? What did that mean for me and our child?

"David's Uncle said his Keeper experienced that with each of his children. It can cause early labor if left unattended."

"Thought Keepers didn't get sick?"

"Normally they don't."

Normally? Ah . . . Being pregnant. Course there was some differences among my kind.

"The doctor who prescribed medication for our female Protectors was contacted and he is sending us the medication you need. Won't be here for a day or two."

How had Anthony managed to get that when no one knew Keepers could get pregnant? Had he sworn the Bombardian to secretiveness?

"David's is a master with Earth spells."

Ah, tricked the doctor. I might have been appalled if I wasn't so pleased David could get the medication. Would have been happier if I could have gotten it quicker.

"Why two days?"

"We had to locate a pharmacy that had it. It's several towns away"

"Blood Pressure medicine?"

"It's not commonly used. Real old, or so the pharmacist said. Even he had to order it. The others in between here and there could not even do that. Their suppliers didn't carry it anymore." Anthony shook his head. "Until it gets here, you are not to worry about anything. David and I will handle your father."

"I need to talk to him." I did, even if I didn't want to. "Please."

"We will see, my Keeper."

"Anthony . . ."

"Honey . . . Do you not recall my way of life that you agreed to?"

Shit. Anthony made the final call when it came to my safety. Safety extended to my life and our child's. I was not going to get my way until that medication arrived. My father wouldn't be happy about that.

"What excuse you going to give him?"

"David's taking care of that."

"Other words . . . You aren't going to tell me."

"Right." Anthony kissed the tip of my nose. "Rest."

"Least tell me you will be partaking in what is going on?"

"I am." Anthony released me and tucked the covers around me. "You've got company." He walked over to the door, opening it and waving in Bryan and Tommy."

"Hey guys."

"You aren't supposed to be scaring me." Bryan came over and dropped a couple of DVD*s* on the bed. "Choose one."

"You two been assigned to babysit my ass?"

"Nope. Volunteered."

Course they had.

"Honey, rest. Enjoy your movies. I'm going to help David, Caleb and Franklin."

"Okay, but try not to . . ." I sighed when he lifted a hand to silence me.

"They can be so bossy." Bryan chuckled. "Still love my David though."

I loved Anthony as well. That would never change.

Chapter 34

Anthony

Franklin pointed at the conference phone when I walked in. The one no one could trace, even if they did the number would lead them overseas.

"You broke our contract."

It was as if Larry was on the other end, but I knew it wasn't. There was no ounce of compassion or common sense. It was all business and even a bit of hatred that flowed from each word the man said. That's why the voice irked me so much I had to shove my wolf down.

"I don't care what you say, you did. You were forbidden from telling the truth about yourself."

"We did not tell the world." David calm persona was excellent. Great thing there weren't any cameras around, or they'd see the clinched fist and flickering eyes.

"Yeah, there was a look alike on the Susan Tinker show with my son, who you are refusing to let me speak to."

"We were there to back up his story, but we did not tell Mrs. Tinker anything until after Larry disclosed the truth about his rescue."

"Yes, well my traitorous son will pay with his life for that."

"The fuck he will." Anthony winced when David shushed him.

"Who the hell is that?"

"I am your son's Bombardian."

"His . . . Fuck it. You are telling me . . . I sent my son to be protected. Not become a Destroyer."

"I have done as your son requested"

"No. You have turned him against his country. You are keeping him from speaking to me. You might as well have left him with the Snipers. Least there he would have died an American hostage by the largest Cartel in the world."

Good thing the jerk was not in front of me. He would have been the one to die and it wouldn't have been an easy death. It was taking all I had not to leave the conference room and enter the White House.

Franklin must have taken note of my frame of mind, because he came over and placed himself in front of me. My wolf was so close that I heard the drops of blooding hitting the carpet. My hands stung as claws dug through multiple levels of skin.

"You have to remain calm. Keep control. None of us will let him harm your Keeper, or anyone he sends this way."

"My son is no Keeper."

"Yes, he is." David's facade held strong, but I wanted to hear rage and distaste from him. The President of the United States forced us into some twisted kind of agreement that made our kind appear to be a dangerous cult. We were not. Most were not dangerous. Although . . . Right then I could have been. "In fact, Larry is a Royal Keeper."

"Fuck!" Silence filled the air before the President screamed at everyone to leave the office. Five more long heartbeats consumed the airwaves before the bastard spoke again. "What is it you hope to achieve from getting my son to commit treason?"

"The moment your son met Anthony he no longer was an American. He became the Royal Keeper of Anthony Lincoln. Therefore, he falls under our jurisdiction. Your son committed no crime."

"If you wish to go along that line to protect my son from his crime then you have broken the agreement. Therefore, you are in breach of a written contract and subject to the retribution facing you."

I bit my jaw so hard that I winced. Didn't know any other way to keep the laughter hidden. What else was I to do. The entire conversation was comical. Each was going into professional mode, trying to wrangle out who and what was going to be the outcome. Both wanted the other to cave. Neither would. Not until they got their desired reaction. For David it was to ensure Larry's safety and ensure there was no backlash from the government. The Bombardians were out of the bag. David and I delivered many documents to Susan Tinker that would prove our existence and the agreement between us and the human government. There was even a recorded session that took place in Theodor's home. It included written consent to being recorded. There was nothing mentioned in that interaction about it being private or confidential.

I found the massive stack of documentation and recording that Theodor had kept on top of his home desk. He might kick my ass for entering the room, then again . . . I doubted the man would leave such laying around in the open. Not even in his home. He had wanted one of us to find them and put them to use. Good method of being on top of your professional game. I'd have to start including such practice in my business.

"He is either a Keeper or my son. He can't have it both ways."

"Wrong." David rolled his eyes at the phone. "Your government made it possible for him to be both."

"How do you think that?" A deep snort pulled the first frown from David. Not at the fact someone got one over on him, nope, it was the President's idiocy. "He cannot be human if he was already a Royal Keeper. Either way, he is guilty, and punishment is due."

"There has been no such crime." David replied. "We simply made ourselves visual after someone with high rank among your kind announced our presence."

"Once again he cannot be both."

"He can. And you made it possible."

"You are ignorant."

"I am not." David bit the words out and stood up taller. "He is your son in the eyes of the Americans, is he not?"

"Was. He's now a traitor."

"He can't be a traitor if he was already a Keeper." I stepped closer to the phone, catching onto what David was aiming to happen. That allowed me to pick up the argument while David took time to control his beast side.

"Then you guys broke your agreement."

"No. In the eyes of the world, Larry was your son, was he not?"

"Yes. My family has and always will help me make decisions." Might have, but Larry had never aided his father in decision making. Nor had his father asked him to.

"Does the world know this?"

"Yes. It's always been that . . ." Silence hung thick in the room and over the phone. I was sure that the President was replaying every time his son stood beside him. Every time he put his arm around his son and wife and told the world how his family was so tight, and that time was always made for them. That he was a devoted husband and father. That his family was like an extension of him. It was all those comments and his actions of showing a devoted happy family that drilled a hole in his own statements. "That does not matter. He is not government."

"Is he not?" Anthony popped his neck. "He is continuously in the press because he is your son. His life is invaded at every turn. He has your ears in all things, according to your own words on national air." There was plenty of proof to back that up. "I believe your words were 'My family will always, and I mean always, help me make my decisions. I trust my family with every aspect involving my life.'" Powerful words. Words that would help people believe Larry.

"He is guilty of treason."

"Once again," David nodded to me. "Refer back to our agreement."

I moved to the fridge, mainly to keep my temper, but retrieved us all cold bottles of water as David and the President went back and forth on when Larry was considered a human and when he became a Keeper. Didn't really matter to me. No one would touch Larry. Hearing the threats against Larry made it ten times difficult to control my wolf.

"I will not stand for this." A hard bang flowed through the phone and into the room. "I want to speak to my son. I want proof that he bares the Destroyer Mark."

"Your visit will take place at our choosing." David's tone bore no room for disagreement, but it did little to detour the President.

"No."

"Yes." There were four voices all with the same response. Hadn't been planned but warmed my entire body to know that my cousins stood at my back.

"Am I to assume that the other two voices are Royal Leaders as well?"

David waved me to take over. "You are."

"Do you guys do nothing alone?"

"Our ways of life has been explained to you."

"Has it? I don't recall an Anthony being involved in the agreement."

"Like you there are changes among our leaders." More than I had meant to say, so I switched the conversation back to the matter at hand. "The meeting you request will take place wherever Larry wishes. There will be no press. Any sign of them and Larry will hold another interview to show his mark. He will be guarded by me, David, and our guards." Hadn't meant to go into that much detail. Shouldn't have since me and my cousins had not discussed it. All I knew was my wolf would settle for no less.

"I will not go for that."

I looked to David, who nodded at me.

"Then Larry will be setting up another interview."

"He will not."

"That is not for you to say."

"It is. He's my son."

"He's an adult." I snarled. "I believe this conversation is over." Or should have been. Loophole that might come back to bite my ass. The United States increased the legal age a few years after the Cult came to life. Then again . . . Once a man or woman became a Keeper or Protector they no longer fell under the realm of the U.S. government. David had made that point, more than once, but the President believed different. I wasn't sure who was right in that matter, but I did know the meeting would go as I said, or there would be none.

David didn't hesitate to hang up the phone.

I flopped back into the chair. "Shit."

"Exactly." Franklin sighed. "That man is . . . Something meaner than I can describe."

"Did we ever decide if Larry was a human, or Keeper at the time?" Caleb chuckled. "Not like it mattered anyway. The world new nothing about him being marked and until the mark is made known he is human."

"That's right, Caleb." David took a huge gulp of his water as I realized it had never been a problem to start with. The world never knew of a Marked One until we alerted them to it. I never did that with Larry since he was the son of the President and was still in danger."

"Then why did we argue that point with him for so long?" Anthony sipped his water.

"To walk him into a circle and get him riled up. Bit of pay back for what he put us through when we created the contract."

"You should have warned me." I groaned and rubbed my temple.

"Didn't know I was going to do it. Sorry." David tossed his empty water bottle into the trash bin. "Doesn't matter. The entire conversation went about like Larry expected it to. That's why Larry has reached out to Mrs. Tinker. Right?"

"Yes, but he's not heard back from her, but he asked her to wait three days." I believed part of Larry's longing for his father to react differently came into play.

"I think that man is worse than Bryan's mother and stepfather."

Had to agree with David on that. Those two had been a work of art in delusion, but the President . . . Took the topper.

"How will you tell him this?" Caleb threw his water bottle into the trash.

"Like anything else." I doubted I'd had have to tell him anything. My man knew his father better than anyone. He knew, no matter how much Larry longed for a different reaction, what would come of the phone call.

"When?"

"After he watches the movies your Keeper brought to him."

"Now, Bryan will keep him hauled up for days if you let him."

"Like you'd let him, David." Franklin snorted. "You hardly last through one movie before you go into check on him."

David waved his hand at Franklin and locked eyes on me. "Until then?"

"Think we need to update Theodor. Has he said what he's up to?"

"Won't until he's ready." David picked his phone up. "If he needed us, he'd reach for us."

True, still . . . Theodor didn't do mystery much. Or he hadn't since I took over for Michael.

Chapter 35

Larry

"Is Theodor joining us for the fun."

Wasn't sure how much fun it would be, but . . . I was going to make sure that I looked my best. Not giving my father the upper hand in any manner. He'd think less of me if I was not dressed properly. He'd blame me being a Royal Keeper as an excuse for such a slack in appearance. Then again . . . A look in the mirror revealed a puffy face. A side-effect from the child I was carrying. Seemed like there were many similarities between pregnant Keepers and women. Huge belly I could handle. Feet swelling, I could manage. Sickness, hadn't been as bad as Bryan's. Thank God I was not having twins. I was sure dad would not guess I was expecting, but he would take note of my appearance. After all, the man took everything around him in. He used what was at his disposal to gain the upper hand. It hadn't worked so well for him after the phone conversation with the Royal Leaders. He'd misjudged my desire to ensure the world knew the truth. He had refused to give into the parameters of a meeting with me. It had taken us releasing more to the press. Dad had called me an hour after the news released the second broadcast. That was why I stood in front of the mirror fretting like a girl. I wasn't, but . . .

"No."

"Do you guys have any idea what he's up to?"

"Your dad?"

"No." No one knew with my dad. "Theodor."

"Wish we did." Anthony took the brush from my hands. "You look amazing."

"Do you think it has to do with the invasion being led by a possible Vampire?"

"Seems like it. What else would make him high-tail it."

I locked eyes with Anthony in the mirror, cursing the sleep lines marring his sexy face. Anthony and the other three had been behind closed doors for hours upon hours for the last three days. Same topic each time. What to bring up to my dad. What they would be willing to release to the humans. President would have restriction on what was told and there was no way Anthony and his cousins would release every detail about their life and world. Wrong information in the wrong hands could lead to deaths. Dad and their meeting weren't the only thing on the agenda. Nope. They were setting up the Pledging Ceremony.

"He is coming tomorrow right?" Our Pledging Ceremony wouldn't be the same without Theodor.

"Has to."

"How's he going to do that?"

"Same way we pop in and out."

Duh. How else? "Will he be staying for the celebration?"

"Yes. He said he wouldn't leave until after we did."

I grinned back at Anthony when he frowned. Not acceptable. Not today. Not the day before we basically marry one another. Nope. Not on my watch.

"Can't wait to see your place."

Anthony led me to believe that we would be staying at David's until they were sure all threats was gone. Then again . . . That might have happened. The other day when David went to take the prisoners meals they were all dead. There was no sign of anyone being in the room they were kept in. They had no way to get to any medication. It was a mystery how the Bombardian's died, but not one the Royal Leaders were concerned about. What bothered David the most was that someone had slipped through his Earth protective shield. That being said . . . Anthony swore it was impossible for someone to do so, so he believed that the Vampire had some kind of mind connection with the Bombardians and whoever they'd gotten into bed with had eliminated the threat to them, as well as the ones the Bombardians hadn't decided on punishment for. Most of them had done turned into some funky half state, which made them unstable to start with. Their debated had been whether to end their lives in a humane manner, or store them all in a confinement house. No reason to worry any more.

"Can't wait to see you in our home."

Our home? Sounded great to me. I'd never had a home since Shawn's family died. I'd always viewed their place as my first home. Shawn's parent's house was always welcoming and homey. Mine was . . . It was anything but a home. I might have considered it one as a child, but the truth behind my parent's marriage and the reason I was born destroyed it.

"You remember your promise about the place?"

"Yes, babe."

"Great. I expect you to change anything and everything you want. Add whatever as well."

"I will." I would too. I'd love to decorate. "We going to do the baby's room together, though."

"We are."

A loud thunk against the door and a shout to get decent was the only warning we had before Bryan walked in.

"Bryan." I smiled as one of my new best friends walked in. Tommy followed right behind him. They reminded me so much of Shawn. They were as strong and as mentally fast as me. They have their Bombardians wrapped around their fingers.

"David says he's going to get your father."

"Okay." Anthony's warm cocooning arms soothed me as blackness surrounded me. Last thing I heard before the bedroom faded into nothingness was a comment of how I best have my medicine. That had been the first thing Anthony shoved into his dress slacks' pocket. No one was sure what all a pregnant Keeper could handle. Seemed like every time I turned around Bryan or I was tossing cookies. That alone . . . As much as I longed to move into Anthony's house and decorate it, I feared going through the pregnancy alone. Wouldn't be, but . . . Something about being around another going through the process with me . . . Anthony would not be able to understand me completely, even though he'd be able to feel my emotional state. Staying with David meant I had someone within reaching distance. Someone experiencing what I was.

"Honey," grass began to form under my feet as the bright sun beat down on my head. "You will be able to contact Bryan whenever you need to. Or want to."

"I know." It wasn't so much leaving David's; it was the upcoming visit with my dad making me doubt myself.

"You scared?"

"Sort of. Would you not be?"

"More than." Anthony ran a hand over my stomach. "I've got your medicine."

Blackness was completely gone and the bright green grass clearing on top of a high hill that overlooked a rich valley was more than stunning. It's beauty almost made me want to change the location of the meeting. No sense in dragging such serenity down with my dad's vile words.

I stepped back from Anthony and smoothed out his white dress shirt. Another fact I loved about my Bombardian. He always dressed for business. Instead of wearing t-shirts like his four cousins, Anthony dressed for success all the times. Since I'd been taught that since I was a young child, it gave me comfort.

"You okay, honey?"

Was he? The area should ease anyone. Not only was there amazing scenery, which included four ducks waddling down the hillside to return to the glistening pond below them. Ducklings trailed behind them. The family eased my mind, just not enough.

"You need a pill?"

"No. I seem to be getting the hang of traveling like that."

"Good." Anthony sealed his lips over mind, nipping my lower as he pulled back. "David should be arriving soon. You got a spot you prefer?"

I moved towards the black metal bench sitting so you stared down at the pond. Such serenity would provide me with strength. My father . . . What a joke. Fatherly visit . . . Mere idea pulled a deep chuckle from me. What lay ahead of me would be the President of the United States. Nothing new to me. There'd been no father figure in my life from the get-go. Difficult fact to swallow and one I never admitted to myself before. A missing father left me with a man who sired me for his own gain. Learning the truth about all that left me heartbroken, giving the desire to understand how any man could be so cold-hearted. That fact alone had me pursing my Masters in Psychology. One of the first questions I asked Anthony was if I could continue my schooling. He promised me I'd finish if I desired to. Also told me that he'd help me open my own practice. That it would be great to have a Keeper running such a business. Someone that could allow other Keepers, Protectors, and Bombardians to express their own issues openly without fear of slipping up and giving away more information than he, or she, should. Made great sense to me. Not to mention I'd be able to help humans who struggled to grasp the idea of another species living among them. There would be lots of people like that. Not to mention the ones who would outright hate Bombardians and their other halves. Others would stand up for them, openly and on the downlow. I'd always dreamed of having my own practice. I only liked one more year before I'd have my Masters. My high IQ had helped me finish homeschooling two years early.

"Perfect choice, honey." Anthony sat down beside me, resting his arm behind my shoulder. "You going to be okay?"

Was I? My mind was everywhere. Not a great state of mind when going against my dad in President mode. The man hated giving into anyone. The meeting being setup by Anthony and rules delivered by David would have ticked my dad off. Worse I'd gone public with more facts about the Bombardians, Keepers, Protectors, Destroyer's' Hermitage, and other fact that had been kept hidden from the world. All that meant I had to have a clear head to face off with my dad. Not going from one topic to the other, mentally. I had to clear my head. I had a major task ahead of me and I would not screw it up.

"Have to be."

"We can go back home."

"No. This has to be done."

"I will not have him upsetting you."

"I can handle him."

"You start feeling lightheaded you tell me. Instantly. We clear?"

"I will."

A blue puff of mist formed two or three feet from the bench. The haze cleared, showing David's hand on my father's back. David pushed him over, making my dad bend at the waist. He was telling him to take slow breaths. First time traveling magically sucked, but once you got used to it, it was neat. Or I thought so. Bryan loved to travel like that. Tommy . . . Not so much. Cain still drove him most places. Tommy said traveling in a car reminded him he was no different than anyone else. Like most Bombardians, Cain gave Tommy whatever he wanted. All Bombardians would bend over backwards to ensure their Keeper or Protector was happy and well. I disagreed with Tommy's belief. Tommy believed he was still human. I did not. I was a Keeper. Belonged to a race created by the government.

"What the fuck - -"

Shit. Clear your mind. Your dad is here. Time to get to work. I took a deep breath and watched as David gripped the backside of my dad's collar.

"Do not charge at him. Do not disrespect him."

"Let me go." My father jerked, failing to break David's hold.

"Calm down and I will."

Unlikely. My dad might pull off faking it. Or at least try to.

"Fine." My dad tugged his fancy suit coat down and stood up taller.

"Walk slowly and calmly to the bench and remember who you are dealing with."

"I know all too damn well."

"That you do not, Sir."

David hit it on the head. My dad believed he knew how to top the Bombardian's leaders. He was so wrong. The Bombardian's never enlightened him to their true power and skills.

"Show me." My father stopped in front of me, frowning.

I pulled my sleeve up and held out my arm. Anthony took hold of forearm, holding it steady for me.

"That is fake."

"I assure you, Mr. President, that is not." Anthony ran his hand across his mark. "As you can see it did not wipe off."

"Then it's a water tattoo."

Anthony hovered his index finger over the mark and conjured up a stream of water while I gently rubbed over the mark.

"You are magically making it appear."

Damn it. Dad would never accept what his eyes told him. I was fed-up with the bullshit. I was on my feet and in my father's face.

"You have seen your proof that I am no longer human. I am no longer under your control. You have no say over what I do. I do not answer to you any longer. Believe it or not, I don't give a fuck." I rested my hand on Anthony's shoulder. My head spun, but tight arms held me up. Sound faded in and out so much I could not understand what was said after Anthony called to me. His tone was soft. Caring. Worried. David's voice was muffled, but what I picked up on told me he was badgering someone. What caught me more off guard was the concern flowing from my father. I had to be reading too much into what I was able to make out. My father never cared about me. There was no way he would start.

"Lay him on the bench."

I thought I was laying. Was sort of. Had to be in Anthony's arms. Didn't matter where I was. I just wanted my head to quit pounding and David's solid and loud tone did not help.

"I told you this was too much for him." Anthony's sharp tone had my arm reach up for him. He rested his head against it and nuzzled my palm.

"I'm fine, babe."

"You are not." Wasn't sure if the words came out or not.

"I am. Relax."

"Has your head eased off?" No way to answer David truthfully. It was better, but not gone. Instead of a continuous loud, repeating gong sound I felt a hard thump, thump, thump.

"What is wrong with my son? What have you done to him?"

"Nothing." Anthony snapped. "This is your doings."

"Babe, look at me." I gripped Anthony's chin, tugging it so he was focused on me. "Feel me deeply. Take note of what is going on inside me."

"Your head is still hurting."

It was, but it was better, so I let that relief flow through me and down the mental connection I had with Anthony.

"I just got too upset. Sorry, I worried you."

Anthony lowered his ear to mine and whispered, "The baby okay?"

"Feel for yourself." I could feel Anthony searching through me. I could feel the love and devotion he felt for our son. Joy rushed through me as I traced the smile stretching across Anthony's face.

"Son, what is going on?"

I turned, gasping at the watery gaze blazing across his brown eyes. The twirling of his fingers bothered me more. My dad never openly showed his worry or concern. I'd never even known him to feel such. The man was always in control and nothing bothered him. When I fell over one of my toys and broke my leg he didn't comfort me. He simply told my mom to call the doctor and then he walked back into his office. I dreamed of having my dad fret over me. Be worried enough about me that his perfect posture broke and real love came my way. Many nights after Shawn died, I longed for him to come ask me how I was coping. Allow me to express my sadness to him. Get advice from him on how to handle all the dark emotions that flowed through me.

"Don't look so shocked."

What did my dad expect me to do? "Why not?"

"I love you. Always have."

"Could have fooled me." Okay, maybe I was a bit too harsh on him, but all the times I desired his comfort and aid rushed through my mind.

"I have not shown it like most fathers, but you are my flesh and blood."

Damn. How did this come up while I'm flat on my back? How was I supposed to believe him after he bombarded me with press right after David rescued me? Days ago he'd considered me a traitor. Told me I deserved death. Went as far as to put my name on the Most Wanted list. Why come at me with the love and a concern front. Not a tactic my dad used.

"Is this some kind of joke?"

"What?" My father came to stand beside Anthony, who snarled at him until I rubbed his cheek. "Why would you ask such?"

"Why? Ha. You were accusing me of treason the other day."

"It was to - -"

"Get the results you wanted."

A deep sigh and my father dropping to his knees, frowning. "Yes." The frown confused me more, but what came next drove the confusion right out of me. Shock consumed me so fast that my head began to pound again. "I was angry. Upset. You could have . . . Most likely did destroy my career. I worked hard to reach the top."

True. He gave up his family to achieve it. Gave up raising me in a loving and caring home. Gave up loving me.

"Why the shift in attitude? Nothing has changed."

"It has."

"What?" I scooted so my back rested against the cool metal. "I still told the world about the Bombardians. Your career is most likely ruined. Nothing has changed."

"I have a second chance."

"At what?"

"Being a father."

"Huh?" Not possible. My mother barely tolerated my dad. They didn't share dinners, breakfast, lunch. Didn't even sleep in the same room. She hardly even spent time in the same house as him. She remained in Florida while dad lived in the White House.

"You know . . . Me and your mom have not been . . . I have . . ."

"Mistress." Course he did. "Still don't explain what that has to do with the change of attitude." Pissed me off that my father seemed pleased about having another child. One he wanted to do better by. By a woman other than his wife.

"She talks to me. Lots. She showed me how I treated you. Told me she did not want our child to be done the same way." My father leaned back on his heels. "I did not see how awful I treated you. How much you were truly on your own when you were younger."

"Then why did you come in hell bent on my mark being faked." Anthony pretty much snarled as his hands came to rest over my rolling stomach. "You upset my Keeper. You put him in danger. You were - -"

"Babe, it's fine."

"It's not." David moved to Anthony's side. "I want to know the answer to that questions."

Okay. David and Anthony had a valid reason to know the answer, but I did not. All I wanted was for my dad to disappear. I had thought he could not hurt me more, but my heart shattered when he expressed his desire to treat his new child better. He longed to give my brother or sister what he should have given me.

"I might be the President, but I am a father. One who sucked, but one who loved his son. One that always believed his son's status kept him from your reach."

"You knew better." David sat down on the arm of the bench. "You now have proof that your son is the Royal Keeper of Commander Anthony Lincoln and the Bombardians have been brought into the light."

"I have." My dad stood. "I'm not happy about it, but it seems my son has already made an agreement with his Bombardian."

"I have."

"Are you happy?"

What! Why did he care? Just because he realized how horrible he treated me and his open desire to do better by his upcoming child. Damn it. Something else was going on. What was my dad's underhanded method? Anthony and David seemed to believe my dad. They could smell the truth. They would not have stood for such betrayal. Didn't change the fact that I could honestly tell my dad that I was deeply in love.

"More than ever."

"Okay." My dad stood. "Nothing left for me to do but cover my ass."

"What's that mean?" I used Anthony's arm to push myself upright and gasped as a cold chill rushed over every nerve in my body.

"You okay, honey?"

"Just tired."

"We end this."

"Not yet, babe. I want to know what his plan is." My decision put a wave of anger through me, but I knew Anthony would let me stay as long as I didn't have another bad blood pressure spell. "Go on, dad."

"It means, I will face whatever comes my way." My dad tugged his suit coat down and ran a hand over his dress shirt. "Not like it matters too much. Election time is next year."

True, but far as I'd known dad was going to run again. "You've changed your mind."

"It's for the best. I cannot recover from this. Nor do I want to cover up my upcoming child."

Took all my control to keep from reaching out and slapping him. I would have if it would have made a difference. The harm done to me was over. I had a whole new life ahead of me. A child of my own to shower with love and affection. My son and Anthony mattered the most. Still, curiosity won out.

"How will you spin this?"

"Think I'll do something I've never done in my life."

My hand went to my chest, rubbing hard. Wasn't sure how much more of my dad's new actions I could handle. Yet . . . The Royal Leaders needed to know what lay ahead for them. I did to. Not so much that I cared . . . Okay, I did. I might not have gotten love from my dad, not the kind I longed for, but I did worry about him. He was my father, after all.

"What's that?"

"Truth."

"Yeah right." I snorted. "You publicist won't allow that."

"She has no choice." My father wiped his hands across his forehead. "I'm the President. What I say is what goes." Wasn't sure how much to trust what my dad said, but once again David and Anthony seemed to believe him, so I would accept what he says. Watch and see how much my dad was able to live up to the change he wanted to make. "David, can you take me back so I can set things into motion? And . . . take my son's name off the Most Wanted List and make sure that everyone knows he broke no laws."

That took a huge weight off my shoulder. Not that I was afraid of being killed by the government, but it meant Anthony would not go after every member among them.

"Great. If you are ready then we will go." David nodded at me and Anthony. "Get home and rest. You have a big day tomorrow."

"What's that mean?"

Wasn't sure if I smiled or floated off the bench, but my heart knitted itself back together as I answered my dad. "I'm getting married."

"Married?"

"Our kind of marriage." Anthony kissed my cheek. "I'm sure David will be willing to transport you to and from the event, if you agree to our arrangement."

"Course I want to see my son get married."

"Then see you tomorrow." Anthony stood and scooped me into his arms. "Ready to go, honey?"

"Yes, please." I gave my father what I hoped to be a genuine smile. Still was a bit skeptical about what he said, but . . . I'd give him a chance to prove himself. "Dad, I hope you achieve treating my brother or sister better." Hardest words I said, but it was pure truth. I never wished the hard life I had onto another one, even if watching my dad devote himself to another child would be hard to swallow.

"Son, I'm sorry I made your life miserable."

"It's fine." Sort of was. Might piss me off from time to time, but the trials I'd faced made me the man I was. "I'm also glad you will be there to watch me enter the next phase of my life."

"See you tomorrow, son."

"Let's go, babe." I looped my arms around Anthony's shoulder. "I'm ready to start our life. Sooner we get the day over with the sooner we can."

"That is so true, honey. So true."

# # #

Dear Reader,

Thank you for reading Marked One Anthony and Larry. Hope you enjoyed and were able to let your imagination soar with each word you read. If you did, make sure you keep an eye out for Theodor's story.

I love to hear from my readers; therefore, I answer all my emails. I'm a firm believer that you can't better yourself if your errors aren't pointed out. So, feel free to contact me and let me know about any you spot or what you thought about the book.

Please keep reading and letting your imagination soar.

Julia Matthews

Website: www.juliamatthews.webs.com[1]

Blog Site https://juliamatthewssp.blogspot.com/

Email: julia.matthews5@gmail.com

---

1. http://www.juliamatthews.webs.com

OTHER BOOKS AVAILABE BY JULIA MATTHEWS
MOON CALLED[2]
HUMAN-SKINNED WOLVES BOOK 1
RED MOON CIRCLE[3]
HUMAN-SKINNED WOLVES BOOK 2
WOLF CLUB[4]
HUMAN-SKINNED WOLVES BOOK 3
HIDDEN WOLF[5]
HUMAN-SKINNED WOLVES BOOK 5
COLLAR OF TRUTH[6]
HUMAN-SKINNED WOLVES BOOK 5
MERCIFUL WOLF[7]
HUMAN-SKINNED WOLVES BOOK 6

---

2. *http://www.amazon.com/Moon-Called-Human-Skinned-Wolves-Book-ebook/dp/ B00RNIX0TK/ref=asap_bc?ie=UTF8*

3. http://www.amazon.com/Red-Moon-Circle-Skinned-Human-Skinned-ebook/dp/ B00VQA75MY/ref=sr_1_1?ie=UTF8&qid=1441370867&sr=8-1&keywords=RED+MOON+CIRCLE+JULIA+MATTHEWS&pebp=1441370869286 &perid=1HTDQKHVJ7Y5CBPWS5MT

4. *https://www.amazon.com/Wolf-Club-Human-Skinned-Wolves-Book-ebook/dp/ B01GDH7P9C/ref=sr_1_1?ie=UTF8&qid=1472482170&sr=8-1&keywords=Wolf+Club+Julia+Matthews*

5. https://www.amazon.com/Hidden-Wolf-Human-Skinned-Wolves-Book-ebook/dp/ B01M1YRKXN/ref=sr_1_1?ie=UTF8&qid=1517755753&sr=8-1&keywords=Hidden+Wolf+by+Julia+Matthew

6. https://www.amazon.com/Collar-Truth-Human-Skinned-Wolves-Book-ebook/dp/ B074TSB2XS/ref=sr_1_1?s=digital-text&ie=UTF8&qid=1517755801&sr=1-1&keywords=Collar+of+Truth+by+Julia+Matthew

7. https://www.amazon.com/Merciful-Wolf-Human-Skinned-Wolves-Book-ebook/dp/ B07H2HKP7X/ ref=sr_1_fkmrnull_1?keywords=merciful+wolf+by+julia+matthews&qid=1551282272&s =gateway&sr=8-1-fkmrnull

<u>WOLF REVELATION</u>[8]
HUMAN-SKINNED WOLVES BOOK 7
<u>JOURNEY TO A MATE</u>[9]
BOOK 1 OF JOURNEY SERIES
(CO-WRITTEN WITH VICKIE MATTHEWS)
<u>ANYTHING FOR A MATE</u>[10]
BOOK 2 OF JOURNEY SERIES
<u>CLAIMING MY MATE</u>[11]
BOOK 3 OF JOURENY SERIES
<u>JOURNEY REVEALED</u>[12]
<u>WITCH & WOLF</u>[13]
(CO-WRITTEN WITH VICKIE MATTHEWS)
<u>WARLORD DEMISE</u>[14]

---

8. https://www.amazon.com/Wolf-Revelation-Human-Skinned-Wolves-Book-ebook/dp/ B07PB8D555/ ref=sr_1_4?keywords=Wolf+Revelation+by+julia+matthews&qid=1557844453&s=gatew ay&sr=8-4-spell

9. *http://www.amazon.com/Journey-Mate-Book-1-ebook/dp/B00C4BSFEQ/ ref=sr_1_1?ie=UTF8&qid=1426082926&sr=8- 1&keywords=Journey+To+A+Mate+Vickie+Matthews*

10. *http://www.amazon.com/Anything-Mate-Journey-Book-2-ebook/dp/B00DRNC4XS/ ref=sr_1_1?ie=UTF8&qid=1426082997&sr=8- 1&keywords=Anything+For+A+Mate+Julia+Matthews*

11. *http://www.amazon.com/Claiming-My-Mate-Journey-Book-ebook/dp/B00GU3817A/ ref=asap_bc?ie=UTF8*

12. *http://www.amazon.com/Journey-Revealed-Conclusion-Julia-Matthews-ebook/dp/ B00ILYDL6W/ref=asap_bc?ie=UTF8*

13. *http://www.amazon.com/Witch-Wolf-Julia-Matthews-ebook/dp/B00IXYPS0C/ ref=asap_bc?ie=UTF8*

14. http://www.amazon.com/Warlord-Demise-Julia-Matthews-ebook/dp/B015E7T3S8/ ref=sr_1_1?ie=UTF8&qid=1461085265&sr=8- 1&keywords=Warlord+Demise+Julia+Matthews

<u>UNRAVELLING</u>[15]
<u>REVEALED BY LOVE</u>[16]
<u>AWAKENING LOVE</u>[17]
<u>MARKED ONES DAVID AND BRYAN</u>[18]

---

15. http://www.amazon.com/Unravelling-Julia-Matthews-ebook/dp/B019MKSD3E/ ref=sr_1_2?ie=UTF8&qid=1461085345&sr=8-2&keywords=Julia+Matthews

16. https://www.amazon.com/Revealed-Love-Julia-Matthews-ebook/dp/B077XNVQB3/ ref=sr_1_1?s=digital-text&ie=UTF8&qid=1517755832&sr=1-1&keywords=Revealed+By+Love+by+Julia+Matthew

17. https://www.amazon.com/Awakening-Love-Julia-Matthews-ebook/dp/B07BD2S4Z1/ ref=sr_1_fkmr0_1?ie=UTF8&qid=1534686290&sr=8-1-fkmr0&keywords=Awakening+Lover+by+Julia+Matthews

18. https://www.amazon.com/Marked-Ones-David-Julia-Matthews-ebook/dp/B07TCZD87T/ ref=sr_1_4?keywords=Marked+Ones+David+and+Bryan&qid=1569157295&sr=8-4

9 7 9 8 2 3 0 1 3 2 0 4 2